"*Seasons of the Heart* is a romance in the grand tradition, spanning the worlds of rich and poor, loved and unloved, desire and destiny itself. If you loved *The Thorn Birds*, you'll adore *Seasons of the Heart*. Garrard's unforgettable heroine will win your heart and her story will stay with you forever."

—Omni *magazine*

"*Seasons of the Heart* has the same compelling feeling as a good TV soap opera. The author gets you immediately involved in the character's lives."

—*Bill Boggs,*
Syndicated Television Host

"*Seasons of the Heart* is a wonderful read with lots of romance between the covers."

—*Nikki Haskell,*
Hollywood Hostess

SEASONS OF THE HEART

JANE GARRARD

LANCASTER LOCKWOOD PRESS

ISBN: 1-887298-13-4

Lancaster Lockwood Press, 277 Park Avenue, 4th floor, New York, NY 10172

Cover design: Janice Rossi Schaus
Text design: Laurie Young

Manufactured in the United States of America
10 9 8 7 6 5 4 3 2 1

ACKNOWLEDGMENTS

To my wonderful parents, William and Ina Marlieb,
for their undying support and belief in me.

To my husband, Mike, and our
three precious children

To my sister Sue Lorimer; Bob Guccione;
and Kathy Keeton.

And special thanks to
Jim Martise
Steven and Sue Geller
Jack Artenstein
Editors Tracy Bernstein and Beth Lieberman
Jackie Markham
Joan Stewart, my agent
Sue Perry
Peter Bloch
Susan Meskil
Rona Cherry
Joan Bowman
Lee Gaynor
Bill Apfelbaum
Bob Costardi
Keith Ferrell
Alan Sonnenschein
Ivan Nesser
Bud Sperry
Ellie Miner

God asks no man whether he will accept life.
That is not the choice. You must take it.
The only choice is how.

—*Henry Ward Beecher*

ꙗ꙼ *Prologue*

*A*lexander Raines, dressed in a navy blue Brooks Brothers suit, sat in the front row, his light-blue eyes fixed steadily on his twenty-two-year-old daughter as she walked up to the podium to accept her college diploma. It was a humid June day, and Alexander could feel the sun warming the top of his graying head. He sat up more erectly in his seat as his only child retrieved the rolled piece of paper that signified her achievement.

Alexander thought of his beautiful Destiny. She had turned out to be everything he ever dreamed she'd be. He couldn't have asked for a more loving daughter. She was a beautiful young woman, the spitting image of her mother, with long dark hair and a curvaceous figure. Except for her deep blue eyes and dimples—they were clearly his. Both of his women were fiery and independent. Alexander could feel the tears well up in his eyes as he thought of her mother, the woman Destiny never had the privilege of knowing, the only woman he had ever truly loved. In his mind's eye, Alexander imagined himself back at the Hotel Dumois in New York City in the summer of 1969.

ꕤ

Alexander spotted Elena going down the hallway of the hotel corridor in her blue maid's uniform with her backpack slung over her shoulder. She was in a hurry, on her way to class. She barely took the time to speak with him. In fact, she didn't even remember who he was. After four years of being in love with her . . . he had found her at last, again, and she was even more beautiful than he had remembered.

He remembered how pigheaded she could be; the way she had acted on their second date when he had offered to give her money. "I don't take handouts from anyone," she said, as she stopped and turned around. She was dressed in jeans and a midriff-length shirt, and they strolled through Central Park holding hands. She looked at him harshly with her dark eyes. "No one. I don't care if I have to get down on my hands and knees and scrub the streets of Manhattan . . . if that's what it takes, I'll do it."

She was determined to make it in the world on her own. She had the most steely resolve he had ever seen, and he knew that nothing would hold her back. She wanted to become a doctor more than anything, and he knew that she had the brains and fortitude to succeed. Alexander sat down on the bench, as she continued to berate him. "You put that checkbook away." He had insulted her honor, when he had only meant to help.

"What do you expect me to do for that money?" she demanded in her slight Spanish accent. "Do you want me to spread my legs for you, right here in the park? Is that what you think of me? Do you think I'm some kind of common whore?"

She was so fiery; yet she could be so passionate and tender, so loving, and Alexander found it terribly exciting. She took life so seriously, but she also had a wonderful sense of humor. "I was only trying to help," said

2

Alexander, gazing up at her. He was so laid back compared to her. "Really. No harm intended. I'm sorry if I insulted you." He had more money than he knew what to do with, money he didn't do a thing for, money that his wealthy father had simply handed to him; while Elena worked so hard for every penny; and he wanted to help where he could. Alexander especially wanted to help those less fortunate, and he felt as though he had a calling to do so. He had a tender heart when it came to the needy and was always eager to give money to charity, to help in any way he could, so he thought, why not give her some? Why not make her life a little easier if he could? He didn't expect anything in return.

❧

"I have an ache, doctor. Could you take a look at it?" He teased her later that afternoon as they lay side by side on the park grass, taking a break from the sun, under a tree, gazing through the leaves at the sky.

"An ache? And where is your ache?" She looked at him in mock concern.

Alexander pointed to his groin, and began to grin. "I'll take off my pants so you can check it," he offered, and she smiled at him wryly.

"You're such a pervert."

"I thought that's what attracted you."

She sat up, pulled up some blades of grass and playfully threw them in his face.

"I'll get you for that," he threatened, as she took off running and laughing. Alexander finally caught her and pulled her with him to the ground. She was overpowered by his strength; his six-foot-two, to her petite five-two. He restrained her, and sat on her holding her down, while he tickled her nose with a blade of grass. A few minutes later he rolled her on top of him and they kissed; the kiss was long and lingering, and he never wanted it to end. He remembered making love to her for the very first time later that day. . . .

❧

Alexander smiled. He liked to think that had been the moment their daughter, Destiny, was conceived. He wished with all his heart Elena could have been here with him today. He would never understand why she left him, and there was a part of him that still deeply resented her for it. For years he had wondered what it was about him that had caused both his mother and the woman he was engaged to marry, to leave him. Why was it that *both* women he had loved so much had abandoned him? It didn't seem fair. At the age of forty-eight he still hadn't gotten over his mother . . . and didn't know if he ever would. He recently discovered an old photo of her in the attic, and as he held it in his hand, he began to tremble.

"Father . . . what's wrong?" Destiny asked him, as he sat numbly in front of the old cedar chest.

"Nothing."

"Who is she?"

"No one." He could barely look at his mother's face in the picture. He quickly tore up the old photo, as his daughter watched in bewilderment.

Alexander imagined Elena sitting there beside him wearing an elegant white suit and hat with her dark hair falling to her shoulders, sharing his pride and joy. She was the only other person who could have truly understood the depth of his feelings at this moment, who could truly have shared in his delight.

She would have been so incredibly proud of their daughter.

✦

"Destiny, I'm so proud of you. Congratulations!" Alexander exclaimed. He rose and embraced his daughter.

She hugged him back. "I can't believe that college is really over. I can't believe I'm officially a teacher." Her blue eyes glimmered in the sun.

✦

"Destiny, are you going to the party?" asked her roommate, Valerie, as she approached them. She was tall and lithe with short-cropped hair, her skin the color of light chocolate.

"Congratulations, Valerie."

"Thank you, Mr. Raines. What do you say, Des?"

"I'll meet you there a little bit later. My father and I are going out to brunch first."

"You know who's going to be there."

"Yes, I know, I know."

Suzanne and Alyssa joined them. "Let's go you two," said Alyssa, throwing back her curly mane of red hair. "We don't want to be late."

"No, I sure don't. Michael is meeting me there," added Suzanne, pinning her straight blond hair behind her ears. Destiny wanted some time alone with her father. "I'll meet you guys. You go ahead," she said, waving on her three closest friends.

✦

Destiny and Hayden left the party early and went to his dorm room for the last time before he cleared out his belongings. Hayden pulled Destiny down with him on his unmade bed. "Are you sure I can't convince you to come with me to Los Angeles?" he said, as he nuzzled her neck.

"We've been through this before. It's a moot point. I told you I want to live in D.C." Their lips met again as she ran her fingers through his strawberry blond hair. He stuck his tongue deep inside her mouth.

"You can always visit your father," he said in between kisses. "What about me . . . I'll be so lonely out there without you."

"It wouldn't be the same."

He began to undo her blouse. He had slipped off his pants. "Baby, please say you'll come."

There was a knock at the door. Destiny went to open it, and a stream of girls burst into the room, giggling away. It was a panty raid. They dispersed, wildly searching the room as Hayden protested and Destiny watched, laughing and cheering them on. "Got a pair," a redheaded girl exclaimed proudly, holding up Hayden's last clean pair.

"Hey, wait," Hayden shouted. He went running down the hall after them in his dirty boxer shorts. "They're brand new."

❧

Destiny knew Hayden had no other choice but to accept the job offer in Los Angeles. She cared deeply for him and hated to see him go so far away, but she never had any desire to accompany him. Her life and family were in Virginia, and she wasn't about to give them up for anyone, not even for her steady boyfriend of one year. Hayden was a brilliant engineer, and the sex they had was terrific. But she clearly wasn't in love with him. He was part of her college experience and nothing more.

❧

Father, I can't believe you did this. You just bought me diamond studs . . . and now this. You're the greatest. You're

the best father anyone could have. I love you so much."
Destiny threw her arms around Alexander and hugged him
tightly. Her father was the one person whom she deeply
loved. Alexander had bought her a beautiful silver
Mercedes for a graduation present. She had discovered it
sitting in the driveway the following morning after graduation. Alexander clearly spoiled his daughter, and Destiny
enjoyed every minute of it.

ॐ

"You're going to need a way to get to work, when you get
that teaching job. Let's take it for a spin." Alexander dug in
his jeans pocket, and threw the keys to his daughter.
Excitedly, Destiny unlocked the door and climbed inside.

"Now remember, this isn't a race car," Alexander said.
He knew his daughter had a propensity for speeding.

"Just sit back and relax. Trust me," she said, laughing.
She zoomed out of the circular driveway while her father
gripped the door handle fearing for his life.

✿ Chapter one

*P*epita stood at the doorway and gasped at the spectacle inside her friend Maria's apartment. She clutched her breasts with both hands. Her body quivering, she forced herself into the living room to retrieve the tiny girl. "Maritza, Maritza. What happened? What happened? Oh, dear Jesus. What happened? she said in her high-pitched voice, scanning the bodies of her best friend, Maria Ortiz, and Maria's fourteen-year-old son, Carlos. She felt the bile rise to her throat and turned her head away. She couldn't believe this was really happening. She bent down and lifted the blood-soaked child in her arms. At least she was unharmed. "Poor baby. . . . Poor baby . . . *todo esta bien, ahora.*" The child began to cry as Pepita scooped her up and ran with her back across the hall.

✿

"What am I going to do? I can't miss another day of work." Pepita said, and sighed, then turned to look at the little girl beside her. "Don't look at me with those big blue eyes." She gazed at the child tenderly. "I can't keep you. I just can't. I can barely afford to put food on the table for my own two boys. What am I going to do with you? No one

9

wants you." She sat up and pulled Maritza onto her lap. The child sucked noisily on her small fingers. Pepita thought long and hard. Alexander Raines, the man Elena had planned to marry, eventually came to mind. She would find him and tell him that little Maritza was his. She would track him down. She knew he lived somewhere in Virginia. She was sure he would take her in. Why hadn't she thought of him before. He was the answer to her problem. Elena had spoken of him often. She said he was kind and compassionate and very rich. Alexander Raines. "I have no other choice but to give you away," Pepita told Maritza, as she stroked the back of the little girl's head. Her hair was as soft as a rose petal.

Maritza babbled away mindlessly as Pepita spoke aloud. She sighed deeply. She stroked the child's tender cheek. "I always wanted a girl . . . and if I had a husband—" She tried to erase such thoughts from her head. She knew it was impossible for her to keep Maritza. Alexander had a lot of money and a kind heart. He could give her a good home.

～

"Mr. Raines? Alexander Raines?" Pepita said into the telephone, with hope in her voice.

"Yes. Speaking."

"Mr. Raines. My name is Pepita Gonzales. I'm a close friend of Elena's."

Alexander almost dropped the phone. He felt his heart jump. "Elena?"

"Yes."

He recalled Elena telling him that Pepita Gonzales had been a close family friend.

"Where is Elena?" He felt a small quiver on the back of his neck. "May I speak with her?" Alexander couldn't believe his good fortune. After two years—perhaps she had reconsidered and wanted to reconcile. He had never stopped loving her for a second. He was willing to take her back under any circumstance.

"Elena . . ." Pepita's voice sobered. "Elena is dead."

"Dead?" Alexander felt his throat constrict, and the tears form in the back of his eyes. "What happened to her?"

"She committed suicide."

Alexander gasped. He felt as if he'd been stabbed in the chest. He fought back tears. He had never imagined anything so awful. "But why?"

"She was a very unhappy person."

Alexander felt a tear escape and moisten his cheek. "What can I do for you?"

"There is something you need to know."

"What is it?"

"You and she had a child . . . a little girl. Her name is Maritza. She's only two."

The receiver slipped out of Alexander's hand and crashed on the table top in the study. His mouth fell open. He was in a state of shock.

"A child?" It couldn't possibly be true. "Why didn't Elena tell me?" Alexander had to admit that it was possible. They had had unprotected sex more than once.

Pepita breathed deeply into the receiver. "She was too ashamed. Elena was a very proud woman."

Is that why she had stopped seeing him? Good God, why hadn't she told him? They could have married and raised their daughter together. It didn't make any sense.

"If you come to the Hotel Dumois tomorrow at ten in the morning you can meet her. I'll bring her to work with me," Pepita said.

"I'll be there." Alexander hung up the phone. He took a deep breath. This was the last thing he ever expected.

11

✧

"Boys, boys . . . Diego, José, get out of bed. It's time to get up," Pepita hollered at her two young sons, who slept on an old couch across the room. She turned to Maritza, sitting on her bed. "I'll clean you up, and make you look real pretty so your daddy can't resist you."

An hour later she put on her blue maid's uniform, combed her thick ebony hair, then wrapped it into a knot and pinned it to the back of her head with a rhinestone comb. She traced her full lips with carmine lipstick and inserted her gold-loop earrings. She looked one last time at her features in the mirror, then turned around to look at the little girl on the bed all dressed up in the frilly pink dress a neighbor had given her. She glanced at the metal crucifix over the bed, mumbled a quick prayer as she crossed herself, then looked back at the child. "You look so pretty." She reached down and lifted the tiny girl in her arms. They both looked into the mirror above the dressing table. "He won't be able to resist you. I just know it."

Pepita balanced the child in her arms as she reached down and dabbed her finger on a bottle of cheap perfume. "Here, some for you and some for me." She touched the child's neck lightly and put a dab behind her ear. "Well," she sighed somewhat reluctantly. "We'd better be going, we have a long walk ahead of us."

The smell of onions filled the bleak hallway of the old tenement and followed Pepita the three flights down to the street. The staircase was filled with the sounds of a wailing baby and the familiar beat of the Spanish music that played nonstop. She stepped outside. It was a muggy, hot July day. Everyone seemed to be outside and the entire block bustled with life. The residents hung out of their windows or sat perched like pigeons on the fire escapes or front stoops. A small group of children played in the water from the fire hydrant. A couple of women Pepita knew waved at her as she made her way down the block.

The Dumois, where she was employed as a chambermaid, was located directly across from Central Park. They would have to take the subway, then walk the rest of the way.

Pepita shifted Maritza to her left hip. She was tiny and frail, but she knew this girl had the inner strength to endure whatever fate had handed her.

Pepita's brow was dotted with perspiration when she arrived at the Dumois a half hour later. She looked up at the Louis XVI-style building, only five stories high and decorated with French windows and balconies. She nervously carried the little girl inside hoping no one would see her. She released the small child from her throbbing arms as she stopped to speak to the desk clerk; and when she turned around Maritza was gone, nowhere in sight. Pepita felt her stomach flutter as she called out to her.

"Maritza . . . Maritza." She began to search the lobby, behind each camel's back sofa, in back of every club chair. She caught sight of the little girl heading through the glass double doors toward the street.

"Maritza! Maritza! Someone . . . please . . . stop her," she yelled, her voice trembling.

A handsome young blond-haired man with a mustache wearing a brown three piece suit quickly caught the child by the arm, just in time. Breathlessly, Pepita approached the man. They moved together back inside the lobby.

"Thank you . . . thank you," she said.

"She's quite a little handful, isn't she?" He gazed down at the child and was suddenly taken aback. *That face.* There was something so incredibly familiar about *that face. She was a beautiful child,* he thought. She held a striking resemblance to his beloved Elena. She had been a woman of extraordinary beauty. This was the first time Alexander had been back to the Dumois in two years, and it brought back bittersweet memories.

Alexander recalled the first time he had seen Elena. She used to work at this very hotel. He remembered her beautiful dark eyes and her lightly tanned skin. "Is this what you're looking for?" she said, holding a foil packet in her hand.

He'd blushed, quickly grabbing the wrapped condom out of her hand. He had been terribly embarrassed. She had been straightening out his room. She worked as a chambermaid on his floor. She was the most beautiful young girl he had ever seen, and he couldn't take his eyes off her. He just stood there immobilized, as if his feet were stuck in cement, thinking of something witty to say.

Alexander thought of the first time they'd made love, her silky nakedness against him; and the overwhelming passion that he felt for her, a passion he'd never felt for anyone before. No other woman had ever made him feel so content, so fulfilled, so happy to be alive.

Alexander had come from Virginia to New York to meet the little girl that Pepita Gonzales claimed was his. He extended his hand and introduced himself.

"Alexander Raines."

Pepita smiled at him, taking Maritza's hand so she wouldn't run off again. He was as handsome and charming as Elena had said he was. "I'm Pepita and this is little Maritza—your daughter."

Alexander found himself stunned by the words—your daughter. He was still in a state of shock. Could this beautiful little girl really be his? All the way up on the train he had considered having her tested to confirm his paternity, but he knew how inconclusive the tests were. He knew it was possible that she indeed was his. Elena told him he was the first and only man she'd ever been with. They had made love on numerous occasions. Alexander couldn't take his eyes off Maritza. He observed her blue eyes and dimples so similar to his own, and was suddenly filled with affection for this little child, and suddenly his lonely life seemed much brighter.

She looked so much like Elena it was uncanny. He still couldn't believe that he had a daughter. That he was someone's father. That he and his beloved Elena had had a child together, an adorable little girl. His only regret was that he hadn't known about her sooner. He wished that he'd been able to raise her since birth. He had already missed two whole years of her precious little life.

"Who's been raising my child the last two years?"

"Elena's mother, Maria."

Alexander thought of the only time he'd met Elena's mother, even though he'd felt as though he knew her well after everything Elena had told him about her. He could still picture the heavyset Spanish woman with the short gray hair standing inside her apartment door telling him that Elena never wanted to see him again. He remembered how upset he was; that horrible feeling in the pit of his stomach. He couldn't believe she was breaking it off with him. He'd thought they were so much in love; he thought they would be together always. Alexander could still hear the door closing shut before him. Maritza looked well cared for and he was grateful for that.

"Does Elena's mother know I'm the father? Where is she now?"

Pepita lowered her eyes and head. "She was murdered a few days ago."

Alexander looked at her, astonished.

"Murdered?"

Pepita exhaled deeply and said, "She was killed along with her fourteen-year-old son, Carlos. He was dealing drugs. He got involved with the wrong people."

Alexander vowed at that moment that he would keep the awful truth from his precious daughter, who was thankfully young enough to forget her past. He would shield her from all the ugliness in the world and give her a good life.

"I'm so happy I found you."

"She's so like her mother," Alexander said, as he gazed down at Maritza who was restlessly holding Pepita's hand. He still couldn't believe that she was his flesh and blood, made from his seed. "Is there a social worker involved in this case?"

Pepita shook her head.

"I'll get in touch with one."

"Please . . . don't," she pleaded. "If they get involved Maritza will end up in foster care. You may never get her. I don't want that."

Alexander agreed. The last thing he wanted was to fight a bureaucracy, for his daughter to be shuffled around from foster home to foster home. "Where can I reach you?"

Pepita gave Alexander her address. Alexander peered at his breathtaking child with the big blue eyes like his own and stroked her soft feathery hair. In response to his gentle touch Maritza began to smile.

🌺 Chapter two

The South Bronx, Two Weeks later

Pepita Gonzales looked wearily at the two-year-old. "We must be going. Your father is waiting outside in the limousine."

"No," Maritza cried.

Pepita studied the little girl carefully. She didn't ever want to forget her. Alexander had asked Pepita not to contact Maritza once he took her to live with him. He thought it best that the girl forget her past. Pepita reluctantly agreed, but it pained her to think that this was the last time she'd ever see the little girl whom she'd grown to love over the last two years.

"Pepe," the child cried.

Pepita's eyes filled with tears and she wrapped her arms around the little girl. "Maritza, you know you can't stay with me as much as I would like you to. You have to go live with your father. Please . . . don't make this any harder. Your father . . . he is a good man. You will have a good life with him." She reached for the little girl's hand. "Come on, grab Oso, your bear. We have to go." Maritza stubbornly refused and buried her head in Pepita's dark skirt. She wrapped her small arms desperately around Pepita's slender thighs and began to sob.

Tears fell from Pepita's eyes, as the child clung to her.

Pepita could sense Maritza's fear, and it tore at her heart. She hoped she had made the right decision by giving her to Alexander. But what other choice did she have? Maritza had no one else. *If only I could keep you,* she thought sadly, once again, but she knew it was impossible. At least her boys were old enough to take care of themselves while she worked.

She released the child's hold and placed her hands gently on Maritza's spare shoulders. "Do you have any idea how lucky you are? You are going to a great big house in the country with lots of green trees and a pond and grass for you to play in. You'll be with a daddy who loves you very much." Alexander Raines was one of the richest men in the state of Virginia. He had even offered to compensate her monetarily for reuniting him with his daughter, but she had refused his generous offer, as much as she needed it.

The official adoption would take a while, Pepita suspected, and in the meantime Maritza could live a decent life with a man who cared deeply for her. Pepita took Maritza's face in her hands. She was a beautiful child. Her hair was long and raven. She had large blue eyes, dimples, a small perfect nose, and lips as full and pink as a tulip in a face shaped like a heart. "We really must go." Pepita picked up Maritza's small suitcase and gave her a tremendous hug and whispered, "I love you very much. You remember that. You're going to have a good life, Maritza." She took the child by the hand and escorted her downstairs.

Pepita wiped a tearstain off the child's cheek as she handed the little girl over to Alexander, who had been leaning against the car. "You look lovely today, Miss Ortiz," Alexander said, as he crouched down to speak to little Maritza.

Maritza just stared at him coldly. In spite of her stand-offishness, Alexander wanted to wrap his arms lovingly around her and immediately claim her as his daughter.

He hadn't forgotten how feisty she'd been the one time he'd taken her and Pepita shopping in New York City shortly after they'd met. He had taken her to F.A.O. Schwarz and let her pick out anything she wanted, and then to De Pinna and Bonwit, where he outfitted her with a collection of party dresses. She had been extremely difficult and had refused to try on anything he'd suggested. She clearly had a mind of her own and was strong-willed for a child of only two.

"Would you like to take a ride with me in the limo?" The strong smell of his cologne wafted into her nostrils. She took an extra long whiff, sniffing him as if he were a strange new food, and Alexander suppressed a grin. "It's a beautiful day," he said and smiled, inhaling the clean air, gazing up at the boundless sky. "We'll have to go for a little ride to the airport. How does that sound?"

Maritza was too busy studying everything about her father to reply. She studied his wavy gold hair with its many peaks and valleys and the thickness of his eyebrows, the brushlike lashes which formed a canopy over his light blue eyes; the lines in his forehead, his strong face, his blond mustache, which was terribly intriguing in itself. Whenever he moved his lips it moved as if it had a life of it's very own. It completely mesmerized her. The temptation to touch him became too great, and he was very close. She poked two fingers into his mustache, then immediately withdrew her hand, breaking into giggles when he tried to bite it. "You try that again, and I'll bite your fingers off." He feigned seriousness but Maritza could see through him. She knew he was teasing her and she laughed, daring to touch it again. She pulled her hand quickly away when he tried to catch it with his mouth. "You're pretty quick, aren't you?" He met her eyes, then glanced at Pepita, who looked amused.

Brazenly, she went after the strange beast that lived on his face for a third time, but to her surprise he caught her fingers in his mouth and pretended to eat them making a silly grumbling noise and she giggled away.

Alexander widened his eyes in mock surprise, releasing her fingers from his mouth.

"More . . . more," she demanded, her eyes glistening in excitement.

"We'll have plenty of time for that. Right now we need to be going. We have a plane to catch."

"Take good care of her," said Pepita with tears in her eyes.

"You can rest assured." Alexander met her eyes and smiled. "She'll get nothing but the best. Thank you, Pepita, for giving me back my daughter."

Alexander tossed the small suitcase into the car, then climbed into it while Pepita gave Maritza a farewell hug.

"Portate bien, niña. Adios." She handed him the small girl and Alexander pulled her onto his lap. They waved good-bye to Pepita as the chauffeur began to drive.

Alexander turned to look at her. She looked so tiny sitting there buckled in beside him. "We're going to take a drive. We'll have a picnic along the way. We're going to drive to the airport and take a plane to Washington, D.C. Then we'll have my chauffeur meet us and drive us to Virginia. Do you have any idea where that is?"

She nodded her head and Alexander laughed, knowing she probably had no idea what he was talking about.

"You are quite bright, aren't you?" Maritza nodded again, and Alexander suppressed a chuckle.

They had a picnic of cheese sandwiches and potato

chips which they ate en route, a menu Alexander had purposely selected because he knew it was one of Maritza's favorites. Maritza's eyelids became heavy, and she rested her head against Alexander's arm.

She reminded him so much of Elena. He was so happy to have a part of the woman he loved. This wonderful little girl had come into his life by the grace of God and he was very grateful.

Maritza snored lightly, and a smile of contentment crossed Alexander's face. He looked out the window and sadly thought of his own childhood and how his mother had abandoned him when he was only six and how lonely and unhappy he had been; how he longed for her; how worthless and unloved he had felt. Maritza's mother, Elena, had done the same thing to her, more or less, and he could empathize deeply with the little girl. There was a part of him that was angry with Elena for doing that to their child. How could she have chosen to leave her? This precious angel. It was an act of pure selfishness, he told himself, and he would never be able to understand it.

No child should have to suffer that kind of loss. Alexander recalled how much he had loved his mother. He looked just like her, everyone said, with his blond hair and blue eyes. So many times he wanted to find her and ask her why, but whenever he broached the subject, his father begged him not to. "Just let her go," he told him, and Alexander felt he owed his father something. He had been the parent who had stood by him, and his loyalty had always been to him first and foremost.

✦

McLean, Virginia, May 1949

"Daddy . . . where's Mommy? She said she was going out for a little while. Where is she? Why hasn't she come back? She has to tuck me in my covers and read me my bedtime story. I want to hear the one about the girl who can make gold out of straw. That's my favorite!" he exclaimed, wide-eyed.

William Raines, wearing his black suit, stared down at his young son, Alexander. He was freshly bathed and sitting on top of his bed. He refused to slip under the covers until his mother returned home.

William was at a loss for words. Cecile, his wife of ten years, had left him today for another man, and she was never coming back. But he didn't have the heart to tell that to young Alexander.

"Where is Mommy? It's getting late. I want her to tell me a story and kiss me goodnight," demanded Alexander, becoming more defiant. "I want Mommy . . . not you!" He made a nasty face and stuck out his tongue at his father, and began to kick his legs and flail his arms.

"Stop that, young man!" William looked down at him furiously. He was thoroughly exhausted from his day and he was short on patience. "I said, stop that! Stop that, this instant!

"William attempted to restrain the boy. Alexander sunk his teeth into his father's shoulder and bit him.

"Ouch!" recoiled William. "You're mother's not coming back!" he said, and stood up and rubbed the painful spot on his shoulder, then walked out of the room and went downstairs to have a late dinner.

Night after night Alexander cried for his mother. "Is she mad at me because I gave away her coins?" Cecile had had a collection of rare old coins given to her by her grandfather, which she had lying on her dresser top, and young Alexander had taken the liberty of giving them all away to the neighborhood kids without asking her permission. Cecile had been furious and had verbally reprimanded her son.

"You didn't do anything wrong," said William. "You're a good boy." He sighed deeply. "Your mother . . . she's a rotten woman . . . a *worm*. You had nothing to do with her leaving. It's between your mother and me."

"Doesn't she love us anymore?"

William looked his son directly in the eye, and sighed, "I suppose not."

Alexander grew up thinking his mother never loved him, wondering how he could have been so unlovable that his own mother didn't even want him. Through an acquaintance he'd learned that his mother had remarried and had a new son, his half brother, whom she told that Alexander had been run over by a car and killed. Alexander had never gotten over it. He was completely devastated. She had wanted him dead—her own son; and she had never loved him. He buried his mother deeply away, as if she'd never existed at all . . . and never spoke of her again.

↙

Alexander watched Maritza peer out the window of the airplane. He squeezed the little girl's hand as the airplane took off. His mind began to wander thinking about the adoption that would not be finalized for a year. He hoped that everything would go as planned.

They arrived in Virginia a little while later. Theodore, Alexander's long-time chauffeur, picked them up at the airport. Theodore exited the main thoroughfare and drove the limo on the lonely stretch of road secluded by trees that led to Alexander's estate.

"Maritza, wake up dear," Alexander shook her gently.

"We've arrived at your new home." The little girl sat up, disoriented. They passed through the black iron gates and drove around the circular driveway with the water fountain toward the two-story mansion.

"Water!" Maritza exclaimed joyfully, peering out the side window.

"It's not for swimming," Alexander said, hating to disappoint her. "But we do have a pond in the back where we can go fishing. Perhaps a little later."

He took a deep breath. "It's been a long trip, and I need to get you situated. "Aren't you anxious to go exploring in the new house?" He met her eyes. "Wouldn't you like to see your new room? It's all yours . . . everything in it."

Theodore pulled the car to the front entrance of the house. Maritza's eyes widened at the size of it. When Theodore walked around to open the door, Maritza grabbed her bear and clutched it tightly.

The house had belonged to Alexander's father, a successful publisher, from whom he'd inherited his wealth. It was built in the late 1700s and was considerably lavish. Maritza immediately discovered the ornate doorbell, which she took the liberty of ringing repeatedly.

Mary's going to have an absolute fit, thought Alexander, as he made his way up the steps to the front door, but she'd better learn to control herself. He did not want anyone frightening Maritza, especially today. He was determined to make her as happy and comfortable as possible. The staff had been thoroughly briefed.

"Who keeps ringing that godforsaken bell. I heard you the first twenty times," grumbled Mary, Alexander's loyal employee for many years. She pulled open the door, was just about to yell at the child, but instead smiled fondly at her, then met Alexander's eyes. "How was the trip, Mr. Raines?" The heavy Irish woman with short red hair bent over to greet the little girl. "And this must be Maritza." She smiled, revealing the empty space between her two front teeth.

"No teeth," Maritza said, as she pointed to Mary's mouth. Alexander suppressed a chuckle. Mary was at a loss for words. She blushed.

"Maritza, you're not supposed to say things like that. Some thoughts we must ponder only in our heads." He could see that Mary was offended. "I'm sorry, Mary. No harm intended. Let's take a tour of the house," he said, trying to distract the child before she had a chance to further incriminate herself. "Come with me, we'll go up to your room first." Maritza's face brightened. She immediately lost interest in Mary's mouth. "It's upstairs." Alexander took her tiny hand in his and together they raced past the Regency long-case clock to the left and up the winding staircase with the beautiful mahogany balusters and intricately twisted white newel posts, stopping only once to observe the glittering chandelier that dangled above the white marble floor like a spider.

Alexander led Maritza into the room at the top of the landing. She seemed not to know what to look at first. In the center of the room was a large canopy bed with a fluffy white eyelet bedspread rimmed with ruffles that swept the floor. The matching canopy stretched like a balloon high over the bed. Soft white pillows in all shapes and sizes, embroidered with roses and trimmed in lace, were scattered on top of the bedspread. Maritza climbed up onto the bed and began to jump up and down, laughing.

The walls were covered in pink flowers and a plush pale carpet covered the hardwood floor. Alexander watched as Maritza climbed off the bed and pulled open a drawer of the white bureau across the room. It was filled with brand-new underwear in lavenders and pinks. There was a large closet filled with dozens of party dresses and

patent leather shoes. She ran into the closet and began trying on the shoes. Then she looked all around the room,
observed Alexander from the doorway, and continued to
explore.

She dashed to the dressing table and tugged on its
hand-sewn white ruffled skirt, then to the two night stands
matching the bureau, which flanked the bed. She seemed
fascinated by the lamps with frilly pink shades and the
bases made out of china, shaped like dolls. There was a
wicker rocking chair and sitting on it was an antique baby
doll dressed in a long white dress. There were shelves
around the room stacked with books, games, and stuffed
animals.

Martiza looked at the books and toys and tore them
from their shelves, and then crossed the room to the rocking
chair, picked up the doll and gently rocked it back and forth
like a baby. She looked at the doll's blue eyes, blond hair,
and long handmaid dress, as Alexander watched quietly
from the doorway.

He was so incredibly happy to have her there. She
filled the emptiness, filled the void in his life. *It was sheer
destiny that had brought them together,* Alexander thought,
and gazed at the child lovingly. "I'm going to call you
Destiny," he said softly. And from that moment on little
Maritza Ortiz became the most important person in
Alexander Raines's life, and one of Virginia's most privi-
leged children . . . Destiny Raines.

❧❋ Chapter three

"W hat's wrong?" Alexander asked Destiny, as she stepped into the house the next morning. "You look as if you've been crying. What happened?"

"I got a 'Dear John' letter from Hayden yesterday." Destiny always confided everything to her father. He was her very best friend. Hayden had found someone else out in L.A.; and even though she didn't love him, she hated the thought of being dumped. She was usually the one handing out the rejection, not receiving it, and she liked it better that way.

Destiny knew, however, that her father would be pleased that it was over between them; she knew he hadn't liked Hayden anyway, and thought he was too conceited. He hadn't liked any of her boyfriends up to date. None of them were ever good enough for her.

Destiny sighed. "I'll tell you the details a little later. Right now I need to get some sleep. It's been a long night. She had spent the night with her best friend, Valerie, and they stayed up all night talking.

Alexander gave his daughter a reassuring look. "I'm sure you'll have a new love by next week."

Destiny stopped on her way up the staircase and turned to him. "None of the guys I date can compare to you," she said with a weak smile.

It tore at Alexander's heart whenever his daughter was unhappy. He felt her pain deeply as if it were his own. It troubled him whenever he thought of how difficult things had been for her before coming to him.

The few times she'd inquired about her background, Alexander had told her that he'd adopted her when she was very young, and that he knew nothing of her prior history. He'd decided never to tell her he was her real father, as difficult as it was for him, fearing that then he'd be forced to tell her that Elena was her mother. He felt the past was better left forgotten. Alexander had always been open about everything else with his daughter, and he hated denying her the truth. There were so many times that he longed to tell her that she was his flesh and blood; a couple of times he'd almost given in, but he realized that it wouldn't have made a difference in their relationship. They were closer than any father and daughter could ever be, biological or not.

Destiny seemed satisfied with his response. She never pressed him further. Nonetheless, each time one of her interrogations was over, Alexander would breathe a sigh of relief. He wondered how long he could get away with telling her so little, and knew that someday she'd demand to know more. Alexander hoped that if she ever learned the truth, she wouldn't hate him for it.

Over the years Alexander had tried his best to make it all up to Destiny by spoiling her and giving her anything she'd ever wanted; but most of all he gave her his undying love and devotion. He instilled the belief in her that she could accomplish anything, as if no obstacle were too great.

There had been no doubt that Destiny had been a strong-willed child and it had taken every ounce of

Alexander's patience to be able to cope with her.

He put down the book he was reading in the study on the table next to him, he thought about Destiny and how trying she had been when she had first come to live with them. She was an active and inquisitive child. She had been like a tornado. Her motto had been search and destroy, and she had swept through the house devastating everything in her path.

⋰⋱

"Maritza . . . Maritza . . . what are you doing?" Alexander stood aghast in the doorway of his daughter's newly decorated bedroom. Destiny had taken the expensive antique doll and had suddenly, without provocation, thrown it to the ground.

He entered the room and picked up the broken doll. "You had no right to break this." She peered defiantly into his eyes, then pivoted around and angrily yanked at the curtains, pulling down the rod and removing the hinges from the wall.

"I won't tolerate this kind of behavior in my house." He looked down at her firmly. She was so tiny. *How could anyone so small and angelic-looking be so destructive?* he thought.

She looked up at him with tearful eyes. "I want Pepe."

"Well you can't have her so you may as well make the best of it."

She collapsed on the floor and began to sob. Alexander crouched beside her and began to stroke her long, silky hair. "Maritza, this is your home now. You never have to leave. I want you here with me always." He pulled her to him and held her for a very long time.

⋰⋱

Destiny and Mary grew very close. Mary was the nearest thing to a mother that Destiny had ever known. Still, Destiny gave Mary the biggest challenge of all.

One morning after the two had a particularly loud standoff, Alexander sat down with Mary in the dining room.

"Mary . . . Mary, you must find another way to deal with her. Toughness is not the answer," said Alexander.

"It's *all* that child understands, Mr. Raines. She's completely out of control—a good wallop would do *both* of us good. Your darling daughter has the face of an angel, but the soul of a devil—she's turned all of our lives upside down in only a matter of days."

"Mary, you must try and be patient—the child has been through a great deal. It's going to take her a while to adjust. We can't expect miracles overnight."

"I'd settle for one moment's peace. You can't take you're eyes off her for *even* a second."

Alexander and Mary suddenly heard a loud crash. Mary ran into the kitchen. Maritza had knocked over a pot of tomato sauce boiling on the stove. "Maritza . . . where are you? I know you're hiding somewhere in here. You just wait until I get my hands on you. You just wait," she grumbled, as she grudgingly began to wipe up the horrendous mess.

༈

Destiny had chosen to become a teacher because she couldn't decide what else to do with her life. She wasn't interested in continuing in school one moment longer than she had to. In fact, she had only attended the university in the first place to placate Alexander. He had insisted that she further her education and wouldn't take no for an answer. Destiny knew she was bright, but in high school and college she had been more interested in men than grades and her mediocre scores reflected her blasé attitude.

"Why don't you pursue teaching? You would make a wonderful teacher," her father said to her when she was forced to declare a major in her junior year.

Destiny gave him a wry look. "I don't know. I don't know what I want to do."

"It's something to fall back on. Later on if you find you don't like it you can do something else."

Destiny finally agreed not knowing what else to do with her life. Education was not a difficult major, would not require too much of her time, and seemed like a reasonable choice.

"You have an unusually special rapport with children," said Alexander. Children seemed to like her. She had always attracted them everywhere she went ever since she was young.

⤳

Destiny bubbled with unbridled enthusiasm the day the secretary from a school in the district called her in for an interview with the principal. "I'm not going to lie to you. Some of these kids can be very demanding," the principal, a middle-aged African-American man with cropped white hair and an ever present smile warned her, "and the families they come from," he frowned and shook his head, "they're not exactly your ideal. Many of them are headed by one parent, usually a mother who is struggling to make ends meet. These kids need a lot of love . . . and an unlimited supply of patience. They try you and try you and see just how far they can push you."

"I want to teach more than anything else," she blurted out. Destiny wondered what made her say that. She wasn't even sure she liked kids. She wasn't sure what she wanted, but she liked the challenge of competing for a job . . . any job, and this *was* her field of expertise. She stared intently into Mr. Devonshire's eyes.

"Please just give me a chance." She couldn't believe what she was saying. Maybe she was going a little overboard. Mr. Devonshire sat silently for several minutes, appearently mulling it over, while Destiny sat nervously crossing and uncrossing her legs.

"School starts in two weeks. That should give you ample time to fix up your room, prepare your lessons, get things in order."

"You mean I have the job?" Destiny had to restrain herself from lunging out of the chair. She had no idea that she'd just won the booby prize, or that she was the one who had just been duped. She didn't know that the last teacher had resigned because the class was too difficult for her to manage. Mr. Devonshire nodded at Destiny and smiled.

"I can start today," she said.

"Good." He rose from his chair. "I'll show you your room."

They walked down the hall, the principal clad in a gray suit with barely a thread of a tie; Destiny wearing flats, a brown leather shoulder bag, a long beige corduroy skirt, and navy turtleneck—all compliments of Garfinkel's. She wanted to look the part.

They came to a halt in front of the room. Destiny's mind began to race with all the things she had learned in her teacher training and was anxious to apply.

She glanced at the door imagining her name on it in bold black letters: **MISS RAINES, FIRST GRADE.** It made her feel special, important, and she felt good about herself. She could hear the chatter of children's voices all around her. She could imagine their eyes bright and attentive, all focused on her, in awe of her.

There was a broad window over the radiator overlooking the playground, a long dusty chalkboard, a big gray teacher's desk, and a handful of small desks with chairs for the children. "It doesn't look like much," Devonshire conceded. "We've ordered some more supplies so you'll at least have the basics."

She had landed her very first job, and she had done it all on her own. She was so proud. She just couldn't wait to run home and tell her father.

⌇

Naturally, Alexander was quite pleased when Destiny shared the good news later that night in the study.

"I'm so happy for you, sweetheart." He rose from the mahogany desk and hugged her tightly.

"I can't believe I really got it, the way he hired me right on the spot," said Destiny. She followed Alexander to the adjacent bar where he took a bottle of Schramsberg champagne from the shelf.

"Where did you say the school *was* in the District?"

Destiny hesitated for a few moments, reluctant to tell him, then quickly rattled off the address.

"That's a pretty rough neighborhood." He looked at her in concern.

"Father," she sighed, "stop worrying. I'll be fine."

"I have a friend who might be able to pull some strings and find you a teaching assignment right here in McLean."

Destiny shook her head.

"I suppose there's no talking you out of it. Well," he said, "I suppose this is cause for celebration." He poured some champagne for both of them.

The study was cluttered with books, and the fireplace was an intricately carved white mantel with crossed sabers above it. Alexander made his way to one of the William IV throne chairs in front of the fireplace and Destiny followed. They both sat down.

This was Alexander's favorite room. He eyed the bold Gallé blowout lamp on the dark table in between the chairs and the fine leather couch across from them. Alexander toasted his daughter.

"I know you'll be a wonderful teacher. You're deeply caring and bright and bubbly . . . and with that temper of yours . . . there's no doubt in my mind that you'll keep those kids in line." He laughed.

Destiny beamed, looking genuinely excited. "I know I can make a difference in these children's lives."

Alexander was suddenly pensive. He took another sip of champagne. Over the years he and his daughter had become the very best of friends; she had become his confidante and he preferred her company exclusively. They discussed everything imaginable; he had shared with her how he had inherited his wealth from his father, a successful magazine publisher; the trials of the businesses he himself had started which had subsequently failed.

It was now time to share with Destiny his most pressing lifelong dream, to someday open a safe house for abused and neglected children. He took a deep breath, then explained it to her.

"Father, that's such a wonderful idea. Why haven't you done it?"

He looked away somewhat ashamed, then sighed. "I've thought of it for quite some time. I just haven't gotten around to implementing it. You know how I tend to procrastinate. It's a terrible fault of mine, I'm the first to admit. Besides, I've started so many things, and they've ended up disastrously."

"But that doesn't mean that this would." She paused

for a moment. "I could even run it for you. I know I could." She met his eyes.

"You wouldn't have the time, not with your job."

She'd momentarily forgotten about it. "I could quit."

Alexander looked at her with surprise. "How can you quit? You haven't even begun. We'll both keep it in mind for a future endeavor, but for now we still have more celebrating to do. Right?"

"Right," Destiny answered and grinned.

୬

At twenty-two Destiny's beauty was unrivaled. At five-feet-six she was slender with a breathtaking face. She was riveting with her creamy skin, sable hair, and blue eyes. Sometimes men stopped on the street just to gaze at her. "You're a teacher? You're much too pretty to be a teacher," was a line she heard all too often from strangers and she wasn't quite sure how to take it.

Whenever Alexander looked at Destiny he was reminded of his beloved Elena and tears began to well in his eyes whenever he thought of how very much he had loved her; how very much he still missed her. He longed to tell his daughter the truth, that the woman he loved was her real mother, but felt it would be too disruptive to her life. Her past was too painful and ugly and he wanted to shield her from it.

For as long as he lived he would never forget Elena; her memory was still as sweet and fresh as a summer flower. He had dated many women over the years, had a few meaningless affairs, but no one could ever come close to her.

He had never loved any human being as much as he had loved her, except for his daughter. He had lost Elena, but he still had his darling Destiny—she was so precious to

35

him. So many young men had tried to steal her away but had been unsuccessful. He knew it was only a matter of time before she'd find someone she would love equal to him or more, and he knew that when that time came, he'd have no other choice but to surrender her or risk losing her forever.

↢

"I don't know how he puts up with me sometimes," Destiny said to Mary one late August afternoon. She knew she had a tendency to be self-involved and difficult and her father had always been so patient and understanding. She and Mary had grown very close over the years in spite of the fact that Destiny could be very outspoken at times and temperamental. But Mary always let her know she was loved.

Mary, her red hair now white, shook her head. "You weren't easy when we took you in. You *were* quite a little handful."

Destiny chuckled. "I remember I liked to have my way. I can't understand why he didn't give me back." Mary didn't say anything. She had been sworn to secrecy years ago.

"Mr. Raines has always been a very tolerant man."

"I can't wait to meet this woman he's been raving about. He's been talking about her for weeks. I keep hearing how talented and beautiful she is . . . how many languages she knows. They ought to be back soon. Father went to pick her up in the limo." Then Destiny leaned over and said in a low voice, "Just between you and me, he told me he's thinking of marrying her. Do you think he'll really go through with it? Of course, even though no one's asked for my opinion, I think it's a little soon for them to be thinking of marriage. They've only been dating a short time. But he keeps saying she's the one. He hasn't been this excited about anybody in years."

Mary's eyes widened in joy and surprise, and she grinned broadly. She looked at Destiny. "It's about time he settled down with someone. He's not getting any younger." Mary looked thoughtful, and chuckled. "He's too good a catch. If I were younger I'd marry him myself."

Destiny laughed. She couldn't picture the two of them together. "Then Theodore would be jealous," Destiny teased.

"My sweet Theo." Mary looked suddenly lost in thought, then smiled.

"I bet he'll announce their engagement tonight."

Mary shook her head as she cut into an avocado and scooped out the pit. "I guess we'll find out when he arrives." Mary looked up at Destiny. "Go run along and get ready. I'll finish up here."

Destiny glanced at the clock above the sink. The kitchen with the high ceiling was stark white. A large window over the sink looked out on the garden filled with summer flowers and a gazebo that overlooked the pond.

A half hour later Destiny came downstairs. She had on a brightly-colored peasant skirt, a white cotton midriff-length shirt, sandals, big gold-loop earrings, and her hair pulled back into a ponytail. She waltzed into the kitchen.

"Mary, has our guest arrived?" Mary tried her best to suppress her reaction. She knew Mr. Raines wouldn't be pleased with his daughter's attire—she wasn't dressed up enough, but Mary knew better than to say anything. After all, the girl was full grown.

"I expect Mr. Raines back momentarily."

୬

"Destiny," Alexander called from the entrance the moment

he stepped into the house. She hurried to meet him. "Destiny, darling," he said, his eyes glowing, his voice racing with excitement. "I want you to meet Julia Stoneworth." Destiny stopped short. Julia was much younger and much more attractive than she had anticipated. Destiny studied Julia carefully, who was not much older than she, maybe thirty at the most. Julia must be eighteen years her father's junior—*much too young for him,* Destiny thought. A bad feeling came over her. She suddenly felt as if she were in competition with this woman for her father.

"This is my daughter, Destiny . . . ." Alexander announced proudly, then wrapped his arm around the pretty blond woman's slender waist. He reeled her in closer, turned his head to look at her, smiling fondly. "Destiny, Julia is my fiancée. I just asked her to marry me, and she said yes. Isn't that wonderful?" Destiny couldn't believe he had really proposed. She'd been secretly hoping that he'd change his mind, and it would just remain the two of them forever. But he was really going to marry her . . . this woman she hardly knew.

In spite of how she felt, Destiny extended her hand graciously, and Julia accepted it. Julia's hand was limp and clammy. She had a cold look in her eyes.

Alexander smiled fondly at his daughter, then looked at Julia again, affectionately. He knew his daughter well enough to detect her disapproval. "I know this may seem a little sudden . . . Julia and I met only a month ago at the National Gallery."

"I was there with some friends for the new exhibit, and as soon as I spotted your father, I was in love," Julia said, the cold gaze she had shown Destiny now gone, replaced by a much softer expression.

"Julia is a gifted painter. You would love her work, Destiny. It's your kind of thing. She's a figurative painter.

You'll have to come to one of her shows. As a matter of fact," Alexander smiled proudly at Julia, "some of her work will be displayed in a new gallery opening up in New York next month." He looked at Julia. "What was the name of that gallery, honey?"

"The Frankin," she replied. She looked at Destiny. "I'd love for you to come to the opening."

"And a friend is trying to get her work into the Whitney."

Who cares? Destiny wanted to shout. Destiny didn't care where this woman's work was displayed. It could have been along the roadside for all she cared. A small smile played around the corners of her mouth at the thought. She imagined Julia and her father sitting alongside the road like two bums trying to solicit passersby. She released a small chuckle.

"What's so amusing?" Alexander asked, smiling.

"It's nothing," she said, waving him off.

How did her father know Julia's work was her kind of thing?

Destiny had her doubts. *Apparently she is your kind of thing,* she thought to herself. She never heard of Julia Stoneworth . . . and wished she never had. Julia was no one special as far as Destiny was concerned, and she resented the fact that her father was treating Julia as if she were Rembrandt or Picasso.

She's just a common mortal like the rest of us, she wanted to blurt out.

"A mutual friend introduced us," he added.

The two of them were engaged to be married. This woman was going to be part of her life whether she agreed to it or not.

Julia Stoneworth hadn't made a good first impression on

him, either, Alexander remembered. There was something Alexander didn't like about Julia when their friend Katharine introduced them—in spite of the fact that he found her very attractive. And then it suddenly dawned on him that by no fault of her own, she reminded him too much of his mother, Cecile, and he found himself wanting to avoid her at all costs.

After they said their hellos, Julia had followed Alexander around the gallery like a loyal pet. She had seemed determined to put him at ease. When the two began to chat further, Alexander found her personality clearly her own—and nothing like his mother's—even though both women were socialites. His attraction to her grew stronger, and he began to find the familiarity strangely appealing.

Both Julia and Alexander shared a love of art. Alexander, who had always had a passion for painting, was completely enthralled with Julia's work, her use of muted colors and unusual shapes. He thought she was a very talented artist and respected her greatly for her ability. She was also brilliant and well read and from a distinguished D.C. family. They shared a lot of the same common interests, and before he knew it, he had proposed marriage, and she had accepted him.

Julia was the total opposite of Elena. Alexander desperately wanted to break free of the past and thought by marrying Julia and starting over he would at last be able to forget Elena.

༄

Destiny watched Julia as she launched into an animated monologue about the exhibit. There was a condescending air about her which Destiny found offensive. Destiny could see that Julia was quite attractive—although her features were small and sharp. She had limpid blue eyes that looked almost surreal. She was a large-framed woman and Destiny guessed her height to be around five-eleven. She dressed smartly in a navy suit, matching pumps, her hair pulled tightly into an elaborately braided knot with large pear-shaped diamond earrings and an engagement ring to match.

Her strong perfume permeated the room; it made Destiny want to gag. She could barely breathe when she followed them into the study where Alexander offered everyone a drink.

"Julia?"

"Vodka on the rocks," she replied. Alexander poured Julia and himself the same and poured a glass of chardonnay for Destiny.

"Before dinner I'll give you a grand tour of the house," Alexander said as he placed an arm around Julia. They walked over to the leather couch in the center of the room and sat down.

Destiny felt like an outsider in her own home. Her father was so gentle and sweet and Julia seemed rather arrogant. She couldn't understand the attraction. Her father wasn't shallow, nor was he stupid; surely he could see beyond this woman's attractive face and expensive clothes.

After they sipped their drinks they went on the grand tour. Julia made few comments about the house, but lots of disapproving faces. Then the three sat down for dinner at the long mahogany table in the formal dining room.

The entire meal was eaten in awkward silence with Alexander struggling to make conversation.

✍

Destiny was restless and unable to sleep the next morning. She climbed out of bed, her blue silk robe tied around her waist, and went down the long gray-carpeted hall to Alexander's bedroom.

"Father . . . Father?" She said as she knocked softly on his door.

Getting no response, she gently pushed open the door and walked into the bedroom. She crossed the room and stood beside the carved oak testered bed. The footboard was carved with panels of foliate strapwork. The motto "Lord have mercy upon me," was carved into the wood near the spot where Alexander slept. *And her father will need the Lord's mercy if he marries Julia,* thought Destiny.

"Father, wake up, we need to talk," she said. Alexander's eyes fluttered open, and he pulled himself upright against the headboard, then glanced at the clock on the matching end table.

"Darling, it's only six A.M., what's troubling you?" He reached over and flicked on the dim light.

"You can't marry her," she blurted. "I don't like her."

"Destiny, how can you even say such a thing? You don't even know her. You have to give Julia a chance. Come sit down."

Destiny lowered herself into the chair next to the bed. She recalled the many times she'd poured out her heart to this man.

"You can't judge someone so quickly. Julia is a wonderful woman. She has a brilliant mind; there's virtually no subject she can't discuss. She's well traveled and educated. As a matter of fact she was graduated from Vassar. She's a fabulous painter and a very gifted artist. And she comes from a very prominent D.C. family. Her father was a senator. She's a little reserved, I'll grant you that. You have to understand that about her. It takes her a while to open up. She's not the open book that you are, my dear." Alexander paused and breathed deeply. "I really think you'll like her

42

once you've spent some time with her and get to know her."

"I don't want to get to know her." Destiny defiantly crossed her arms.

"Don't be so judgmental. She's just a little shy."

"Arrogant would be more accurate."

"I'm sorry you don't approve, but then again I don't recall asking for your consent," said Alexander firmly. "I'm going to marry Julia at Christmastime. You'll just have to adjust to the idea."

Destiny could feel tears forming in her eyes, and she turned her head away from her father.

"I've waited a long time for this, for someone special to come along. Please . . . try and understand. Just because I've fallen in love with Julia doesn't mean I love *you* any less." Hearing him confess his love made her feel even more vulnerable and she gulped down a sob.

"You will always be very important to me," he said.

But it's been just the two of us for so long . . . she wanted to say. *I don't want to share you with anyone, especially someone like her.*

"I'm convinced that once you two get to know each other— every friendship takes time." Destiny rose from the chair and quickly left the room.

"Destiny . . . please . . . don't be so unreasonable," he called out to her.

❧ *Chapter four*

"*I* don't think your daughter approves of our getting married. I don't think she approves of me, *period*," Julia told Alexander as they ate dinner a few nights later at the Willard Intercontinental Hotel. Julia didn't care for Destiny, either. It was obvious to Julia that Destiny was a spoiled brat, who was used to getting everything her own way. And she wasn't exactly Miss Cordial. She had made her feel very unwelcome the night they met. It was obvious that the girl felt threatened.

"Give her time. She's probably a little jealous. After all, she's had me all to herself for quite some time. I'm sure you two will be great friends once you get to know each other."

Julia seriously doubted it. "I'm not so sure."

"Julia, don't look so dejected. My daughter, I'll admit, can be a little headstrong at times but always comes around to her senses, trust me. I'm not worried in the least. Let's not dwell on it. It's a beautiful night. Let's take advantage of it and go for a walk. I might even buy you a present." He grinned at her. "That is, if you're good."

Julia met his eyes, smiling back wryly. "I'm always good, Alex. I thought I already proved that to you."

"What do you say?"

"I say let's go for a walk and then get a room."

Alexander rose from his chair and went to help his

fiancée. Their eyes met and held. She was a beautiful and exciting woman. He took the liberty of running his hand through her mane of long blond hair. He placed his hand gently on the small of her back.

"Skip the walk," she mumbled playfully into his ear. And he smiled.

Alexander admired her elegant white suit and studied her from head to toe. She had wonderful taste in clothes and was a very sophisticated woman. He was proud to be in her presence. He wrapped an arm around her waist, and they left the dining room together.

～

"I need to look for a new job," Destiny told Valerie during a break in the teachers' lounge. She was totally exasperated with the kids in her class. They wouldn't listen to a thing she said. The noise level was unbearable. She had absolutely no control over them. They were like a herd of wild animals.

"I can't do this another day," she said. "Every night I leave with a splitting headache."

"That's why they invented aspirin—for teachers."

"I'm just not cut out for this profession. Those little monsters are really getting to me."

Valerie was busily grading papers and not looking up as she spoke. She took a bite of her tuna sandwhich, which was lying on a piece of crinkled foil next to her. "Teaching takes a lot of patience, I'll give you that," she said.

"I don't think I have any left. I didn't have much to begin with," said Destiny. She took a sip from her can of soda, which by now was lukewarm and fizzless.

"What am I going to do with my life?" Destiny thought a moment, then said, "What about a career in fashion?"

Valerie shook her head. "Nope, Des . . . you'd better try again. I don't think fashion's your thing."

"Are you implying that I have no taste?"

Valerie looked up from her work, pushed her black-rimmed glasses to the end of her nose and looked over the top. "Take it from me, girl, you'd better stick to teaching."

Destiny laughed. She appreciated her friend's brutal honesty, even though sometimes it hurt her feelings.

"How do *you* do it?"

"Drugs, tranquilizers . . . whatever I can get my hands on," teased Valerie.

I need my own apartment, thought Destiny. *I need my own space.* That would be a good place to start . . . then definitely a change of career. But who else would ever hire her? She wasn't qualified to do anything else but teach.

✒

Alexander pulled Julia closer to him in bed and ran his fingers through her flowing hair. They had just finished making love. She looked wonderful nude. Her small breasts were firm and round and her slender body was fit as a result of her many years of training at the Royal Academy of Ballet. He loved the taste and feel of her milky flesh. He loved her mind, listening to her romance him in three languages, and the idea that they were married.

After all these years he was at last beginning to put Elena behind him. *Mrs. Alexander Raines*—he loved the sound of it—and he was filled with pride and joy to have someone as special as Julia as his wife.

Julia was truly gifted in the art of lovemaking and went out of her way to please her new husband.

She turned to look at him, her translucent blue eyes meeting his. "Don't you think it's about time Destiny moved out of the house?"

The two women hadn't gotten along since Julia moved in five months ago. They either didn't talk or when they did an altercation always ensued. They didn't seem to see eye to eye on anything. Destiny didn't seem willing to accept another woman into her father's life. She had seen Julia as a rival from the start.

"Destiny will move out when she's ready," Alexander said and planted a small kiss on the top of Julia's sweet-smelling head. "Besides I like having her around. I'll miss her when she's gone."

He smiled at that comment, and Julia rolled onto her back. *God help me,* she thought, as she gazed at the ceiling. If only Destiny were gone everything would be perfect. That girl was nothing but trouble. Girl, that was exactly what she was. She didn't deserve to be called a lady.

She didn't deserve one half of all she had. All those fancy schools and lessons didn't fool her. Destiny ought to be cleaning the mansion, not living in it. Alexander had confided in her about his daughter's past. He had even told Julia things Destiny herself did not know, swearing her to secrecy. The girl had been born trash, and that's what she always will be. *You are what you're born and nothing can change that,* thought Julia, with a self-satisfied look on her face.

How could he have ever taken in that gutter rat? she thought, placing one hand under the satin pillow.

৵

"I just came to say good-bye," said Mary, her eyes red-rimmed with tears as she wandered into the garden. Destiny put down the pink begonia she was just about to plant and looked up at the old woman in surprise. Mary was dressed in her best black outfit and looked like she were about to attend a funeral.

48

"Good-bye?" Destiny stood up, her legs and tennis shorts stained with dirt. "Good-bye? Mary, what are you talking about? Why are you all dressed up like that? Where are you going?"

Mary turned her eyes away and answered in a somber voice. "Mrs. Raines has fired me and Theodore. She asked us to leave by noon."

"Fired? By noon?" Destiny felt a bolt of anger shoot through her. She took a deep breath. She could feel the blood rush to her face. "She can't do that. She doesn't have the authority." Destiny met Mary's eyes. "Does my father know?"

"She told me she makes the household decisions. She said she has people of her own she wants to employ."

Destiny held her tongue. The expletives that came to mind about her stepmother were less than flattering, and she knew Mary did not condone her swearing. "Where is my father?" Destiny began to march angrily toward the house.

"It's no use. He flew to New York for the day; some urgent financial matter he had to attend to."

"Where is she?" Destiny's face contorted in anger. She threw open the French doors. "Julia," she hollered. "Julia, where are you?" She glanced at Theodore who stood with his bags packed by the front door. "I'll take care of this," she reassured him, attempting a smile.

Julia stood at the top of the stairway in her creamy silk peignoir. It was past noon and she wasn't dressed yet. "Is it necessary to scream at the top of your lungs?" The two women's eyes locked. "Civilized people communicate in a quiet manner face to face. If there is something you want to discuss with me then please come upstairs, " she said coolly, and turned and walked away.

Destiny, infuriated by the snide remark, stomped up

the winding staircase. She could feel her heart pounding as she entered her stepmother's room without the courtesy of knocking.

"Don't you believe in knocking? It *is* the polite thing to do. I don't think it's too much to ask," said Julia in her icy-sweet southern voice.

"Why did you fire them?" Destiny demanded, glaring at her. "You had no right to do that. I won't allow it."

"It's already been done," shrugged Julia matter-of-factly. "I have a staff of my own that your father agreed I could bring with me once we were married."

"My father agreed to this?" Destiny's eyes widened in astonishment. "He would never agree to firing Mary and Theodore. They're like family. He's not the kind of man to just discard people. He would never agree to such a thing. You must have misunderstood."

"No, I'm afraid he left these matters up to me. They're not any of your concern."

"But it *is* my concern when you insist on throwing my family out into the street. How can you be so ruthless?"

"I gave them a full month's pay." Julia glanced at the clock. "I'd love to stand here and chat," she said, as she feigned a small smile, "but my decorator's coming at twelve-thirty." Julia turned to go to the bathroom, then pivoted back around. "Would you mind asking Mary to prepare something for lunch before she leaves? The new cook won't be arriving until tomorrow, and Mr. Frank, the decorator, likes a good snack before he begins working. Helps his creativity. I'm sure you understand. I don't want him thinking about food. I want him concentrating on wallpaper." She flashed Destiny a forced smile as she slipped off her robe, tossed it carelessly on the Louis XV chair, and disappeared into the bathroom.

"Bitch," growled Destiny through the door. Her temper

flared. She could feel her heart pound and face flush and she suddenly had an overwhelming urge to hurl something at the woman. The blue and white early Ming ewer on the bureau only an arm's length away, one of Julia's prize possessions, was just too tempting. Out of anger Destiny deliberately knocked it off the top.

She scurried out of the room as it crashed on the polished wood floor.

Destiny begged Mary and Theodore to stay. "Please . . ." she begged them as they stood at the front door waiting for a cab. "There's been a misunderstanding. Believe me, my father would never approve of this. He'll be absolutely heartbroken if you leave. Please reconsider. Please say you'll at least think about it. Stay at least until he gets back. We love you both very much." She threw her arms around them, one at a time, and they both held back tears.

"She would make it impossible for us to be happy here anymore," said Mary, and Theodore nodded in agreement. "We can't stay in a place where we're not wanted, where we're treated like nothing more than servants."

"But we *do* want you. Father and I want you very much."

"But before you know it," Mary heaved a sigh, "you'll be getting married and going away, your father will be off on some new business venture, and we'll be left at Julia's mercy. Julia doesn't want us and wouldn't treat us well." She grabbed Destiny's hand. "Sweet child . . . please try and understand."

"Cab's here." Destiny choked back a sob as Theodore opened the door and carried out the luggage. Mary pulled Destiny into her soft embrace and held her. "We love you very much." Destiny, tears rolling down her cheeks, held Mary tightly.

"I love you, too," Mary said, her voice quivering.

Destiny ran to hug Theodore who stood waiting outside the cab. She hugged him with deep affection.

"Come and visit us. We'll let you know where we'll be staying," said Mary, wiping a stray tear off her cheek.

Destiny clenched her mouth and nodded as they climbed into the car and drove away; her hatred for Julia escalating with each passing moment.

～

The limousine met Alexander at the airport, and to his surprise, Theodore wasn't there as usual to greet him. There was another man named Nicholas, a much younger man, with platinum blond hair instead of gray.

"Where's Theodore?" asked Alexander, looking around as if he expected him to pop up from behind the car at any moment. He thought it odd he wasn't there.

In over forty years he hadn't missed one day and Alexander missed the warm reassuring smile that always welcomed him home from a trip.

"I'm driving for him tonight."

Alexander's brow wrinkled in concern. "He hasn't been taken ill, has he?" Nicholas helped Alexander into the back seat and took his black leather briefcase and suitcase. He'd been instructed by Julia not to say anything.

"He's fine, sir. Nothing to worry about. How was your flight?"

"Tiring." He was unwilling to share his woes with the strange young man, guessing that Theodore simply had another matter to attend to. "It's been a long day."

Less than an hour later they arrived at the mansion. It was a warm spring night and the air was fragrant and still. Alexander, clad in a dark suit, entered the front door, and Nicholas followed with his briefcase and small suitcase.

Destiny scampered in from the study to greet him.

"How was your trip?" she asked quickly. "I'm sorry to burden you like this, the minute you step in, but I must talk to you right away. Before Julia comes down." She glanced at Nicholas as if he were intruding; he took the hint and went back outside.

"Is something wrong? You look upset." He reached out to stroke the side of her face. "You've been crying."

Destiny lowered her head, then lifted her chin. "Julia fired Mary and Theodore. I tried to talk them into staying but they wouldn't hear of it; they said they didn't want to stay where they weren't wanted. You didn't agree to such a thing did you?"

Alexander's face grew pale. He looked at her, aghast. "She *fired* Mary and Theodore? Of course I didn't agree. You know I would never agree to such a thing." He could feel his stomach tighten. "Whatever possessed her to do such a thing?"

"I didn't think so. She's bringing in her own staff."

"I see," said Alexander. "She asked if it would be all right if she could bring some of her staff here, but she never mentioned firing Mary and Theodore." Alexander felt terrible; he couldn't believe Julia would do such a thing. He specifically recalled telling her how much Mary and Theodore had meant to him, how they were like family. He looked down at Destiny, who was about to cry. "Don't worry, I'll just call them and tell them it was a terrible mistake, that Julia didn't mean to fire them. I'm sure they'll understand." Alexander took a deep breath. He was completely exhausted after a long day of trying to sell a new invention he'd come up with—he dabbled in so many different projects—and didn't really feel like dealing with any of this right now.

Destiny forced a weak smile. "Don't look so sad." Alexander wiped a tear off her cheek. "Things always have a way of working out." Tiredly, Alexander dragged himself up the winding staircase, which seemed to go on indefinitely, looking for Julia.

Julia threw open the bedroom door, facing Alexander as if he were the matador and she the bull, as soon as she heard him coming. "Look what she did. Look what that precious daughter of yours did. I purposely left it for you to see." She pointed to the mess on the floor. "Out of anger she broke my Ming ewer. You know how much that piece meant to me," Julia said, as she glared at Alexander. "You do know it's irreplaceable. It's one of a kind. You've got to make her move out before she destroys everything that means anything to me. I can't live like this!"

"Calm down, Julia, please, calm down, get control of yourself," Alexander reached out to her, and she recoiled. "I'm terribly sorry. I know how much it meant to you, but Mary and Theodore were equally important to Destiny and me . . . they're also irreplaceable."

Julia looked away from him, then met his eyes. "Let me explain . . ."

"There is nothing to explain." He cut her off. "You did fire them, didn't you?"

Julia nodded. "There was no longer a place for them here."

"I beg to differ with you. There *is* a place for them . . . there still is."

"You can't be serious. You're not thinking of hiring them back?" She looked at him in disbelief.

"I suspect it's already too late for that." He looked away fighting back emotion. "But I'm certainly going to try."

"But we don't need them. Besides, I've already replaced them."

"They'll always be needed here. They're my family and I love them. And as far as I'm concerned, they're welcome just to live here."

Julia looked appalled. "You've got to be joking!"

"I've never been more serious."

"You're completely out of your mind." She huffed. "Well, it seems as if your mind's made up. She crossed her arms. "Then there's nothing more to say." She took a deep breath. "You're always siding with that girl against me. It's been that way since the moment I moved in."

"That's not true," said Alexander, shaking his head. "But in this particular instance I happen to agree with my daughter. You had no right to do what you did. And about the vase . . . I'll talk to her about it. She'll have to make it up to you somehow. That kind of behavior, I agree, is inexcusable. Now, if you don't mind I've had a difficult day and I'd like to unwind." Alexander loosened his blue silk tie.

"I'll go down and fix you a drink," Julia said.

᛭

Julia and Destiny were constantly fighting; and it seemed as though every night after work or play, whichever demanded Alexander's attention, he had to settle some matter or another. He hadn't had a day's peace since the two women met, and he wondered if he ever would. He was sick of being the referee in their battles. He collapsed onto the bed and buried his throbbing head under the pillow.

❧ Chapter five

"**Y**ou taste so good," whispered Nicholas, as he worked his lips down Julia's milky flesh.

Almost frantically, she hoisted herself on top of him, leaned over to grab his head with both hands and stuck her tongue deep inside his mouth. He held onto her hips. "Oh, God," she moaned, rocking herself back and forth, digging her long fingernails into his upper chest. He flinched in pain. "Don't stop," she cried, "not now." Her muscles began to spasm and contract as her back arched, and Nicholas did all he could just to hold on to her.

❧

With the after school meeting canceled and rescheduled for another day, Destiny was able to return home earlier than she'd anticipated. It was late afternoon and after grabbing a quick snack from the kitchen, feeling fatigued, she decided to lay down for a short nap before dinner and before she began grading papers and preparing her lesson plans for the next day.

On the way to her room she remembered that her father had asked her to tell Julia that he would be delayed in California an extra day. She dreaded telling Julia anything at all; she still hadn't forgiven her for firing Mary and Theodore who refused to come back even after

Alexander had made a personal visit to their new residence to plead his case. And it riled her that she had to recompense Julia for the piece she'd broken by paying her a little bit each month, even though Destiny knew she'd been wrong.

Destiny knocked on the door of Julia's room, but there was no answer so she took the liberty of walking in unannounced, guessing that Julia was probably taking a bath as she usually did in the late afternoon after hours of painting in her studio. She wasn't the least bit prepared for the sight that greeted her—Julia, stark naked on top of Nicholas, her head thrown back, her long blond mane sweeping his legs as she cried out in pleasure. The two lovers failed to notice Destiny. She quietly slipped out of the room and bolted to her bedroom. *Poor Father,* she thought. *How could she do that to him?* He loved Julia so much, gave her everything she wanted, and she had made a mockery of their marriage. Destiny had to tell him, even though she knew he would be devastated. She had to show him what Julia really was—a deceitful, self-involved tramp. How could he have married her? Destiny could see through her from the beginning. She sat down on the edge of her bed trying to catch her breath. *How will I break it to him?* she thought. There was simply no way of telling him without breaking his heart, but as far as she was concerned she had no other choice.

ﾐ

"Father, I must talk to you alone, tonight after dinner," said Destiny, the night her father returned from his trip, as he lumbered up the endless steps to change into something more comfortable. "Meet me out in the gazebo at eight," whispered Destiny, fearing that Julia who was somewhere in the large house might overhear.

"Is there a problem at school?"

"No."

Alexander sighed. "Are you two at it again?

❧

At eight o'clock sharp Destiny stood in the gazebo gazing at the pond. The water glistened beneath the muted sky. She crossed her arms over her black T-shirt and paced nervously back and forth. She absolutely hated to tell him, but she simply had to . . . he had a right to know.

She tried to imagine his reaction. Knowing her father he would receive the news calmly and not say anything much at all. But inside she knew he'd be terribly hurt.

At ten after eight, Destiny heard her father walking toward her. She turned around and noticed that he looked much more relaxed than he had earlier. He wore his tan Bermuda shorts and a blue Ralph Lauren shirt.

"I just love these spring nights," said Alexander, inhaling the fresh air as he joined her. They sat down together on the bench. Destiny couldn't seem to sit still and got up and began to pace. "Father," she took a deep breath, "I have something to tell you and it's very difficult for me to say. I really don't know how to say it at all." She looked away from him, agitated.

"The direct approach has always worked well in the past, so why don't you try it this time."

Destiny lowered her chin, crossed her arms again. "Julia . . . Julia is not what you think. She's not what you think she is at all."

Alexander met her eyes curiously.

Destiny exhaled. "Julia is sleeping around on you."

Alexander suppressed a grin. He didn't believe her. He knew Destiny hated her stepmother, but this was really sinking low. Anything to discredit her. "What makes you say a thing like that?"

"I'm telling you the truth." She could tell he didn't believe her. "I caught her in the act. I walked in on them . . . her and Nicholas." Tears filled Destiny's eyes.

Alexander could see she was serious, that she meant what she said. A lump formed in his throat. He couldn't believe what he was hearing.

"I didn't want to have to tell you." She rubbed her forehead. "But I thought I should. I thought you should know. I thought you would want to know." She looked at him, tears cascading down her cheeks.

Alexander was at a loss for words. He stood up and turned away from her. He needed time to think. Julia and Nicholas. Julia and . . . anyone. He felt terribly hurt and angry—betrayed. How could she do this to him? He had put all his trust in her. Why did the women he loved always betray him, cause him such heartache? Hadn't he been through enough? First his mother, then Elena . . . now Julia. He had been a fool to believe in her, believe that somehow she'd be loyal to him and that things would be different this time. He put his hands in his pockets and began to pace.

"I'm so sorry. This must be so difficult for you. She'll probably deny the whole thing. That's just like her."

"You'll have to excuse me." Alexander left before his daughter had a chance to say anything else.

She followed him into the house and fifteen minutes later she could hear him yelling behind the closed bedroom door. She could hear Julia crying, asking him how he found out, pleading for forgiveness, telling him it was a terrible mistake and that she would never do it again. Destiny went to her room, changed into her nightgown, and climbed into bed hoping she would fall asleep.

ॐ

The next morning Julia, her face red and blotchy from all the crying she'd done the night before, and looking as if she'd just stepped back from the edge of insanity, stormed into Destiny's unlocked bedroom. "You stinking little bitch," she breathed into Destiny's face, and Destiny's deep blue eyes sprung open in alarm. Julia's face was so flushed and contorted she looked as if she might commit murder. Destiny, her heart caught in her throat, suddenly feared for her life. She immediately pulled herself up and recoiled against the headboard.

"Are you happy you little bitch? It's what you've wanted all along, isn't it?" Some of Julia's spittle landed on Destiny's cheek, and she wiped it away with the back of her hand. "You think you're so righteous, you little gutter rat." Julia plopped herself down on the bed. "You think you're Miss Prim and Proper, that you're so perfect. You never do anything wrong, do you? Well," she huffed, "let me tell you something . . . you're trash because you come from trash . . . and nothing can ever change that."

"What are you talking about?"

"What are you talking about?" Julia mimicked her, contorting her face. "You've always wanted to know about your background, right? But no one would ever tell you anything? Aren't you just a little curious why? Hasn't it ever dawned on you? You really are a stupid bitch. Well, guess what," she stuck her neck out like a goose, "it's your lucky day. I'm going to have the distinct pleasure of telling you."

"You know?" Destiny clutched her chest. She could feel her heart beating a mile a minute. *Father knew all along but never told me? Why would he do a thing like that? He's always been so honest.* "How do you know? My father doesn't even know."

"Like hell he doesn't. Of course he knows. You're even more naive than I thought if you really believe that. He

61

knows all right. And now I know, too. Everyone knows but you, princess. How does that make you feel? Dear Daddy never told you the truth."

Destiny couldn't believe what she was hearing. She could feel the anger course through her veins. How could her father have denied her the truth about her background? She had asked him to tell her on more than one occasion, and he always said he didn't know. Why did he want to keep it from her?

"He never wanted you to know. He thought it would be too painful for his little precious baby . . . I mean *Maritza Ortiz*.

"You were born in the South Bronx in a slum. Your grandmother was a factory worker and your uncle a drug dealer."

Destiny could feel the tears well up in her eyes. Was Julia really telling her the truth? It seemed too awful to believe.

"But the best part is yet to come. Your mother was some Spanish chambermaid that your father knocked up. Yes, you probably didn't know this, but dearest Alexander is your real father, but, of course, he was never planning to tell you that."

My father is my *real* father. Why hadn't he told her? How could he keep something like that from her? Destiny felt her anger surging. "No! You don't know what you're talking about." She couldn't believe that he would blatantly lie to her. He was too good a man—had always confided in her.

"Stop," cried Destiny, tears clouding her eyes. She couldn't bear to hear any more.

Julia laughed viciously. "Your grandmother and uncle were murdered right before your very eyes. Don't you remember? Now try and think back. Dig deep into your memory. You must remember something. The smell . . . perhaps the taste of the blood. You were found sitting in a puddle of it. You were playing in your dead grandmother's blood. Don't you remember? Come on, search your mind. You must recall something. Think of all that red all over the place." She smiled the smile of a devil. "Pretty gruesome, wasn't it?"

"You're crazy. You're insane. Get out of my room! Get out of here!" Destiny began to shriek.

Julia rose from the bed. "Gladly. I only wish whoever did it had finished the job. You piece of trash." She thundered out of the room slamming the door behind her.

ॐ

"Is it true? Damn it. Is it true?" demanded Destiny, tears filling her eyes. She threw open the double doors to the study and marched across the room to Alexander who sat in his favorite black leather wing chair reading a novel.

He removed his wire-rimmed glasses, looked up from the book, and met her eyes in surprise.

"Is what true? Is what? Destiny calm down. Try and pull yourself together. You're babbling."

Destiny could feel her pulse race. She felt as if she might explode at any minute. "Sit down. Try and relax." He motioned to the couch. Destiny lowered herself into the chair. She was so upset she was still trembling. "Did you and Julia have it out again?"

Destiny burst into sobs. Alexander reached into his shirt pocket, retrieved a handkerchief, and handed it to her. She took it and wiped her eyes, but the tears kept flowing. "She told me everything. Why didn't you tell me? How could you have lied to me, Father? I trusted you—" her voice trailed off.

"Destiny, I'm still not quite clear what you're talking

about. He looked at her sympathetically.

"Julia told me all about my background, every ugly detail."

"She *what?*" Alexander almost lunged out of the chair. He was mortified. He stood up quite agitated and began to pace, stuffing his hands into his pockets. How could she do such a thing? He had trusted her. She'd been sworn to secrecy. "What exactly did she tell you?" Alexander tried to remain calm. Someone had to remain rational.

"Everything." Destiny's face was filled with pain and anger.

"What do you mean by everything? Tell me word by word."

Every time Destiny recalled the words she burst into tears. She dabbed the corners of her eyes with her handkerchief. "She said I was trash," her voice quivered, "that I came from trash. She told me I came from the South Bronx, from a slum, that my grandmother worked in a factory and my uncle was a drug dealer." She again burst into sobs. "She said I saw them murdered."

Every inch of Alexander filled with fury.

Destiny was in such agony. How could Julia have been so cruel, so filled with hatred? He literally wanted to strangle her.

"She said my mother was a chambermaid . . . and that *you* are my real father." Alexander's eyes widened in alarm. "How could you not tell me that? That you are my father? I thought we were so close." Destiny couldn't wipe away all the tears that gushed from her eyes.

"But we are. . . ." Alexander went to embrace her and angrily she pulled away. "Nothing's changed that."

Julia hadn't spared her a thing. Destiny tried to pull herself together and sat up more erectly. "But what hurts me so deeply is that you told me you didn't know these things when all along you did. Why did you lie to me? Why didn't you tell me? It would have been much easier coming from you."

Alexander exhaled deeply, sat back down, and rubbed his forehead. "So many times I wanted to tell you . . . but I couldn't. This may be difficult for you to understand but I did it out of love. I wanted to protect you from exactly this kind of thing."

"How can you call that *love?*" Destiny looked at him with disdain. "You taught me to be open and honest, but yet *you* were living by a different set of rules all along."

"If you believe nothing else, believe that I did what I felt was right, what I truly believed was best for you. I love you more than anything. I always have. You're my daughter. You mean the world to me."

"All these years I've been your *adopted* daughter," she said bitterly.

Tenderly, Alexander went to embrace Destiny again, and she pulled away. She rose up from the chair.

"Who is my mother?" She wanted to know desperately, now more than ever. "I hope it's not too much trouble, but do you think you could at least tell me that much?"

Her father met her eyes. "I was deeply in love with her." Alexander had a faraway look in his eyes. "Elena . . . my beautiful Elena," he said softly. He could see her clearly, as if she were standing there before him . . . and he wished she were. "Elena Ortiz. I met her at the Hotel Dumois. She worked as a chambermaid there during the day and went to school at night." He paused for a moment. "She's—" He couldn't bring himself to say the words. "She's dead."

"Dead?" It wasn't what Destiny expected to hear. She felt herself fill with disappointment. Now she would never be able to meet her.

"She committed suicide."

She looked at him sadly.

"I loved your mother with all of my heart. We were going to be married. She was a wonderful woman. You remind me so much of her."

Destiny refused to listen to any more. She didn't feel sympathetic. She turned around to look at him before leaving the room and said coldly, "I'm moving out." Alexander felt his heart throb in his chest.

"Please don't go, not like this, not under these circumstances. Don't do anything rash, Destiny."

Suddenly, he became angry. A fire of emotion rose in him from the depth of his being. *No one walks out on me. I can't take anyone else walking out on me.* "Anything you might regret later on." *He was only six. It was like his mother leaving all over again and the pain was much too severe. He felt so unworthy, so unloved. His mommy didn't want him, and if she didn't want him no one else ever would. He had been such a bad boy to make her go away. He wanted to break down and cry. No mommy, please don't go! Don't leave me! Come back! Mommy, I promise I'll be good. Just give me one more chance.*

Alexander had to refrain from losing total control. "Please believe me. I only meant to protect you. I did what I did out of love. And I can assure you, I plan to have it out with Julia. If anyone should leave, it should be her. I'll never be able to trust the woman again."

Destiny refused to answer him. She felt so terribly betrayed. She left the room to go pack her belongings not knowing if she'd ever be able to trust or look at her father again.

～

"I should have thrown you out immediately." Alexander

said, shaking his head in exasperation. Nicholas . . . and now this. What kind of a fool do you take me for? To think that I even contemplated a reconciliation." Alexander paced back and forth across the bedroom, his brow tensed in fury, his hands locked in his pockets. Julia sat on the large bed in her pink satin robe, her legs crossed and tucked under, her long blond hair forming a cape over her shoulders, eyes red-rimmed with tears. "What astounds me is that I ever trusted you. I should have known better. Pure lunacy on my part. How could I have been so damn blind not to see you for what you really are?"

"Destiny drove me to it."

"Perhaps you should have thought of that *before* you went to bed with the chauffeur . . . *before* you betrayed my trust . . . *before* you told my daughter news about her background that you knew would devastate her. Julia, you're much too smart for that."

"I didn't want to lose you, Alex—"

"So this is how you thought you'd keep me . . . by betraying my trust? Julia, come on, surely you're not that naive?"

"The thought of losing you drove me to the edge. I lost it. I'm only human with human frailties. Haven't you ever come close to falling off a cliff? Haven't you ever done anything you've regretted?" she asked tearfully.

"I *think* before I act. I consider the consequences of my actions. I take *nothing* for granted."

"Alex, please, you haven't given me a chance to explain. You haven't even heard my side. At least give me that, if nothing else."

He preferred the *nothing else*. That was what she deserved. Alexander stopped and glared at her with unforgiving eyes. "I don't know what you could possibly say. I was fool enough to even consider accepting your apology for the first offense." He exhaled deeply. "I'm afraid you'll have to leave."

"I know we can work it out," pleaded Julia, rising to her knees as if in prayer.

"Not this time. This time you've gone too far. Destiny is down the hall packing her things because of you." He was equally hurt because of his daughter and deeply angry at her for walking out on him—just like her mother, Elena, and his mother, Cecile.

They were all the same. Every one of them. Each one ripped out a piece of his heart and took it with her. "My relationship with my daughter will never be the same." He didn't know if he'd be able to forgive Destiny for leaving him. How could she do this?

"Perhaps if you had told her the truth from the beginning. You had no right to keep it from her."

Alexander immediately cut her off. "You're in no position to preach. I did what I thought was best. I did it out of love. I tried to protect her. You can see for yourself that I was right. She's absolutely devastated."

"Destiny is a resilient young woman. I'm sure she'll recover," Julia said.

But I don't know if I ever will, thought Alexander. How much can one man take?

"If you'd only let me explain and try to make it up to you," Julia sobbed.

Alexander approached the bed and Julia grabbed him desperately around the waist and begged, "I love you, Alex. Please don't do this to us."

"*You* did this to us."

"Please."

"You're wasting your breath." Alexander loosened himself from her grasp and crossed the room to her closet, retrieved a piece of luggage, and brought it to her. "Pack your things and get out." Julia climbed off the bed and tearfully threw her arms around him again.

"Please, Alex, no one is perfect. People make mistakes . . . I love you."

He pushed her away. "You can't charm your way out of this one."

"She drove me to it," Julia repeated. Alexander opened the bureau drawer and grabbed a handful of expensive lingerie. With the other hand he threw the suitcase on the bed and unzipped it. He stuffed her best silk garments into the case wrinkling them intentionally. She watched him do it cringing at the thought of her best undergarments being treated with such disrespect. "I couldn't help it. I lost my temper. Sometimes it gets the best of me. If I could do it over I would never have said those things. You must believe me." She threw herself to the floor in front of him pleading for forgiveness. She began to kiss his legs and attempted to unzip his pants.

"That won't work, either, this time." He unloosened her hands, and she fell to the floor. "You have half an hour."

"Alex, I can't possibly collect all my things in so little time. You know how much I have."

"Well, then," he took a second to mull it over, "if that's the case, I guess you won't be able to take everything. Whatever you leave behind I'll just donate to charity. I'm sure they'd love to have your things."

Julia was appalled. She pulled herself up, straightening her bathrobe, and began to race around to room trying to collect her belongings as quickly as possible.

~

"Destiny, don't be so rash. Please don't go like this," Alexander said as he walked into her room. She hovered over her suitcase, tears blinding her eyes. "You leave like this and things will never be the same, I'm warning you," said Alexander.

"Is that a threat?"

"Take it however you like. I'm telling you you're making a grave mistake. You can't run away from your problems. It's not the adult thing to do," he stated.

"How the hell would you know?" She turned and glared at him. "Why should I listen to anything you have to say?"

Destiny was too distraught to think clearly. She didn't even know where she'd go. All she knew was that she had to get out of there immediately.

She was too hurt with her father to even look at him. "I don't belong here. I never did." Her voice trailed off.

"Destiny, for God's sake, come to your senses. I know you're hurt and I'm sorry. I'm sorry that you had to find out the way you did. Of course you belong here; that's utter nonsense, and you know it isn't true." Alexander grabbed her shoulders and turned her around to face him. A tear rolled down her cheek. Alexander wiped it away with his finger. "Of course you belong here. You are my daughter. Please . . . reconsider. Where would you even go?"

Destiny didn't answer. A feeling of sudden fear washed over her. She didn't know. She hadn't given it much thought.

Julia's words slipped back into her head. She couldn't seem to release them. She met her father's eyes again and felt another urge to cry. It saddened her to think that she'd never feel the same way about anything again. "I need to finish packing." She turned away from him and resumed stuffing her strewn belongings into the small suitcase.

"Will you at least let me know where you're staying?"

"Yes," she replied flatly, wishing he would leave. She

had no intention of contacting him. Alexander crossed the room. "I'll have Raymond drive you to your destination."

"That won't be necessary." She choked back a sob. "I'd rather take a cab."

Alexander nodded. *Now please leave,* she thought. And as if in direct reply, he walked out of her room.

Chapter six

Chase Braddon peered out the window in anxious anticipation as the train rolled into Union Station. All his life he had dreamed of visiting Washington, D.C., the white city—that was what his grandmother, Etta, called it—ever since he was a little boy. It was where things happened, where all the country's monumental decisions were made. It was one of the most exciting cities in the world.

Chase needed something to lift his spirits. He was feeling depressed and needed time to collect his thoughts before heading back to eastern Oregon—before facing his family to tell them that he had been ousted from the academy at West Point only a few days before for cheating on a military science exam. At the time he'd thought he'd been pretty ingenious inserting the tiny pieces of pencil lead under his fingernails and changing the answers he'd missed as the instructor called them out. He never really believed he'd get caught.

Cadets will not lie, cheat, or steal or tolerate those who do. The honor code kept reverberating in his head. There was no question that he had violated the code, but he had enjoyed attempting to outwit the system. He disdained authority. Always had. Always would. No one who knew him back home thought he'd last a week at the place and instead he lasted years. He was too much a free spirit, too carefree to be able to withstand the rigid, conformist attitude that was pervasive at the Point. But it had been too good an opportunity for Chase to turn down. He had excelled in math in high school with little effort and a college-educated neighbor of his, aware of his desire to leave Milltown, urged him to apply. He never thought he'd really get in and was thrilled when he learned of his acceptance. A free education, the prestige of being a West Point cadet, a career where he could see the world—it sounded too good.

It was amazing that he'd been able to play their little game for as long as he had. He deserved some credit for that, he told himself.

The academy had asked Chase to resign, but he had boldly contested it. He wasn't afraid of taking chances. He'd always been a daredevil. What did he have to lose anyway?

A few days later, the honor committee had reviewed his case and he was found guilty. He was out! That was it. There was no second chance. No apology necessary. He still couldn't believe he was no longer part of the cadet corps. He figured it would probably take a little while for reality to set in.

Chase hadn't told a soul yet about his being booted from the academy. He couldn't bear the thought of telling his grandmother; he knew she'd be devastated. For her his acceptance had been a dream come true. Her grandson, Chase Braddon, golden-haired hauler of wood, a West Point cadet. Her light blue eyes always lit up whenever she bragged to her friends about him and it saddened him to think of her finding out the truth. He had blown it, a dream of a lifetime, a chance to make something of himself. How could he have been so stupid? With only one more year to go—and now he was out.

How could he have been so naive? What was he going to do with his life now? At least the academy gave him some direction, some purpose.

He came from a small town in eastern Oregon where everyone knew his business. He could imagine this bit of information spreading like chickweed.

The whole town had known about his father, how he used to drink and beat him, how his mother had died of breast cancer when he was only a toddler, leaving his paternal grandmother, Etta, to raise him and his older brother, Jeff, while his dad worked long hours on the railroad. They knew about his rivalry with Jeff, who had graduated from Stanford and had become a psychologist and the founder of a small private school in town for disturbed kids. He hated Jeff for being smarter, for always being better at everything.

As far as he was concerned the only things he had over his brother were his strapping good looks—he was tall and blond and muscular from all the years of chopping and hauling wood; his eyes as blue as two bright beams in the dead of night—and the fact that he'd been accepted into the academy.

༒

Valerie stretched her arms as she rose from the couch. With her dark velvety skin, boy-short hair, and long features she was as elegant as a cougar.

"I really appreciate you taking me in," Destiny said for the third time.

Valerie waved her hand and shot her a "no problem" look as she picked up the classified section of the *Post* to scan the apartment ads. "Here's one you might be interested in," she said. Destiny pulled herself upright from her slouching position on the couch so she could listen. "It's a one bedroom not too far from here on Quebec Street off Connecticut Avenue." Valerie met her friend and colleague's eyes and smiled. "Only about four blocks and the rent isn't too outrageous, but I guess you don't have to worry about that. . . ."

"I've decided to live completely off my teaching salary. I'm not taking any money from my father. I don't need his donation."

Valerie flashed her a look of surprise, thinking she was nuts. Washington was an expensive city. She would have been happy to have any financial help. She crossed the small living room to the phone and began to dial, balancing the receiver under her chin. "I'll call and see if we can go look at it. If I were you I wouldn't waste any time. If it looks as good as it sounds it may be gone by this afternoon."

The thought of her own apartment excited Destiny. After a minute of conversation with whoever answered the call, Valerie hung up and turned to Destiny. "He said now's a good time to look at it. Grab your purse."

ॐ

"It's perfect," beamed Destiny. "I'll give you two months' rent right now." She withdrew her checkbook from her purse as Valerie hugged her victoriously. "It's just what I wanted. Well," whispered Destiny, as the manager momentarily slipped away, "it is a little smaller than I had in mind but it's too good to turn down." One room on the first floor; a tiny kitchen off to the far right; a walk-in closet and bathroom to the immediate right.

On their way out a few minutes later, Destiny stopped, gazing at the glass entrance and beyond to the grass and trees. "I can't believe it was this easy."

"It's usually not." It was late afternoon and the air was

still stiflingly hot. "Let's celebrate with a hot dog on the mall. My treat. I'm anxious to see the latest exhibition at the Air and Space. You know what a fanatic I am. It's supposed to really be something," Valerie gushed.

Later Destiny stood in line waiting for a hot dog, while Valerie went back to the Smithsonian for a book she'd discovered earlier in the gift shop and simply had to have. Her jacket was draped casually over her right arm, since she was attempting to stay cool, which was almost an impossible task, in her sleeveless white shirt and matching white jeans skirt.

"Don't order the last hot dog. I'm famished," a man with a slight western accent said. Destiny pivoted and discovered the owner of the voice standing directly behind her. She was taken aback by his rugged handsomeness and felt an immediate chemistry. She began to blush, hoped she wasn't being too obvious, and quickly turned her eyes away. She felt terribly conspicuous, as if he could read her mind. Destiny felt as if she were wearing a neon sign on her chest that read: I find you incredibly handsome. Please take me home with you. She snickered at the thought and cupped a hand over her mouth.

She met his riveting blue eyes. "Did you say something to me?"

"I said not to order the last hot dog," he said and smiled.

He had an incredible smile with perfect white teeth.

Destiny couldn't take her eyes off him. She kept glancing back at him. Strangely, there was something familiar about him, as if she'd known him before.

"Lady, what would you like?" the teenage vendor asked impatiently.

"Uh." She smiled. "One hot dog, please."

"Make mine a chili dog with extra cheese." He moved

up to the counter beside her. She felt his bare arm brush against hers and a chill crawled up her back. She wanted him to touch her again. "They're both on me." Chase dug into his jeans pocket and gave the vendor the appropriate change before Destiny had time to protest.

"You didn't need to do that."

"I know, but I wanted to." As they walked away from the line and came to a stop only a few feet from the concession stand, Chase looked at Destiny. She was the most beautiful dark-haired woman he'd ever seen and Chase had a weakness for beautiful women. He'd been spoiled at the academy—women from all over came in droves to see him on the weekends. Especially the ladycliffers, the students at the all women's college next door; they couldn't seem to get enough of him. He had screwed so many of them that he'd lost count.

It was widespread knowledge among the corps that the "cliffdwellers" had an insatiable appetite for the young studs in gray. Many of the girls daringly climbed over the fence between the two schools at night to meet their cadet lovers. He himself had snuck out of his room more than once to meet a ladycliffer in the woods for a quick romp in the leaves.

Chase enjoyed all the "free fruit" that fell from the trees and rolled his way. Women had always been wildly attracted to him and he reveled in it. He spent many a night in heated passion rolling with his cadet gray trousers down, his butt naked to the moon in the leaves and twigs off the main path of Flirtation Walk, pumping some girl he hardly knew.

"I take it you're new to this area?" Destiny said, as she licked the mustard off her hot dog. Chase watched her and could feel his manhood stiffening beneath his jeans. There was something incredibly sensual about her.

"Arrived here just yesterday morning, took the train from New York."

"Are you from New York?"

"No, actually, I was born and raised in Milltown."

"Milltown?"

Chase gestured with his hands. "It's in eastern Oregon. It's only a couple of blocks in size. It's an out of the way little place, and there's a river nearby and train tracks."

"Sounds quaint."

Chase chuckled. "I don't know if I'd call it quaint. You'd have to see it."

"Destiny," called Valerie as she caught up with them.

Chase turned to look away from Destiny's hypnotic gaze.

"I'd like to introduce you to my best friend, Valerie Morgan." Valerie extended her hand and Chase smiled graciously as he shook it.

"What were you doing in New York?" Destiny asked. She found Chase Braddon surprisingly easy to talk to for someone with such intimidating good looks, and he didn't seem as full of himself as a lot of the guys she had dated, and she found that refreshing.

Chase looked away and hesitated, then met her eyes. "I just resigned from the academy."

Valerie looked at Destiny disapprovingly. Destiny and Valerie were the first ones he had told.

"The naval academy?"

"West Point."

A cadet. Destiny was impressed. A cousin of her father's had graduated Annapolis. She knew how difficult it was to become a cadet, how hard academy life was, how bright one had to be to be accepted in the first place. She wondered what the reason was for his resignation, but didn't have the guts to ask.

"I didn't get your name."

"Destiny Raines." She extended her hand.

"Chase Braddon." His handshake was firm and strong. He was so masculine, and the touch of him sent tingles up the back of her legs.

"Destiny," Chase repeated it again, and she blushed.

"We need to be getting back," said Valerie.

"I'd like to see you again soon." He didn't know how long he could stand to wait. He imagined himself naked with her. "Can I have your phone number?"

Destiny smiled at him, flattered. "I don't have a number yet. Valerie, do you mind if I give him yours?"

"Yeah, well, I guess," Valerie hesitantly agreed and Destiny reached into her purse, found a pen, tore the corner off one of her checks and scribbled down the number.

"Where are you staying?"

"In a motel downtown. I'll call you." Chase gave her a mock salute and Destiny chuckled as she watched him sling his backpack over his strong shoulders and wander off.

⁓

The two women dropped their paintbrushes down on the cloth in exhaustion. "That's definitely an improvement. Don't you think?" Destiny wiped her hands on her paint covered jeans and admired the walls. She was so incredibly proud of herself and her eyes glowed. It was the first time in her life she had painted anything. She hadn't hired anybody to do it for her. She did it herself and liked the feeling of satisfaction it gave her.

"No, it's off a shade. Let's redo it," Valerie said, then collapsed on the floor. Destiny surveyed the room with a look of contentment. "It really makes all the difference in the world."

"Now if you only had some furniture. Why don't you

call your father, let him know where you are and while
you're at it ask him to furnish the place? You know he
must be worried sick about you. It's been two weeks since
you left. Don't you think you oughta call him?"

"Why hasn't he called *me* if he's so upset?"

"He doesn't know where you are. You didn't tell him."

"Valerie, he's not stupid. It shouldn't have taken him
long to figure out that I would let *you* know."

Frankly, Destiny didn't care how worried or upset he
was. She didn't feel sorry for him one bit. She was only
concerned with her own feelings, how *she* felt. "I wasn't
planning on it. I'm still too angry. I'm not ready to forgive
him. I don't know if I'll ever be."

"What? You're not serious." Valerie went on, "Look,
granted the guy made a big mistake. He should have told
you everything. You shouldn't have had to hear it from the
bitch. I'd write her off totally. She's made your life hell
from the start. Your father, he made a mistake. Give the
guy another chance."

"Why are you so soft on him anyway?"

Valerie thought of her own father. She had grown up
in a middle-class D.C. neighborhood, the oldest of three
children. Her father was a workaholic. He was a civil ser-
vice worker, a GS 13, who worked for the Department of
Defense, and she hardly ever saw him. He was always at
the office working late into the night and on the weekends. The little time he was home was spent coddling her
two brothers, living vicariously through them and their
sports, and ignoring or constantly criticizing her. She
would've given anything to have a doting father like
Alexander.

"You know how much he cares for you." Valerie
remembered Alexander watching proudly at their college
graduation; her own father had been away on a business

trip. "He's spent so much time with you. He'd do anything
for you."

"Anything but tell me what I wanted to know—the
truth." The thought of having anything to do with her
father still riled Destiny. She hadn't even begun to forgive
him. "Forget him. What do you say we order a pizza?"

"No thanks. I'm going to make it an early night so
have enough energy left to deal with the little convicts
tomorrow."

Destiny laughed as Valerie stood up. She loved when
Valerie called them the little convicts.

"Thanks again. You don't know how much I appreci
ate everything," Destiny said. Valerie always came through
for her. She was always there when she needed her most
She hugged her friend.

As soon as Valerie left, Destiny collapsed onto the
floor, her face and hair speckled with white paint. Thank
God she had at least rented a bed, she thought, as a wave
of fatigue hit her. All she could think of was climbing on
top of the bare mattress and going to sleep.

ॐ

The next morning the doorbell rang rousing her from the
comfort of her bed. She dragged her exhausted body from
the warm shell of covers and reluctantly went to answer it
Destiny glanced at the clock. *Who could it be this early*
she thought. She released a sigh. It was almost time to ge
up for work, anyway, she reasoned. Half asleep, dressed in
a white T-shirt, she opened the door and found Chase
Braddon confidently leaning against the door frame. She
felt a bit embarrassed about her disheveled appearance
Rodeo scenes flitted through her mind, as he stood before
her wearing jeans and a fringed cowboy shirt and boots
His blond hair was slicked neatly back. He smelled o

lightly scented men's aftershave.

"These are for you." From behind his back he withdrew a bouquet of supermarket daisies.

"Chase . . . how did you find me? How did you know where I lived?"

"I called your friend. She was hesitant at first about giving me your new address, but I'm pretty persistent when I wanna be. I wore her down. I hope you don't mind my just showing up . . . especially this early, but I wanted to catch you before you went to work." Destiny thought his coming over this early was a bit odd, but nevertheless was happy to see him. "She said you didn't have a phone yet." He hesitated a moment. "May I come in?"

Destiny gestured for him to enter, wishing she'd had at least some notice so she could have fixed herself up. Embarrassed by her unkempt appearance, she pushed back a loose wisp of hair. "Excuse the mess." Chase surveyed the room as he crossed it, then boldly sat down on the edge of the unmade bed and made himself comfortable as if he planned to stay awhile.

"Would you like half a can of coke? I think I have one left in the frig."

"No, I just came to see if you'd like to join me for breakfast."

Destiny smiled. "I'd love too, but I don't have time. I have to get ready for work."

She thought of her students and groaned. She didn't feel as though she had the energy to deal with them today, and wished she could go out with him instead.

"Can't you show up a little late?"

"I don't think so."

"Call in sick?"

"I'd love it. As a matter of fact, I'd love to call in sick every day, but I'd better not."

"Lunch?"

"I only get a half hour. Not enough time."

"What do you do?"

"I teach."

"A respectable profession."

"That's me, respectable."

"Dinner tonight?"

Destiny nodded in agreement. "Tonight will be fine." She glanced again at the clock. "I hate to be rude but I've got to jump into the shower."

"Want company?" he teased.

Destiny made a wry grin, then asked, "what time tonight?"

"I'll be by around seven."

"Thank you for the flowers. They're beautiful. Daisies are my favorite."

"Lucky guess." Chase stopped in the doorway. Their eyes met and Destiny smiled softly. "I have the sudden urge to kiss you. Do you mind?" He planted a flutter of a kiss on her lips which she enjoyed.

Destiny watched him go down the empty hall, anxiously looking forward to dinner.

⁓

They had had a wonderful time together at dinner. Chase had taken her to the Charter House on the water, and had spent a fortune on their meal. He had ordered lobster, which Destiny found quite extravagant, but nevertheless ate voraciously. She served coffee to Chase in her apartment afterward as they chatted the evening away. Chase was full of stories, filled with adventure. He lived life on the edge, and there was practically nothing he wouldn't do for a thrill. The guy was virtually fearless and absolutely reckless.

The phone rang an hour later and when Destiny went to answer it, her expression immediately sobered. It was her father, who had gotten her phone number from Valerie. He couldn't have called at a worse time. She still wasn't in a mood to speak to him. Hearing his voice filled her with sadness and anger.

"Destiny, I've been worried sick about you. I was about to send out a search party. You said you'd call. Why didn't you let me know where you were? I've missed you terribly. Please come home for a visit so that we can begin to resolve this. I can't go on with things this way between us. We've always been so close."

Destiny was still too irate to resolve anything. As far as she was concerned she was the one who was suffering— the only victim. "I don't know what more there is to say. What's done is done."

"I've found it in my heart to forgive Julia after all she's done. I may be a damn fool, but I've taken her back."

Destiny almost dropped the receiver. Was her father insane? How could he take back that woman after what she'd done to both of them? She couldn't believe it. "Can't you do the same for me?" he pressed on.

"You've taken her back?" You jerk. Destiny could feel her whole body flush in anger. She slammed down the phone. She was so angry she wanted to beat her fists into her father's chest, but instead she threw up her hands in exasperation and began mumbling to herself as if Chase wasn't there. She groaned, and her heart was beating fiercely. "I can't believe he took her back." She began to pace the room, the smell of the day-old paint made her dizzy.

Chase observed how upset she was. "Who?" he asked, hurrying over to her. He pulled her into his arms and she didn't resist. She needed someone. Anyone. And he happened to be there. She fell into him crying. He knew how vulnerable she was and selfishly seized the moment. He began to kiss her salty lips.

"Everything's gonna be all right." He began to kiss her harder, running his strong hands through her silky hair down to the small of her back.

Destiny lost herself in his kisses. She didn't care about anything anymore, only the way he made her feel. He was the only one who could take her away. Chase tore off her dress, her bra, and panties. And then he slipped off his shirt and jeans. Her body quivered with desire. She wanted him more than she'd ever wanted anyone. His body was incredibly strong, his muscles impenetrable as he pulled her down onto the bed, sucking and fondling her breasts and then he climbed on top of her.

His lovemaking was aggressive. Exciting. Furious. He seemed to devour her. Her mind was numb, but her flesh was alive, vibrating with pleasure and desire as he pried open her legs and inserted himself into her.

After they'd made love, she nestled in his arms and listened as he told her of his dreams to travel the country by foot with only his backpack in tow. Money and material possessions meant little to him. Chase was carefree and uninhibited. He brought Destiny to sexual heights she'd never known. He was so strong, he made her feel secure and incredibly feminine. He was just what she needed. She was in bed with a virtual stranger, a man she'd only met days before, but it seemed as if she'd known him a lifetime.

He turned to look at her, then rubbed his stomach like a little boy. "I think you've earned dessert."

Destiny laughed. "I thought it was supposed to be the other way around—first dessert, then we go to bed."

Chase leaned over and kissed her lips again. "I've

never been with anyone like you before. You're different from the girls back home."

Destiny's grip on the sheet covering her breasts tightened. Chase met her eyes and gently pried opened her hand, letting the sheet fall to her waist. "You've got beautiful breasts. Don't hide them." He began to play with her and she could feel her whole body shiver, as he moved his lips slowly over each erect nipple. She leaned back her head and began to moan. He was so incredibly good. They began to make love again.

❧❋ *Chapter seven*

"*I* can't believe she finally agreed to come. Did you have to get down on your hands and knees?" Julia asked, then took a deep breath. "How very kind of her."

"Now, now, Julia." Alexander buttoned his white tailored shirt before putting on his black dinner jacket. "You promised me you'd be on your best behavior." He studied himself in the full length antique mirror, which stood in the right corner of the spacious room. "All I need is for Destiny to walk in and for you to jump all over her. You must learn to control yourself; you've already made your feelings about my daughter obvious enough."

Julia turned her back to Alexander so he could zip up her dress. It was a royal blue silk with a low V neck and long contoured sleeves. He ran his fingertips teasingly up her back and she turned to face him. "Julia, you know I love you." He kissed her gently on the lips. "You're an incredible woman, but sometimes, my dear, you can be a royal pain in the ass."

She peered into his eyes. "I just don't understand it. After all you've done for that girl . . . she has no right to torture you. You're too good a man, too good a father for her to treat you the way she does and get away with it."

"I'm sure that after today everything will be resolved." Just like you and I worked out our differences, Destiny and I will do the same."

The eternal optimist, thought Julia. He was too good a man. She didn't deserve him. She was thankful that he'd decided to reconcile after what she'd done to him. After all, how many men would have taken her back?

Alex was one of the most forgiving and gentle men she knew, and she loved him for it. Julia had learned her lesson the hard way and she didn't want to risk ever losing him again. She realized just how precious he really was. He was a jewel. She was determined to be a better wife, to never cause him such heartache again. She pulled back to give him a full view of her dress. "Well, what do you think?"

"I think you look absolutely scrumptious."

"Good enough to—" A mischievous smile crossed her face.

There was a knock at the bedroom door. Alexander hesitated, then said, "Yes, come in."

Julia frowned, annoyed by the interruption. She crossed her arms and walked over to the window. It was early November; it was snowing outside and the trees and ground were already blanketed in white. The pond was like opaque glass.

"Sorry to bother you, sir, but Miss Raines and a friend have just arrived. They're waiting for you in the study."

"Thank you, Helen. Tell them we'll be down momentarily.

Helen, a slight young woman with premature gray hair, nodded obediently. Now they were out of time, thought Julia, annoyed. She didn't think she'd live to see the day when that girl didn't come between them.

Alexander detected her disgust and attempted to quell it with a compliment. "You look ravishing, Julia." She smiled vainly. "Lets go downstairs." He offered his hand and she accepted it.

✌

"Destiny, darling, we're so happy you agreed to join us for an early holiday dinner, since, as you know, we'll be away for Thanksgiving. Julia perfunctorily threw her arms around her stepdaughter, then released them quickly. The hug, devoid of any real warmth, was nothing more than a formality. Destiny tried to suppress her revulsion. She had made up her mind to be civil.

"And who is this charming young man?" Julia cooed.

Cut the crap, Destiny thought. Julia and her exaggerated southern accent were so saccharine it was sickening.

"Chase Braddon, I'd like to introduce you to my father, Alexander Raines, and his wife, Julia Stoneworth Raines." Alexander and Chase shook hands. Alexander curiously eyed Chase's western-style blue shirt with the white fringes, the brown leather jacket, faded jeans, and pointed cowboy boots.

"Can I offer you a drink?" Alexander led Chase over to the bar.

"Do you have a beer?" Alexander and Julia traded glances.

"Beer sounds refreshing for a change," said Julia.

"I'm afraid I don't have any on hand. Is there something else I could offer you? A glass of Scotch perhaps?"

"Scotch would be fine for both of us," said Destiny.

Alexander retrieved four glasses and began to pour the liquid gold. "So Chase, tell me a little about yourself."

"I'm from eastern Oregon." Chase was at a loss for words. Destiny could see him struggling, and attempting to bail him out, interjected. "Chase went to the academy." It was the first thing that came to mind. A second later she wondered if she should have said it, but it was too late.

"Congratulations. That's quite an accomplishment." Alexander smiled at the young man. He breathed a sigh of relief.

"You just graduated?" asked Julia.

Chase hesitated and looked away, averting their stares. "No . . . well . . . actually, I resigned."

"You resigned from the naval academy?" asked Alexander, his eyes widening in disapproval.

Oh, no, thought Destiny. She had really put him on the spot, and she was sorry.

Chase shook his head. "West Point."

An academy dropout. Alexander wasn't impressed. He had always been good at sizing up his daughter's boyfriends and he was right once again.

The word resignation echoed in his head. He tried to conceal his disappointment, but the look in Chase's eyes and the sound of his voice when he announced his resignation only confirmed what he already knew. This young man whom his daughter had brought home was an obvious loser.

Of course, he had to have something on the ball mentally, thought Alexander, to have been accepted into the academy in the first place. It was no easy task to get in—but then to resign. Alexander tried to imagine what the cause might have been. He wanted to know more but didn't feel it was his place to ask. The fact that Chase hadn't volunteered the information only confirmed his guilt. He could only surmise the worst—that Chase had had no other choice but to leave.

Alexander took a sip of his drink, then motioned for everyone to sit down. Destiny lowered herself next to Chase on the couch. Chase took a big swallow of Scotch.

"What are your future plans?" Alexander didn't waste any time. Not where his precious daughter was concerned.

"I'm planning to move back to eastern Oregon, where I was born and raised. I'll try to find work there either at the local lumber mill or on the railroad. I plan on attending night school and completing my degree as time permits.

"Degree?"

"In engineering." Alexander downed more of his Scotch and tried not to reveal his dismay. This man was not what he'd had in mind for his only child. At least he was pursuing a degree. Education had always been terribly important to him.

He couldn't believe his daughter had fallen for someone like Chase. They were so different. In all fairness, Alexander could see how Destiny could be physically attracted to Chase Braddon; he was tall and blond and muscular, seemed friendly enough; but other than that, he couldn't for the life of him understand the appeal. They were from some totally different backgrounds.

⌁

Julia smiled broadly at Chase. She found him ruggedly handsome and wonderfully direct and thought he'd make an exquisite subject for her to paint. He looked like Adonis, but with a down-home boy touch.

"So, how long have you and Destiny been friends?" asked Julia, her smile soldered in place.

Chase smiled back, then said. "Not very long as a matter of fact."

Destiny glanced at Chase. "We've been seeing each other pretty regularly," she added.

"How would you like it if I showed you around the estate?" said Julia. She sensed that Chase wanted to get away from Alexander's scrutiny.

"I'd like that, ma'am." He rose from the couch, relieved to leave behind Alexander and his impenetrable stare.

⌁

Destiny found it difficult to look her father in the eye. She was still so terribly angry with him. And seeing Julia in the flesh only infuriated her more.

"I'm so happy you came." Alexander gazed at his daughter affectionately.

"I only came because you wouldn't stop bugging me," she replied coolly. "And because it's a holiday."

"How serious is it between you and Chase? . . . Are you having an affair?"

"If you want to know if we're sleeping together . . . yes, we are." Alexander lowered his eyes. Destiny was intentionally trying to hurt him, and it gave her a certain pleasure seeing how displeased he looked. "Is there anything else you'd like to know?"

Destiny knew her father would never approve of Chase, that was one of the things that had attracted her most. She knew he'd think he wasn't good enough. No man ever was. She enjoyed tormenting her father, to get even with him for all the pain he'd caused her.

"Destiny, please try and get over your hostility," Alexander said. "You mean the world to me, and if I wronged you I'm so terribly sorry. Please find it in your heart to forgive me . . . to forgive both Julia and me."

"I'm afraid I just can't forget everything, just like that, as if it never happened." She stood up and crossed her arms guardedly over her sweater. Her faded jeans skirt swished around her leather boots as she walked.

"At least try and forgive, try and understand."

Destiny looked away tearfully. "It's not that easy. A person's lost identity is not something one can regain overnight."

"Take all the time you need. Please just come back into my life. I miss you." Alexander stood up. He could feel his eyes become glassy. He went to embrace his daughter, but like a defiant child she pushed him away.

"You would make an exquisite subject," Julia said, as she and Chase walked down the upstairs hall. "How do you feel about posing nude? You don't strike me as the shy type." Julia turned Chase to face her and their eyes met and held. His strong physique made her want him. Just one last time . . . one last fling, she thought, and then she'd remain faithful to Alexander forever.

After all, she had needs that Alexander couldn't fully satisfy. It was an impossible task for one man. Julia found Chase irresistible. She studied him with her eyes and fingered his strong angular face. "Amazing bone structure." She peered at him and smiled. "It would be a chance for you to earn some extra cash."

Chase's bank account was almost depleted and Julia's offer sounded like an easy way to make some quick money. "This is my studio," she said. Chase surveyed the room filled with paintings, some of them still works in progress. Paints and brushes and white drop cloths were strewn around the unfinished attic.

"Did you do all these?" He could see that Julia was a talented artist, even though he knew little about art. "You're good."

"You have no idea how good." She looked at him wryly and laughed. "Alexander rarely comes up here. Sometimes I get so lonely." Julia ran her hand over an old dusty trunk tucked beneath the slanted ceiling.

Chase eyed the magnificent pear-shaped diamond she wore on her wedding-ring finger. Julia moved closer to Chase and ran her hands over his strong shoulders and down his muscular arms.

Chase had a terrible weakness for beautiful women, and it had gotten him in trouble on more than one occasion.

He had gotten Andy Bray, head cheerleader and student body president at Milltown high school, pregnant in her senior year. She had ended up leaving town and moving to Boise, where he'd heard she'd given up his newborn son for adoption.

He had received a "slug," many demerits, and had to walk the area at the academy every weekend for months as his punishment after he'd been discovered with a naked ladycliffer in his bed.

Julia was incredibly attractive, and from what he could tell, quite experienced and easily accessible.

"Unzip me." She turned her back to him. The dress clung to her like a second skin and he ran his hands up and down her back. He pulled down the zipper. Her skin was as flawless and soft as an infant's; and he watched her step out of the dress and toss it onto a chair. She stood before him in her black lace bra and garter belt, which accentuated the paleness of her flesh. With one hand he unlocked her golden-fairy hair from its comb and let it fall loosely past her shoulders. She unclasped her pearl earrings and tossed them carefully onto her dress. They met each other's eyes only briefly before they were passionately entwined, their lips firmly engaged, their tongues meeting for the first time inside each other's mouth.

After breathless kisses and plenty of mutual fondling, Chase, feeling as if he might explode, momentarily freed himself from the confines of his pants. He lifted Julia, who was by now completely nude, into his strong arms, her small breasts swelling against his chest, her legs securely wrapped around his waist, and pressed her into the door. He entered her, pounding away at her until she could no longer contain her joy and began to shriek in pleasure.

"Where could they have gone? I can't find them anywhere," said Destiny, coming down the main staircase.

Alexander stood waiting for her at the bottom.

"She probably took Chase outside to show him the grounds. I'm sure they'll be back momentarily."

A few minutes later Julia and Chase appeared on the upstairs landing.

"Where were you?" demanded Alexander. "Destiny's been looking all over."

"I wanted to show Chase every detail, and he found it fascinating." She turned to him. "Didn't you, Chase?"

"Quite a place," he agreed. "And your wife, she's quite the hostess."

"Yes, Julia has many admirable qualities," said Alexander. "We better go sit down for dinner. Helen says she's ready to serve."

"Smells good." The smell of roasted turkey assailed Chase's senses. His appetite always increased after sex. He took a deep breath. He could easily get used to this. He smiled at Destiny. She looked even more radiant than she ever had before.

ॐ

"Destiny, I love you. Let's get married," said Chase, tenderly caressing her back after they made love in her apartment on a biting December day. Destiny rolled over to look at him. He had caught her totally off guard.

"Married?" The thought had never occurred to her. Chase was absolutely wonderful in bed, he was good company, and made her laugh. He treated her like royalty, always buying her little presents, always full of compliments, but she never once considered marrying him. The relationship was perfect just the way it was. They each had their own space, own lives; she had her teaching career. He had found a small apartment near hers and a temporary job as a security guard in the area. He thought he could convince her to return to eastern Oregon with him. She had no idea that he was having an affair with Julia, too, and posing as her nude model twice a week.

Julia paid Chase well, better than he'd ever dreamed, and knew how to make him feel like a man. Chase recalled the first assignment he'd had as her model. He had to stand completely nude in front of her, while she examined him carefully with her eyes. He could see the lust in her eyes the minute she looked at him, and he enjoyed the attention. She couldn't seem to resist his strong muscular body standing vulnerably before her, and each time she began to position him she began to fondle him expertly. She took him into her mouth and seconds later he came. They made love in every position he could imagine; and afterward, each time as if she were newly inspired, Julia would throw on her smock and begin to paint. Chase wondered how long they could go on in this fashion without being discovered by Alexander, but Julia assured them that they had nothing to worry about. Alexander never bothered her while she worked, and she had instructed Chase to enter the studio through a private entrance in the back and to only come to model at designated times—times she knew her husband would be preoccupied or away.

Chase pressed his lips into Destiny's. "Please, baby, say you'll marry me. I love you so much. I can't live without you. I want you to be my wife. I'll do anything, just say yes," he persisted.

"Chase, look, I'm flattered, but I'm not in love with you."

"I'm willing to live with it. I'm willing to take the chance. I need you, baby." He began to kiss her.

"Chase, we spend every moment in bed. I don't feel as if we really even know each other."

"What's to know." He began to nuzzle her throat. "I'm

a simple country boy with nothing to hide. I've told you everything there is to know about me."

Destiny gazed as Chase began to make love to her. "You're distracting me. I can't think."

"I just want to make you happy."

"Chase—" Destiny tried to speak, but he clamped his mouth down over hers to shut her up.

"I'll take you far away from your daddy so he can't hurt you anymore," he said, coming up for air.

He knew he had hit a cord with her. He knew moving far away appealed to her immensely.

After they were finished, he rolled onto his side so that he could look at her. He would have agreed to anything, whatever she wanted. He put his hand under his head and began to calculate her worth. He could live in the nicest part of town, in a big house up on the hill. He could hear the folks around town now: "That Chase Braddon, he became quite a success back east. Look at him now. He ain't no loser no more." He could spend all his time fishing at the river, catching crawdad, basking lazily in the sun. Chase could feel the hot sun on his face, smell the crappie and bass, the catfish; he could hear the ripple of the water beneath the boat. It was a life that would suit him well. It was a life he wanted. It was a life that only Destiny Raines was able to provide.

✌

Alexander paced back and forth in his study. "I can't believe Destiny would do such a thing. I can't believe she would run off and elope with someone like Chase Braddon. What could she have been thinking? Doesn't she realize that she's made a terrible mistake? He'll never make her happy. She's ruined her life." He paced back and forth in the bedroom in his silk robe as Julia watched him from the bed. "Did she do this just to spite me? To get even? Is that what this is all about?"

Julia felt more sorry for herself than for Alexander and tried to hide her disappointment. Destiny's leaving the area was the best news she'd had in a long time, but she hated to see Chase go. She would miss her trysts with him.

He had been such an exquisite model. He'd had the body of a god and had inspired her work. She was painting better than ever before, thanks to him. He had added excitement to her life. She loved Alex, but the truth was that he bored her in bed. He did the same predictable thing every time and never seemed to want sex as often as she. He frustrated her and left her unfulfilled, wanting more. Chase had been able to completely satisfy her, to make her feel whole.

With Chase, unlike Alex who would have politely rejected her saying, "I just can't do that. I'm sorry, Julia," there was nothing she couldn't initiate or suggest, nothing Chase wouldn't do . . . couldn't do. He was as bold and as adventurous as she, and she adored him for it and paid him handsomely with gifts and money for giving her such pleasure.

Alexander threw up his hands. "That child is my flesh and blood. I've raised her since she was two years old and I thought I knew her, but I guess I was wrong. I never thought she'd resort to something like this. Doesn't she realize what's she's done? She doesn't love him." He met Julia's eyes. "I'm convinced of that. She couldn't possibly fall for a man like Chase. He's totally wrong for her. She could do much better than that."

"No one will ever be good enough for Destiny, Alex." Alexander had put Destiny on a pedestal years before, a pedestal she didn't deserve, thought Julia. He had treated her like a queen and her payback was to torture him.

It was a rare occasion that Julia saw Alexander so visibly upset, and she took a certain delight in it. The last time she recalled seeing him this way was when he demanded she move out. He had always prided himself on being a man of great self-control.

Destiny had called a few minutes ago from the airport. She didn't even have the decency to say good-bye in person, thought Julia.

"How could she do this to me? You spend years raising a child, giving all of yourself, and this is what you get in the end— nothing but aggravation and torment."

✥

Destiny and Chase held hands as they sat on board the jumbo jet headed for Boise. Destiny still couldn't believe what she'd done, how impulsive, how reckless she had been just to run off with Chase and get married. Only a day after his proposal she had quit her job, packed her few valuable belongings, and found herself standing in front of a justice of the peace, beside a virtual stranger, saying, "I do." The shock and hurt in her father's voice still reiterated in her head.

"We'll have two glasses of wine," Chase told the flight attendant. "We just got married."

"Congratulations." She smiled, her eyes moving from Chase to Destiny. She reached into her portable ice box and retrieved two small bottles of wine. She balanced two plastic cups on the cart and poured them each a drink.

Chase handed her the bill. It was some of the money Julia had given him. Julia. He would miss the money and the kinky sex.

"To my beautiful bride." Chase raised his glass. Destiny smiled, then took a small sip. Chase grabbed Destiny's hand and squeezed it. "We're gonna have a great life, you and I." Suddenly, Destiny felt her stomach tighten and a feeling of uneasiness washed over her.

At that moment she wasn't quite as sure.

❧ *Chapter eight*

*M*illtown was just as Chase described it, an out of the way little place only a couple of blocks in size, so small it was almost an illusion. It looked as if it didn't really belong, as if it had been abandoned by the rest of the state of Oregon, the way it sat virtually alone surrounded by mountains. Their long drive from the airport finally ended as Chase's father swung the green pickup into the dirt driveway.

Henry Braddon was even worse than Destiny had imagined. He was like something out of a bad dream. He was loud and crass, overweight, bald, and reeked of stale beer. He was rigid and domineering, and bored Chase and Destiny with his sermon about the country still being in the midst of a depression, which lasted the three long hours he drove them back from the Boise airport.

Destiny eyed the small pea-colored house with the pointed roof and weather vane on top in the shape of a rooster. She could feel that same ill feeling in the pit of her stomach return, the same feeling she'd had upon meeting Chase's fifty-six-year-old father. She seriously wondered if she'd been temporarily insane when she agreed to marry Chase Braddon in the first place.

"This is it, it ain't no mansion but it's home," said Henry, lifting Destiny's suitcase out of the back of the truck.

"Just head into the house, little lady. Grandma's anxious to meet you." Destiny nodded and walked wearily toward the house, glancing back at Chase who was helping with the luggage. She climbed the three creaky wooden steps. The air was biting cold, and her breath was like a cloud of smoke in front of her. She opened the screen door and knocked hesitantly. She looked down at the ground to the right of the porch; it was hard and cracked with sparse patches of yellow grass. A shriveled old woman with hair like soft snow opened the door. A smile illuminated her face; she looked as if she'd been revived from the dead. Her skin was thick with lines like a well-traveled map.

"Destiny." She threw out her arms and embraced her, an unexpected strength reeling Destiny into the house. She smiled at the young woman. "You is even prettier than my grandson said." Etta Braddon stepped back to admire her.

"Thank you." Destiny caught a glimpse of the loose flesh dangling from Etta's arms. She was dressed in a summer blouse decorated with tiny pink tulips that buttoned down the front, and her pants were a flesh-colored polyester.

Etta helped Destiny slip her arms out of her coat. She ran her fingers over the black mink in awe. Her flesh was thin and transparent like a white rubber glove. Destiny could see her veins, and her nails were clipped short and square. All she wore was a tarnished gold wedding ring on her left hand. "Don't want this to wrinkle none." She placed the coat carefully on the guest bed in the room to the immediate left.

Destiny scanned the interior of the living room. Despite the freezing weather outside, the house was stifling hot like a sauna. She was overdressed in her colorful wool sweater and matching skirt. The wood stove, which sat on a yellow linoleum floor to the left of them, heated the entire building including the three bedrooms. Destiny sat down on the faded gold couch. She eyed the two out-dated magazines strewn on the wood coffee table in front of her. The brand-new color television set with remote control directly across from her seemed strangely out of place.

Etta sat down in an old brown chair with a round tombstone back that rocked and swiveled. Destiny noticed the photo in the cheap square frame on the wall by the door and released a small chuckle. "Is that Chase?" she asked. The dated-looking picture was of two boys; Chase, the smaller one to the right, looked like a medieval squire. His hairdo didn't seem to fit his face, and Destiny found it amusing.

"Why . . . yes, that's Chase and his big brother, Jeffrey." Etta smiled. "I keep forgettin', it's Jeff, now. He hates to be called Jeffrey anymore. It's so hard to get used ta. And my memory . . . it ain't so good no more. That was taken some time ago."

Destiny studied the photo further, intrigued by the picture of Jeff, smiling, with his arm around his baby brother. "What's Jeff like?"

"He's the total opposite of Chase. Jeff has always been a good student; he got straight A's through school," said Etta proudly. "He never got into a lick of trouble . . . unlike his little brother. He couldn't seem to stay out of it. Jeff pretty much kept to himself. He was always a good kid; worked at Hank Ritter's grocery store every day after school. He even earned enough money to buy a motorcy-cle. Of course he wrecked it. Slid on wet pavement, but thankfully he didn't get hurt, just a couple of scrapes and bruises. He was never real interested in the girls, kinda just kept to himself. Did I tell ya he got the most valuable player in high school award? He was quite the baseball player, that one. He was so modest about it, too. Never cared to show the trophy to no one." She shrugged her arthritic shoulders. "It's just the way he is, I guess. They're all so different. Sorry, I just seem ta ramble away, once you get me started. Enough about them boys. You must be hungry?"

Destiny nodded. She was famished. Anything sounded good. The old woman rose from her chair and walked straight ahead through an arch that separated the living room from the dining room. Destiny followed her past the round antique oak table and chairs and the old buffet that held pictures of relatives in small inexpensive frames.

Destiny entered the kitchen and sat down at the small metal rimmed table to the right under a window with homemade tieback curtains and two wilted plants on a small metal stand in front. "How 'bout some ice cold milk?" Etta opened the stained refrigerator, took out a quart of milk; then crossed the room past the wood stove to a small single sink. She retrieved a clean glass from the large white freshly painted cabinet. She poured Destiny a glass of milk as if she were a small child, then took out a tin half filled with store bought cookies from the pantry to the left of the sink and offered her one.

"Thank you." Destiny smiled politely, retrieving a cookie from the tin. "You betcha," said Etta. The cookies were chipped and stale as if Chase's grandmother had been storing them for years. She took a small bite. Henry and Chase came in the front door with the bags.

"Chase, I'm so glad you're home safe. You know how I worry about you flying in those big air birds. Every time I watch the news there's a crash." She embraced her grandson. She looked at his brown leather jacket. "You're not dressed properly. Don'tja have a warmer coat?" she asked in concern, her dusty blue eyes fixed on him as Destiny looked on.

"Grandma, I'm fine," replied Chase.

She caressed the leather. "This is awfully thin fer round here. You know how cold it gits. It's been below freezin'." The scent was strong. The jacket smelled new. "Where are your cadet grays? You know how I like you to wear them when you come home." She crossed her arms over her chest. "Makes me so proud. You know how I like to show you off to my friends."

"Do you have any of your peach pie?" Chase asked his grandmother, feigning a smile, feeling his stomach knot. He dreaded having to tell his grandmother the truth. He knew it would break her heart. But he had to. He'd always told her everything. She had such a hold over him. She was the one person he had always confided in. She was the only one who could ever bring him back to his senses when he was about to fall off the edge. She was the only person he had ever really loved. His grandma deserved to know. He had no other choice but to tell her. He hated for Destiny to find out he lied, but there was no other way out.

"Isn't she something?" Chase said to his grandmother, gesturing to Destiny.

Destiny looked away, blushing. Etta gazed at her, approvingly. "She is."

"Destiny and I were recently married."

Etta looked at her grandson in surprise.

"Married?"

"Isn't it great?"

Etta didn't know what to say. She could see that her grandson, like always, sought her approval. He'd told her about Destiny in a letter; she knew that they'd been dating . . . but she had no idea that he'd went ahead and married her. "I didn't know cadets was *allowed* to get married. Seems to me you once told me there was some rule against it."

Chase turned his eyes shamefully away.

"Grandma, I've got something to tell you." Chase took hold of his grandmother's hand. "Sit down on the couch." Etta's face filled with worry as she lowered herself on the cushion. She pulled herself up to the edge of the couch as Destiny and Chase sat down beside her.

"Grandma . . . I resigned from the academy."

Etta felt her heart flutter. She suddenly felt as if she couldn't breathe and clutched her chest.

"Resigned? Why? Why wouldja do a thing like that? You worked so hard to git in. You only have one year left til you graduate."

"Grandma, believe me, it's not what I wanted." Chase guiltily lowered his eyes, then met hers again, as Destiny watched in silence. "I didn't have a choice in the matter. Do you think I would make the decision to quit with just one year left?"

Destiny perked up, listening more intently.

"What happened?" Etta's eyes filled with tears.

"I made a mistake, Grandma—a big mistake."

"What kind of mistake? What happened?"

"What?" repeated Destiny, her posture stiffening.

Chase looked at Destiny, then back at his grandmother. "I cheated on a military science exam and got caught. I broke the honor code."

Destiny was momentarily speechless. "Chase . . . you didn't tell me the truth. You told me you resigned because academy life wasn't for you. You said it was too rigid, too confining. Chase . . . why didn't you tell me the truth?" Destiny sunk into the couch with her arms guardedly crossed.

Etta began to sob into the palms of her hands. "How could you have done such a thing?" His grandmother looked at him. "You know better."

"I'm sorry, Grandma. I know I've disappointed you, how I've hurt you."

"What about me? Destiny interjected. "You lied to me."

Chase looked at her. He exhaled deeply.

"Now, I don't know if I'll ever be able to trust you," Destiny said.

"You ruined your own life . . . not mine." Etta peered at her grandson. "You have a wife to support. How do you reckon to do it?" She looked at Destiny, then back at Chase. "What are you gonna do?"

"I'm going to try and get a job on the railroad or at the mill."

Etta looked away.

～

The elk steak was as tough as leather and tasted gamey, even with the brown sauce on top which was supposed to make it more palatable. Destiny didn't care for the taste. She had difficulty swallowing it and thought she might gag. She was afraid to say anything and risk being offensive. These people and their ways seemed so foreign to her; it was as if she were on another planet. She struggled to fight back tears when she thought of sitting at her father's table eating food that was recognizable. She knew she didn't fit in with Chase's family and she didn't like the feeling of being so awkwardly out of place.

"Always knew you was a loser, ever since you was a small boy," Chase's father said, looking directly at him. Destiny could see the hurt in her husband's eyes, even though he tried his best to hide it. "Gettin' thrown out of the academy. You put this family to shame."

"Don't be so hard on the boy," said Etta. "It wasn't easy fer him to tell us. He must feel bad enough without you making it worse."

"We may not be rich folk, but we ain't no cheaters or liars."

"Henry, I don't see where this is headin'."

"Is there some more elk steak?" Henry gnawed away at the piece on his fork. Etta got up from her seat at the table and crossed the room to the wood stove. She took a piece of wood from the adjacent stack and shoved it inside grumbling to herself. Earlier in the day Chase's grandmother made it quite clear to Destiny that she hated cooking on a wood stove. As the two women prepared dinner, Destiny had asked her why she didn't have a more modern stove.

"Because Henry's too darn cheap . . . we have ten thousand dollars in the bank." Destiny looked at her in surprise. She never thought they had even that much. "If he don't want it, it don't get bought." She sighed deeply. "Liftin' the wood is puttin' an awful strain on my back. I just can't do this no more. I just can't do the things I used ta."

"Have you seen a doctor about your back?"

"He won't take me . . . and he won't pay fer it."

Destiny was appalled. She'd only known Henry Braddon for a couple of hours, and she already despised him. The similarities between Chase and Henry flitted through her mind. They had the same face and mannerisms. She shuddered at the thought of what Chase might become, what she had married.

Etta rejoined the table with a second helping of elk for her son. She placed it down in front of him and after licking his fork clean, he used it to lift and examine each piece of meat. Destiny's appetite disappeared.

"Excuse me." She rose from her chair.

"Are you gonna use the commode?" asked Henry, trying to impress her with his fancy vocabulary, revealing the partially-chewed food in his mouth. She nodded. "Don' flush, I'll clean it out with a shovel later." Destiny blushed in embarrassment and smiled weakly.

"He refuses to have the plumbing hooked up. You should see how I have to take a bath," groused Etta. "You see those two tin buckets by the stove?" Destiny turned to look. "We have to fill 'um with boiling water and carry 'em." Destiny held her tongue. She no longer had to go to the bathroom and she sat back down.

"No longer got the urge," chuckled Henry.

"The guest bed has clean sheets, washed 'um this morning," said Etta. Earlier she had shown Destiny how she washed their things with a scrub board in the backyard. Destiny couldn't believe that they lived so primitively.

Guest bed. The words rang alarmingly in Destiny's head. Surely we're not spending the night here, she thought. She bit her bottom lip. Feeling suddenly restless she rose up and carried some of the plastic dinnerware to the sink.

"Everything was delicious." Etta knew that Destiny didn't like the elk but did not take offense. "I'm going out for some fresh air. Chase, would you like to join me?" She peered at him.

"Good meal, Grandma." He rose up. Destiny supposed it was all that he was used to.

Destiny grabbed her coat from the guest bed and went outside. The sky was as gray as she felt. They wandered away from the house. "I'm not spending one night in that house," she said. "I want to go to a hotel."

Chase laughed. "There's only one motel in town," he paused, "and it's being renovated."

"You'll have to find somewhere else for us to stay."

"Look, Sweet Thing," he looked down at her with his handsome face flushed by the cold.

"Don't call me that."

"Destiny, just say you'll stay one night and tomorrow I'll find somewhere else, okay?" Destiny met his eyes, fighting back tears, her cheeks flushed. Chase thought a moment. "Daddy does have an RV locked in the garage. He might let us sleep in there, but of course we wouldn't have any heat."

Destiny exhaled deeply, the vapor like steam from a kettle pouring from her mouth and nose. "Just one night." She peered at him. At least the house was warm, she told herself; it was better than sleeping in a cold garage.

"That's my girl." Chase patted her back. "Come on, let's head back in, it's cold out here."

At seven-thirty the sky was pitch black and Etta and Henry kept fighting back yawns as they all sat in front of the TV watching the local news. Henry gulped the last drops of beer from the can. "It's time for all of us to hit the sheets," he announced to Destiny's surprise.

Etta read the look on her face. "He always makes everyone else round here go to bed when *he's* tired. You don't know how many times I just lay there and stare at the ceiling all night long 'cause I can't fall asleep."

"Stop complainin', Mama. A good night's sleep ain't never hurt no one," snapped Henry.

"Daddy's right, Grandma. We've all had a long day. Come on Destiny."

Henry flipped off the television with the remote, as if he had some kind of mystical power. "Get up at four every day. Can't seem to sleep past." He looked at Destiny and smiled, revealing his broken yellow teeth. She shuddered inside.

"There are extre blankets in the bureau drawer," said Etta, "if you need 'em." Chase and Destiny stood up and Chase grabbed Destiny's hand. Etta stood before them as

Henry waved good night and headed to bed. "If you kids need anythin', jus' holler." Etta smiled softly at Destiny. "Chase, why don't you go and use the bathroom first. I want some time with Destiny." Chase nodded, leaving the two women alone.

"I imagine the way we live here must be quite different from where you come from."

Destiny nodded. Etta had hit a nerve. Destiny suddenly felt terribly vulnerable, and her eyes began to fill with tears. "Now, now, Honey, things is gonna be all right." Etta hugged her.

A few seconds later Destiny pulled gently away. She wiped her eyes. "I guess I'm just over tired."

"And newly married and in a strange place with *very* strange people," said Etta, and Destiny chuckled.

"I'll be fine. I just need a good night's sleep . . . and thank you, thank you for everything." She smiled softly.

"If you need me, hon, I'm right next door."

Destiny was exhausted and confused as she fell into bed wondering desperately how she had gotten herself into such a predicament. She just wanted to fall asleep, but Chase wouldn't stop pawing her.

"Baby, you're not really going to sleep are you?" He pulled her into him. She could feel his hardness poking into her lower back.

"Yes . . . I'm tired." She wished he would roll over and leave her alone. Anyone could walk in on us."

"Not those two, they sleep like two bears in the dead of winter." Destiny was too tired to argue. "You're bought and paid for, Sweet Thing," he persisted. She hated when he called her that and didn't find the comment particularly amusing. "Come on, just a quick one. Where's the wild woman I married?" He began to fondle her in an attempt to arouse her and in spite of her exhaustion she felt a small quiver of excitement. He wouldn't relent, and her excitement began to grow. She felt more awake and turned to face him. He pulled her closer teasing her with his lips. "I love you. I need you," he whispered as he kissed her.

"But, what if—" He pressed his mouth against hers to quiet her, then mumbled, "Don't worry, once their heads hit the pillow, trust me, they're out cold. Pretty soon you'll here them rattling the house with their snores." Destiny chuckled at the thought. They began to make love and suddenly Destiny forgot about everything else, losing herself in him; and neither of them had any idea that Henry Braddon was watching them through a hole in the door that adjoined the two rooms.

❧ *Chapter nine*

"*L*ast week you said *only one* night; it's already been seven days," said Destiny, anger furrowing her dark brows.

She was so damned demanding, Chase thought. Nothing pleased her. Who the hell did she think she was? She was treating him like one of her servants and he resented it. Her rich father had spoiled her, and she was used to getting everything her own way. "We don't have any money—or jobs. We can't afford to move out right yet," Chase lashed back at her. He had expected Destiny to have a large bank account, but to his dismay she was completely broke, and refused to ask her father for a penny. He was sorry he had married her, as beautiful as she was. She had turned out to be a real bitch. "If you would just ask your father to help us out . . . at least until we got on our feet."

She was also incredibly stubborn. "I refuse to ask my father for anything." Destiny fought back tears and began to pace. "I can't live *here* another day."

"We have no choice. Do you think I like this any better than you do? Do you think I enjoy having to see that bastard every day? Listening to his boring monologues about the depression for hours on end? Hearing him tell me how worthless I am, that I'm a failure? I know you're unhappy. You're not too hard to read, but what do you expect me to do?" For the first time in a week they had the house to themselves, and now they could really have it out. Henry and Etta had made their monthly trip into town for some groceries.

"You said your brother Jeff had some kind of a school. You said I'd be able to get a job."

"I haven't had a chance to talk to him yet, all right?" He hated to ask his brother for anything and he didn't want Jeff to know he had been thrown out of the academy, so he'd been putting off seeing him for as long as he could. "We'll go over there tomorrow, okay?" he said to appease her; to get her off his back, then he grabbed his jacket off the chair.

"Where are you going?"

"Out to look for a job. If that's all right with you."

She flipped him the bird when his back was turned.

A feeling of loneliness and utter misery washed over Destiny as she wandered into the backyard and looked to the mountains for solace. All week she and Chase had done nothing but fight and she was emotionally spent. They couldn't seem to agree on anything. She gulped down a sob, and tears began to cloud her eyes.

Smoke spewed from the neighboring chimneys; there was the smell of hickory in the air. Gray clouds sailed across the dim sky. The December wind was brutal, and she tightened her gray cashmere scarf around her head and neck and adjusted her matching wool gloves. She had to get out of that oppressive house, had to get away from Chase and his family if only for a little while to clear her head, to mull over the terrible mistake she'd made eloping with him.

She had run off with a virtual stranger and now she was paying the price. He wasn't the person she thought he was, and she felt so disillusioned. Lately he'd become cold and distant and treated her as if she were the enemy—and that was what she felt like. What a fool she'd been. She knew in her heart that their relationship could never survive, that it was unsalvageable. They were vastly different—like the sun and the moon. They came from such different worlds. She knew she would never be a part of his, and she realized that in trying to hurt her father she had only hurt herself.

She missed her father and Virginia, longed for the comfort of his home, the familiarity, his love, and wanted to find it in her heart to forgive him, but something still held her back. She hoped that in time her ill feelings would wane and pass. As much as she wanted to go home, it saddened her to think that things would never be the same, that she couldn't go back to the way things once were; that she could never be Daddy's little girl again. She was a grown woman now; she had to take charge of her own life. She couldn't depend on him to solve all her problems anymore. She knew as difficult as it was that it was time for her to strike out on her own, to make her mark on the world.

Fifteen minutes passed quickly as Destiny stood there in the piercing wind lost in reverie. Soon the reality of the cold brought her back, and shivering, she headed back toward the house. The stifling heat immediately warmed her as she stripped off her coat, scarf, and gloves and threw them carelessly on the guest bed. She wandered into the living room in her jeans and red sweater and rubbed the circulation back into her hands in front of the wood stove. She yawned, and out of boredom ambled lazily back to her bedroom and climbed onto the bed. She felt herself dozing off to sleep when she was suddenly startled by a creaking floorboard. Her eyes sprung open in alarm. What was that? She reassured herself that it was nothing but the ghostly sounds an old house makes, and she lay back down and closed her eyes.

Henry Braddon had waited for the perfect moment. He had taken Etta to visit a friend, an unexpected treat, and she was thoroughly delighted to have the opportunity to spend time with Rose Thurman, an old girlfriend whom she'd known since the thirties. They rarely went to town to see anyone, rarely went outside at all. Chase would be out most of the day in search of a job; an old friend from the mill had picked him up around noon. Henry snuck back into the house and watched Destiny doze just like she did every afternoon the past week. He figured it'd be easier this way, that she'd be less resistant to his advances. She was so beautiful, he thought as she lay there, so beautiful and exotic with her dark hair spread like an angel's wing on the hand-stitched pillowcase. For the last week he had watched the two of them make love. She seemed to like it enough, he thought; he could tell the way she moaned, the way she squirmed around on the bed; so the idea of her doing it with him might even appeal to her. That was what he hoped. He wasn't sure how she'd react but he'd never know unless he tried. He hoped that she'd want it as much as he did. Ever since the first time he saw them do it, he couldn't sleep because he thought about it so much.

After downing his fourth beer Henry finally got up the nerve and cracked open the door between the two rooms. Destiny didn't even flinch. Tiptoeing, he made his way across the room to the bed. He held his hand tightly over his mouth to keep from belching too loudly. Thinking about it made him hard. He hadn't had a woman in so long he couldn't remember.

Destiny's eyes sprung open in fear the moment she

felt Henry's heavy frame crushing her chest, and she struggled to breathe. Her heart pounded and she was stunned when he attempted to kiss her. She tried to scream but his dirty hand clamped down on her mouth. He began to kiss her throat and spewed her with his fetid breath. She used all her strength to push him off, but couldn't budge him. With no other recourse, Destiny caught the inside flesh of his hand with her teeth and bit him as hard as she could.

Henry recoiled and looked disbelievingly at the blood trickling down his hand. "What'd you do that fer?" His astonished blue eyes met her frightened ones. He wiped his hand on the pillowcase and resumed slobbering all over her face.

The sweet smell of his saliva nauseated her.

"What are you doing? Are you crazy? Stop it! Get off me!" She freed her lips from his and shrieked.

Henry drew up her sweater and attempted to remove her bra. "I thought we could have a little fun this afternoon. You know you want it, too. I seen how much you like it." She spat in his face and began to beat his back with her fists. "Now, come on, little lady," he said, holding one hand over her head and pinning the other one to her side. "Don't make me git rough with ya." All the hatred she had inside for Henry surfaced at that moment, and if she'd had a knife she would have killed him. She tried to squirm beneath him but he had her locked in place.

"You sonofabitch . . . *get off me*." Destiny's eyes began to tear when she realized she was powerless and that there was nothing more she could do to help herself.

"Just try and enjoy yourself . . . this'll probably be the best you had."

⤳

Chase had forgotten his wallet and unexpectedly entered the house while his friend Bobby George Brenner waited in his red pickup with the motor running. He immediately heard the commotion and bolted into the bedroom. Chase was stunned. "Daddy, *what are you doing?*" He couldn't believe it. He was dizzy with anger and felt his pulse race. "Get off her! *Are you crazy?* he hollered; and with some effort pulled Henry off Destiny.

Henry, a bit wobbly, looked Chase directly in the eye. "She didn't want to give me none." He didn't know what he was saying. His breath reeked of beer. Chase knew he was drunk. Charged with anger he punched his father in the face, knocking him down flat.

"Are you all right?" Chase lowered himself next to Destiny whose heart was pounding furiously. Tears gushed from her eyes.

"Yes," she said, trembling.

"I'm sorry." Tenderly he placed his arm around her. He could see how shaken she was. He pulled her closer. "Daddy becomes someone else when he drinks." He exhaled deeply, then glanced at his father sprawled on the floor. "Pack up your things. We're leaving." That was the best news Destiny had heard in a week.

"I never want to see that man for as long as I live," she said scornfully, glaring down at Henry unconscious on the floor.

"Come on, we'll stay with my brother Jeff." Chase helped Destiny off the bed. She was still quivering. She readjusted her red sweater and jeans.

"I want to wash."

"Later." Chase retrieved her suitcase from beneath the bed, opened the bureau drawers, and threw her thing carelessly inside; then he took a few minutes to pack his own things while Destiny watched. "You can shower at Jeff's." Destiny began to sob into her hands.

Chase pulled her gently into his arms. He didn't know what else to say other than, "I'm sorry."

⚘* Chapter ten

Destiny sat wedged in between the two men in the front of the pickup looking out the dashboard window. Her mind whirled in confusion as she tried to recover from the shock of what had happened. Her head was throbbing and she felt sick to her stomach. How could Henry Braddon have done that to her? She still couldn't believe he had tried to rape her; it seemed too bizarre to be true. There was something terribly wrong with that man, she thought. He was more disturbed than she had given him credit for and desperately needed to seek psychological help.

The attempted rape replayed in her mind, and she felt as if she might throw up. "Open the window. I think I'm going to be sick." Chase looked at her with worry and quickly rolled it down. Destiny felt the cold winter air rush at her face, and thankfully found some temporary relief.

Henry Braddon was the most repulsive man she'd ever known and she wished she'd never met him . . . or his son. She wished she'd never set foot in Milltown. It was the biggest mistake she'd ever made. She wished Henry were dead; and if she'd had a weapon she would have killed him. She had never despised anyone as much as she despised him.

She longed to go home. It was the only place she

123

could feel safe and secure. In her mind's eye she imagined being in the mansion, tucked safely away in her room surrounded by all her possessions, where no one could hurt her.

She wanted her father. He no longer was the enemy but her only ally. He was the only one who could comfort her now. He had always had a way of making her feel better, of easing the pain . . . except for the last time, she thought. The memories came rushing back at her. She wished she were anywhere in the world but where she was right now.

She felt so desperately unhappy and alone.

They rode from lower to upper Milltown with Bobby George Brenner, a friend of Chase's since they were both boys. Chase stared silently out the window at the tall pine trees that lined the mountain road. He kept mulling over what had happened, the image of his father on top of his wife, playing over and over in his head. Chase felt the blood rush to his face. He was filled with anger and regretted not seizing the moment and killing his father when he had had the chance. His hatred for his father had festered over the years; every beating, each caustic word played repeatedly in his mind. The few pleasant memories had faded like old cloth over time. His father was a despicable human being, there was no denying it, and he knew he would never change. The man was better off dead.

If it hadn't been for his grandmother Etta he didn't know what he would have done, how he would have survived over the years. She loved him in spite of all his shortcomings . . . and there were many.

He knew her intentions had always been good. She had tried to make the best life she could for her two young grandsons under the circumstances.

He remembered the long walks that she took with him and Jeff in the woods up in the surrounding mountains;

the wonderful picnic lunches she would make. She taught him how to drive the pickup and to fish and plant crawdad traps in the murky river. She had always been there to comfort him after the beatings from Henry.

His grandmother had always been proud of her heritage, proud to have been reared in Milltown, and she vowed to never leave. This had been her home for as long as she could remember, and she couldn't ever imagine herself anywhere else. Chase recalled sitting around the campfire with his grandmother and older brother telling jokes under a starlit sky on the riverbank, frying crappie over an open flame. He remembered the hours of fun he had water skiing and snow skiing.

They sped past the local sawmill, where Milltown got its name, and where Bobby George had been employed for most of his adult life. The steam spewed from the mill's chimney stacks like water from a hose polluting the crisp blueness with gray.

In less than half an hour they arrived at Jeff Braddon's house in upper Milltown, a middle class suburb—much nicer than lower Milltown. They approached what was commonly referred to by the locals as "the rich part of town," away from the trailer parks. Here the residents lived in single family dwellings.

The town was comprised of predominately blue collar workers who were generally employed by either the lumber mill or the railroad. Milltown, once a saloon town, was conservative and small. Hunting and fishing on the river, meeting at the bowling alley every Thursday night, was a life so diametrically opposed to the life Destiny had known.

"Thanks," said Chase, helping Destiny out of the truck as soon as they pulled into the sloped driveway. Bobby George had a full lumberjack beard, dark brown with specks of gray, kind eyes and a round face. He nodded as he drove off. "The key should be under the side doormat." Jeff's habits were always calculable, Chase knew. Chase left Destiny trembling at the front door as he went in search of the key.

"Did you tell him we were coming?" Destiny watched as Chase fidgeted with the lock on the front door of the modest yellow ranch.

"Not exactly."

Destiny looked at him disapprovingly.

"He said any time I needed a place to stay—"

"You're sure he won't mind coming home from work and finding us here?"

Chase hesitated. "He might be a little surprised at first. He doesn't know I'm in town." Destiny looked at him in disbelief. "He and Daddy don't speak—and I really haven't kept up with him."

Destiny surveyed the living room as they stepped inside. The furniture was gold plaid and there were lots of plants, colorful framed prints on the wall, shelves cluttered with books and a stereo system. It was light and airy with a big picture window straight ahead above the couch; and she felt comfortable there. She followed Chase down the short hall on the right to the guest room. She had spotted a small sunny kitchen with a door to the left of the living room. There was a small bathroom to the immediate left followed by a master bedroom. Across the hall was the guest room which held a double bed and dresser next to a bedroom converted into an office.

"I'm going to shower."

Chase put down the two suitcases. "I'm starved. Gonna go see if there's anything to eat."

"Don't you think you should call your brother at work?"

Chase shook his head. "Destiny, stop worrying. He'll

be home in a couple of hours. Go take your shower."

She nodded reluctantly, then stepped into the cheery bathroom.

Destiny couldn't seem to scrub herself thoroughly enough; no matter how hard she tried she could still smell Henry all over her; she could still feel his rough calloused hands pawing her; still smell his sweet slobber on her face. She opened her mouth for the third time and let the steamy spray of water rinse her tongue and teeth, but it didn't seem to help. She bit into the soap but it only left a bitter aftertaste.

A few minutes later she emerged from the bathroom wrapped in a thick white terry towel, her long dark hair dripping like icicles down her back. Chase was in the living room with the stereo blasting, listening to country western as he gobbled down his second ham sandwich. She crossed the hall to the guest room, slipped into clean underwear, fresh jeans, and a blue sweater; then took her old clothes, wrapped them in a tight ball and tossed them into the kitchen trash. She knew she'd never be able to wear them again.

Chase found her in the sunny kitchen. He was searching for a bag of chips to accompany his sandwich. "What are you throwing away your clothes for?" He looked at her in astonishment. "We can't afford to just go out and buy new things like you're used to." Chase retrieved the clothes. "You can't throw these out. They're still wearable."

"I'll never wear them again," she protested.

"I'll wash 'um."

"Chase, just throw them away." She turned her head. She couldn't bear to look at them. They made her ill.

"Some people were not brought up with a silver spoon in their mouth."

Destiny frowned.

"You hungry?" he asked, ripping open a bag of potato chips he'd found in the cabinet.

"No." She shook her head.

She went into the bedroom to lie down, her head throbbing. In a few minutes Chase joyfully announced that they had the house all to themselves. He climbed onto the bed and began kissing the back of her neck.

His insensitivity angered her, and she could feel her body become rigid. She curled into a fetal position and hoped he'd take the hint and go away. Didn't he realize what she'd just been through? How upset and shaken she was? She had almost been raped. It wasn't something she took lightly. It wasn't something she forgot about the next minute. Chase seemed oblivious of her feelings. That son of a bitch. All he cared about was food and sex. He was incredibly self-serving. How could he be so selfish? So single-minded? He obviously didn't care how she felt. How could he possibly expect her to be in the mood to make love so soon after what had happened?

He began to roam her body freely as if he owned it. Destiny's fury rose.

"Don't touch me. Leave me alone." She pushed him away.

"Don't tell me you're acting like this just cause of Daddy? You're not gonna let him get to you, are you?"

Destiny could feel her blood boil. Chase Braddon was the most insensitive jerk she'd ever met. How could she have been so blind? How could she have been so taken in by his rugged good looks? She crossed her arms and sat up against the pine headboard. She looked at him disbelievingly. "You know you're really something." She breathed deeply. "There's only one person that matters to Chase Braddon and that's Chase Braddon. You really don't give a good damn about anyone else, do you?"

"Destiny, what are you talking about? You know that

isn't true," said Chase defensively, peering into her eyes.

"It *is* true, Chase. Get your hands off me." She pried one of his hands off her thigh. "I think it would be best if I went back to Virginia. This whole thing was obviously a major mistake." She shook her head. "This is never going to work." She had given the matter considerable thought over the last week. She wanted to rectify the terrible mistake she'd made—if it wasn't too late.

He looked at her in astonishment. "Are you talking about a *divorce*? That's crazy. We just got married."

"It's not crazy. It's what I want. I never should have married you. I never should have come here."

"Calm down, Destiny. You're just a little upset."

"A *little* upset?" Her blue eyes grew wide.

"I know that little thing with Daddy upset you . . . but what we have . . . it's special. I love you, baby."

"Little thing!" She looked directly into his eyes. "You call what happened a little thing?" she yelled. He was incapable of loving anyone but himself, she thought. Her body froze and she stared fixedly ahead.

"Please . . . Destiny . . ." Chase put his finger to her lips to quiet her. "I'm sorry if I said the wrong thing. I don't always know what to say. Don't hold it against me. Don't talk about divorce, okay?" His voice softened, and he reached for her tenderly. Angrily, she jerked away.

He was suddenly angered by her rejection and used his strength to pin her down. Without warning he had turned on her, and her face filled with terror. What kind of family had she married into? Chase was as crazy as his father. She began to tremble in fear. "You're my wife and you're gonna do what I say." He peered at her with steel blue eyes, then began to kiss her. She tightened her lips. It was like being with Henry all over again.

Destiny tore away from him and began to scream at

the top of her lungs. "Get off me you son of a bitch! Get your filthy hands off me!" She began to dig her long nails into his back. Tears poured from her eyes, and she began to smack him.

"All right, calm down, just calm down, don't go crazy, okay, okay . . ." Chase pulled away, looking at Destiny in astonishment, her face contorted as if she'd totally gone mad.

"When I say leave me alone I *mean* it!" She rose from the bed, grabbed her coat from the open closet rattling the hangers, and went thundering down the hall and out of the house.

࿐

Jeff came home shortly after four and was completely stunned to find his younger brother, whom he'd barely spoken to in the last year, spread out on his couch watching TV as if he'd taken up permanent residence. "Chase—" a smile appeared on Jeff's face after the initial shock subsided, "I didn't know you were in town."

"Only been in town about a few days," he lied. "I've been meaning to call. Was staying with Daddy, but you know how that is." He met his brother's eyes. "Thought you wouldn't mind if I camped out here awhile."

"No," Jeff shook his head, "no problem." I have plenty of room. I'm happy to have you. Are you on leave from the academy?" He lowered his leather briefcase.

Chase was reluctant to answer. "Permanent leave, you might say. I resigned."

Jeff looked at him in surprise.

Chase quickly changed the subject. "Picked me up a beautiful bride when I was stationed east." Jeff's eyes widened and he smiled. "Daddy thought she was pretty, too. Couldn't keep his hands off her. Caught him slobbering all over her, the son of a bitch."

Jeff looked at him, alarmed.

"He tried to rape her. . . ."

Jeff's eyes widened in horror. "The bastard was as drunk as they come, reeked of beer. Should have shot him when I had the chance."

"He's really crazy," breathed Jeff. "Is she okay . . . your wife? He didn't hurt her?"

"I came in just in time. He was so polluted he didn't know what was going on. I knocked him flat."

Jeff hadn't seen their father in many months; the sight of the man disgusted him. He shook his head and breathed. "He's needed help for years. Grandma knows that . . . but she can't make him get it. He thinks he's fine just the way he is." He met his brother's eyes. "He's a pathetic excuse for a human being. I just keep my distance from him."

"My wife—her name is Destiny. She's a schoolteacher from McLean, Virginia. She needs a job and we could sure use the money. I thought maybe you had an opening at your school."

Jeff nodded. "I'd be happy to talk to her."

"She should be back soon. She went out for a walk."

"Congratulations, little brother," said Jeff. He shook Chase's hand.

⌇

Destiny returned. She'd been outside trying to walk off her anger for the last couple of hours, stopping only once to visit with a lonely neighbor who'd invited her in for coffee. Her cheeks were flushed.

"I suppose a congratulation is in order. Jeff said as he extended his hand to Destiny.

"Thank you," she said. There was something about Jeff

131

she immediately liked. Apparently, Chase hadn't told him she was planning to divorce him, that she felt her marriage to him had been a mistake. He seemed to know nothing about it.

"I'm really sorry about what happened. Chase told me about Daddy." Destiny clenched her jaw and looked away. "The man is mentally ill," Jeff added. "He needs help. I'm glad to have you in the family."

Destiny smiled weakly, laughing to herself. She bet he was. Look what he had to choose from. Any addition would have been a welcome improvement.

Strangely, she found Jeff Braddon's presence comforting. She was glad he was there and she didn't have to be alone with Chase. Jeff seemed so normal compared to the rest of them. He was warmer than his younger brother; not quite as handsome, but there was something very appealing about him. He had a certain charm.

He was different than she had expected. He was well-mannered and polite, gentle and soft-spoken. At five-eleven and at the age of thirty he was a couple of inches shorter than his baby brother. He had straight brown hair and green eyes. His face was strong and his neatly trimmed beard and mustache made him quite pleasant looking. He seemed genuine, and Destiny admired that quality about him.

Jeff helped Destiny slip off her coat and hung it in the tiny closet by the front door. Destiny admired the way he dressed. He was clad in a beige corduroy jacket, light blue tailored shirt, and matching slacks. His shoes were a rugged-looking suede and looked as though they'd been used for hiking.

"How about if I take you both to dinner?"

"I could cook something," Destiny offered.

Chase looked at Destiny in disbelief. "It would probably be safer to eat out," he said, chuckling.

Destiny grinned wryly. She didn't know what had possessed her to offer to cook. She didn't have an inkling as to how to prepare food and never cared to learn. She had helped Mary on occasion in the kitchen, cutting up vegetables, but that was the extent of it. As long as there were restaurants that could do it better . . . who was she to compete? Her specialty was ordering a pizza. She didn't know why she had said that. She supposed because she liked Chase's brother and had wanted to impress him with her culinary skills? What culinary skills?

"I appreciate the offer and I'm sure you're a terrific cook." Chase rolled his eyes and Destiny suppressed a grin. "Perhaps another night would be better. Right now I'm starved and don't have much food in the house." Jeff never kept the kitchen well stocked and usually grabbed fast-food on his way home from work. "I know this great little Chinese place in town. My treat."

Chase was happy that his brother had offered to treat, since he was running out of money, and Destiny could eat like a stray animal. "What do you both say? Unless you would prefer something else?"

"Destiny?" Chase waited for her approval. He didn't want to upset her in any way. He was relieved that she was back in control of herself.

"I love Chinese," Destiny replied.

Two hours later they returned from the Chinese restaurant, Destiny and Jeff laughing, standing at the front door as Jeff searched his pocket for his house key, their bodies unwittingly close, as Chase looked on.

"This is the best time I've had in weeks," said Destiny, smiling, looking at Jeff, acting as if her husband weren't even there. The two of them seemed to like each other a little too much, thought Chase. They had seemed to really hit it off, more than he would have preferred.

Chase had been unusually quiet during dinner. He'd been too busy observing the interplay between his brother and his wife. They seemed to be having too good a time. At times he'd felt left out, as if he were invisible when they discussed subjects he had no interest in.

"What grades did you say you taught?" asked Jeff, as they approached the house and he unlocked the front door.

"I taught first grade in the District, but only for a short time."

"You wouldn't happen to be looking for a job?" Destiny had planned on leaving town right away, but after meeting Jeff—she couldn't believe it herself—she was having second thoughts.

Her face brightened. "Chase told you?"

Jeff nodded his head as he took her mink coat and hung it up. He eyed the coat and laughed. "You just look needy."

Destiny laughed. Jeff gestured for Destiny and Chase to come into the living room and sit down. He lowered himself comfortably on the couch, and Destiny sat next to him. Chase sat on the brown leather easy chair across from them and flipped on the TV. "You have a job if you want it. I could always use another good teacher. Finding dedicated teachers is a challenge these days."

"I'm very flattered."

Jeff explained how he obtained a degree in child psychology and founded the Braddon School, a school that catered to the needs of abused children. It was the only school like that in the area. Children came from all over the surrounding towns to go there.

"I brought home some of the children's art work. Would you be interested in seeing it? It's really quite revealing." Chase yawned again. This teaching mumbo jumbo bored him to tears. He played with the remote, flipping from channel to channel until he stumbled upon an old John Wayne movie.

Destiny nodded enthusiastically and Jeff retrieved his briefcase by the front door. Destiny moved closer to him to examine the pictures. "Typically, children find it easier to express themselves by drawing, rather than by verbal communication. They draw the elements that are the most important in their lives and omit those that aren't.

"Here for example. As you can see in this first one, the child is anxious and withdrawn. The drawing is quite small and up in the right corner of the paper.

"She's only five. The small figure represents her feelings of inadequacy. The lack of feet indicate her feeling of helplessness."

"Was she a victim of abuse?"

"Not directly, but she watched her father who was an alcoholic and drug addict repeatedly rape and beat her mother." Destiny looked shocked. "I like to refer to her as *emotionally* abused. In this next one you can see quite the opposite." Destiny studied the drawing carefully finding it fascinating. "This child is much more aggressive. The drawing of this person is significantly bigger and dominates the paper. Delinquent children frequently draw soldiers or cowboys as a sign of status gained through aggression. Many of the boys that grow up in abused homes adopt the role of aggressor; sort of as a defense mechanism and they grow up to become abusers later on; the girls tend to identify with the victims, most of the time their mothers, and frequently become victims themselves. Unfortunately, the pattern of abuse is cyclical."

Destiny sighed deeply, distressed. "So how do we stop it?"

"If we can detect it early enough, then we can help

these children rehabilitate and arrest the cycle. These drawings are a projection of their inner selves. In addition to the physical self, you can see a depiction of the psychological self." Jeff showed Destiny a third example done by a six-year-old girl who'd been sexually abused. Tears welled up in Destiny's eyes. "As you can see in the picture her bottom half is shaped like a phallic symbol, and she has noticeable breasts and the neck is large and elongated. The thick neck indicates a struggle to maintain control over her body. As you can clearly see domestic violence has a distressing effect on children. Many of the kids at my school suffer from depression, anxiety, low self-esteem and feelings of helplessness; some are timid, while others are overtly aggressive." Jeff paused. "Have you read any work by Koppitz?"

"No, I'm afraid I haven't."

In the short time they had spent together Destiny had learned so much and she found it all fascinating.

"How would you like to come out and visit the school tomorrow?"

Destiny smiled brightly. "I'd like that very much."

"In all fairness I must tell you that if you accept a job with us that the pay isn't great. We're on a limited budget."

"I didn't go into the teaching profession for the money. I went into it because I care about the kids, because I want to help them, because I know I can make a difference."

"Great. Then tommorrow, I'll drive you in."

"Are you sure you don't mind us camping out here for a little while?"

"Not at all." Jeff smiled as Chase looked on distrustfully. He didn't appreciate the way his brother looked at his wife, nor the way she responded to him; the way the two of them had so much in common; the way Destiny seemed so at ease in his brother's company, so interested in everything he had to say. They had only known each other for a couple of hours, and it was obvious that they were becoming fast friends. The minute he could afford it, he was going to move out of his brother's house.

Destiny had risen especially early that morning. She was so anxious to see Jeff's school that she couldn't sleep all night thinking about it. She also kept thinking of Jeff and how much she liked him, how attractive he was. Ever since the moment they'd met, he'd lingered pleasantly in her thoughts. She was relieved and happy to be spending the day with him. She snuck quietly out of bed leaving her husband fast asleep, hoping for a few stolen moments with his brother.

She heard Jeff tinkering around in the kitchen and threw on her robe, went into the bathroom to brush her teeth, wash her face, and comb her hair.

"Good morning." Jeff's back was turned. He was standing in front of the kitchen sink pouring water into the coffee pot.

"Coffee drinker?" He glanced at her as he inserted the pot into its holder and flipped the switch.

She nodded, thinking he looked so cute puttering around in the kitchen. He looked like someone's husband and for a fleeting moment she happily imagined that he was hers; that the two of them were married and Chase Braddon didn't exist at all.

"In just a few minutes you'll have the best coffee you ever tasted."

Destiny laughed. Jeff turned completely around and their eyes met and held. He looked quite handsome in his casual work attire—jeans and a pale blue button down shirt. His tan corduroy blazer was thrown over a kitchen chair. She felt so at ease with him, even half dressed.

"You look fresh and pretty this morning."

Destiny chuckled, flattered by the compliment, but a bit embarrassed. "I don't have a stitch of makeup on." She combed her fingers through her hair.

"You don't need any. You have that wholesome, yet exotic, look," he said with a twinkle in his eye.

She grinned broadly. "You made my day. "Please . . . go on."

Jeff laughed. "Eggs?" He smiled warmly, and his green eyes glimmered. They were the prettiest color green Destiny had ever seen; they reminded her of a tabby cat.

"Just black coffee."

"Pull up a chair. Make yourself at home."

"We already have," she chuckled.

Destiny sat down at the kitchen table as Jeff stood in front of the stove making scrambled eggs. "Help yourself to some orange juice; it's freshly squeezed. It's in the frig." Jeff had gone out to the convenience store a half hour ago for breakfast supplies.

"You seem to know your way around the kitchen. I like that in a man."

"I'm good at making breakfast, but that's about it. Chase is a pretty decent cook."

Destiny preferred not to think about him. She was enjoying Jeff's company too much. Jeff poured her some coffee, then lowered himself across from her with his plate of eggs. She watched the steam rise in front of her.

"Sure I can't interest you in the best scrambled eggs in town?"

"They do look good, but I rarely eat breakfast." She slowly sipped her coffee. It was strong—the way she liked it. Destiny couldn't believe that Jeff was really Henry's son and Chase's brother. He didn't belong with them.

꒰ঌ

"So how did you and my little brother meet?"

There was a foreboding chill in the air as Destiny slid into Jeff's blue Camaro next to him. She could tell by the look of things that a winter storm was approaching. The sky was a feathery gray, and the wind was biting. They didn't pull out of Jeff's driveway until a quarter of nine. Jeff thought it would be best to go in a little later than normal so that Destiny could see the classes already in session. He was quite anxious to show her all that he had accomplished in the one year since the school first opened. Destiny longed to meet the children she'd heard so much about.

The school, a refurbished red farmhouse, sat on an open field on the edge of town. It was warm and homey inside, Destiny thought, as she entered the house. The floors were carpeted in pale blue, and the walls and furniture were painted in soft easy colors. "I need to stop by my office for a second," said Jeff. "If you want to, go ahead and look around." Destiny, clad in a colorful sweater and peasant skirt peeked into the first classroom to the immediate right.

"Come in if you'd like," said the teacher, an attractive well dressed blond woman around Destiny's age. The children looked young, five or six she guessed, and they were busy drawing. The atmosphere was friendly and safe. The room was divided into learning centers. There were soft colorful cushions and an array of toys and children's drawings on the walls. There was a sunny playhouse, bookshelves, an ample supply of paints, nails to hammer into wood, and a big heaping mound of clay. Destiny smiled at the teacher as she left a little girl drawing at a round table and crossed the small cozy room to introduce herself. "Samantha Peters," she extended her hand. "This is our kindergarten/first grade. We have five children; one is absent today." Destiny introduced herself and informed Samantha that Jeff was her brother-in-law and that he had offered her a job. The young woman looked pleased.

"Where do these children come from?"

Samantha looked empathetically around the room. "From different places. Most of them were referred to us by social services. Some are local and some of them have come from the surrounding towns."

"Where are their parents?" Destiny looked at her quizzically.

"Some are in prison; the others are in safe homes getting counseling. Our goal is to try and rehabilitate these kids while their parents are being rehabilitated. Some kids are already in foster care." She gestured. "You see that little boy over there?" She pointed to the table on the left. "He's quite aggressive, doesn't interact well with the other children." Destiny stared at the cute little dark-haired boy. "His father is an alcoholic and used to beat him and his mother. He has lashes all over his little body." Destiny looked stunned. "His mother was so emotionally scarred herself, she was incapable of nurturing him, which is another reason for why he acts the way he does. He's terribly frustrated and starved for affection."

"How could he hurt his *own* child?"

"It happens more than you know. The violence between spouses extends to the children in the home in at least fifty percent of the cases. It may take the form of either physical or sexual abuse, or what is referred to as, 'rough' play."

"What exactly do you do with them?"

"In our school we use art as a form of expression. We also role-play with the children, use puppetry, and behavior modification. We do *all* this in addition to teaching them the basics."

Destiny wanted to throw her arms around each child.

She knew inside she had so much to give. Samantha met Destiny's eyes. "Times are tough . . . we all know that, but so many people take out their problems and frustrations on their children. I wonder why people can't seek help *before* they ruin their children's lives. They're only perpetuating the ugly cycle of domestic violence."

"Tell me about that little blond girl you were working with when I came in. What's her story?"

"Tiffany." She sighed and shook her head regretfully. "That poor little thing has the self-esteem of a fly. Go over and look at her drawing and see for yourself—it's so small you can barely see it." Destiny crossed the room to the tiny girl with the blond ponytail and big hazel eyes. She appeared depressed and very shy. When Destiny spoke to her, she whispered so softly that she could barely hear her. She refused to make eye contact with Destiny even when she crouched down and spoke to her directly.

"Tiffany, that's a very pretty picture. Would you like to tell me about it?" The little girl shook her head. It was clear to Destiny that she wanted to be left alone.

Jeff watched Destiny from the doorway, appreciating her sensitivity, admiring how he respected the child's privacy and didn't try and push her. She was the most beautiful woman he'd ever seen, and he was envious of his little brother for finding her first. She was warm and kind, and he could see that she was a very special person, who was deeply caring. He was confident that he'd done the right thing by hiring her and knew she would be an asset to the school. He knew the children would love her. He was beginning to have feelings for her that he knew he shouldn't have, and he didn't know quite what to do about them. He kept trying to resist what he felt for her, and kept reminding himself each time she crept into his thoughts . . . that she was his brother's wife.

"Would you like to see the rest of the school?" he asked. Destiny looked up at him and nodded, tears filling her eyes.

"These kids . . . they need so much," she said, and shook her head. "And they've gotten so little. It just isn't fair. Why do people have kids if they don't really want them? If they're going to treat them this way?"

⅄

Destiny began working at the school the following day. Jeff had assigned her some of the sixth graders, and she found that they had similar problems as the younger children, but on a larger scale. They had lived as victims of abuse for much longer and were even more scarred and more difficult to contend with; and each day her patience was exhausted, but in spite of it all, she still found the experience quite rewarding. If she could reach only *one* child, the experience would all be worth it.

She had never forgotten little Tiffany who pulled at her heartstrings the very first day. She had made a special effort to get to know her and spent much of her free time talking to the little girl; and after a period of time Tiffany began to trust Destiny and her somber little face lit up whenever she saw her favorite teacher coming.

One afternoon during her break, Destiny went into her classroom and pulled the quiet little girl onto her lap while Miss Peters read them a story. Tiffany allowed Destiny to stroke her hair. She squeezed the little girl. "I love you . . . and I think you're the best."

⅄

"Tiffany's enamored with you. What's your secret?" Jeff asked that afternoon, as Destiny was busily packing up her things to leave.

"I just pretend she's mine." She met his eyes and smiled warmly. "I really wish she were." She shrugged her shoulders. "I just give her loads of hugs and kisses. I hope I have a little girl of my very own just like her someday."

Jeff walked over to Destiny and rested his hands on her shoulders. His forwardness surprised her, and she didn't know quite how to respond. She felt somewhat uneasy. It seemed so intimate. It was the first time he had ever touched her, that they'd been this close, and she liked his touch; but she didn't know what the gesture really meant. She had the sudden urge to kiss him.

He looked her directly in the eye. "You are a terrific asset and a gifted teacher. I'm so glad I hired you. You're doing a great job. The kids and the staff all love you."

She gazed into his eyes. She knew she was falling in love with him. She'd never felt like this before. This was the real thing. She couldn't help herself. She wondered if he sensed it and hoped he felt the same. "I'm glad you hired me, too. I love working here at the school. I love the kids." I love being with you, she wanted so desperately to say to him. She wanted to spend all her time with him; she couldn't get enough of him.

"You keep up the great work." He released his hands from her shoulders. She tried to hide her disappointment. She wished he'd attempted more. Destiny didn't want Jeff to leave. "See you later." He gave her the thumbs up sign.

$\boldsymbol{\kappa^*}$ *Chapter eleven*

*I*t was the middle of March. Milltown's air was still biting, the flower buds still hidden in the hard ground. The children were indeed a challenge, but it didn't take Jeff, and Destiny's three coworkers, long to discover that she had an uncanny way with them, that she could work magic.

Young Samuel, a twelve-year-old boy, a victim of a broken home and child abuse, had kicked Destiny in the legs as hard as he could one day at school, leaving her aching and bruised for a week. After kicking her he had picked up his chair and had thrown it at her—luckily missing her only by inches. Destiny's immediate inclination had been to throw the chair back at him, he had infuriated her so. But she knew better—she knew that that was not the solution. What he needed was her love and understanding and an inordinate amount of patience.

Another child, Glenda Sue, was eleven. She refused to do her work, couldn't stay on a task, distracted the other children, and called Destiny every unflattering name she could think of. During those first months there were many times that Destiny wondered why she had subjected herself to this kind of harassment; why she had agreed to teach these kids . . . the kids no one else wanted.

Jeff had told her how amazed he was with her perseverance and dedication. She refused to give up on a single child in her classroom. In spite of all their abuse she still found it in her heart to love each and every one, and with Jeff's continuous support and aid, she devised innovative ways to teach them.

Many days Destiny worked late into the evening. She was truly dedicated and there just weren't enough hours in the school day to accomplish all her work. She and Chase were living in their own place now, a small apartment near Jeff's in upper Milltown.

⁊

Jeff was getting ready to leave when he noticed the light still on in Destiny's classroom. "Don't you ever go home?" he said, poking his head in the door.

She looked up at him from grading papers at her desk, glad to see him, which didn't happen so often anymore, and she smiled. "I'm happier when I'm here. Besides, I have plenty to do."

"I thought my brother worked nights."

"He does. He usually gets home around two in the morning . . . drunk as can be. He tries to wake me up, but I pretend I'm fast asleep. He mumbles to himself, stumbles a few feet and then collapses on the floor. He rarely makes it to the bedroom."

"I'm sorry. Is there anything I can do?"

Destiny watched Jeff sit on the edge of her desk and face her squarely. *Take me home with you,* she wanted to say. She couldn't bear the thought of returning to her apartment. She longed for Jeff to reach over and touch her. He was all she thought about day and night.

"I can think of a few things." She wanted to tell him exactly how she felt . . . that she was very much in love with him.

"Jeff . . . I—" She was about to tell him, but suddenly she lost her nerve. She was disappointed in herself. There was a stack of books next to her chair on the tile floor. "You can help me carry these books out to my car—if it's not too much trouble."

"Sure." Jeff began piling the textbooks into his arms. Destiny rose from her desk and followed him out to her car.

⚘

Destiny and Jeff spent many evenings working side by side, eating fast food together and talking away the hours. It was the only time when she could have him all to herself, and she cherished it.

She had fallen deeply in love with Jeff and was planning to ask Chase for a divorce. She had never loved Chase, and regretted marrying him. She could no longer bear to live with him and had been sleeping on the couch for some time, because she could no longer bear to have him touch her. Chase had become cynical and angry, despised his job at the mill where he worked the swing shift. He felt it was beneath him after the academy and complained constantly about how miserable he was.

When Chase wasn't working his shift at the mill he sat glued in front of the TV with the remote locked in his left hand, flipping channels, feeling terribly sorry for himself and noisily slurping beer after beer.

His temper flared when he drank and his tongue became acrid. With no one else to take out his frustrations on, he took them out on Destiny. "I've seen the way you and Jeff look at each other. You spend an awful lot of time together, and I don't like it. I don't want you working at that school anymore," said Chase angrily, the minute Destiny stepped into the apartment early one night before he left for work.

"What are you talking about?" Destiny glared back at him. "Jeff and I are good friends. And if you think I'm quitting my job because you tell me to, you're crazy. I make my own decisions, remember?"

Coming home to this small dismal apartment she shared with a husband she didn't love and no longer even liked, depressed her. She missed the luxury of the mansion. She missed being surrounded by beautiful things. If her father had been able to see the way she was living, she knew he would have died. A few times she'd thought of calling him, but each time she'd lost her nerve. Too much time had gone by.

"You don't even know what you're saying, Chase. You're drunk, as usual."

"You've been working awfully long hours for a teacher. School's over at three. What are you doing there so late? Coloring?" He laughed, then quaffed another beer.

Destiny chose to ignore the hostile remark and placed her book bag, heavy with textbooks, onto the kitchen table. She brought home the work she still hadn't finished.

She surveyed the room in disbelief. The entire apartment which she had decorated in wicker and pale colors had been trashed. Old plates of food and empty beer cans were strewn everywhere. Chase didn't seem to care about anything anymore. He had once promised her that he would keep things picked up while she worked, but he had fallen back on his word.

The sight of Chase in his deteriorated condition repulsed her. He was unshaven and reeked of booze, sat around in tight blue jeans and a torn sleeveless undershirt. He was becoming the spitting image of Henry and there was little she could do about it. She had been thinking of leaving him for some time, and knew she had to get out of there. "I can't live here anymore, Chase. I'm leaving."

He approached her, his large muscular frame towering over hers. "You are not going anywhere. You're staying right here."

"You have no control over me. You can't make me do anything I don't want to do."

"Oh, no?"

To her astonishment, he scooped her up in his arms and carried her off to the bedroom. "Put me down," she said, trying to struggle loose, beating him with her flailing arms. He pinned her down on the bed. She thought he was going to rape her. He breathed right into her face. "You do as I say, or I'll have to lock you in the closet."

"You wouldn't dare," she yelled.

"I don't want to hear another word about your leaving, do you understand? I'm sick of it."

"I can say whatever I like," she threw the words at him angrily.

"Okay . . . have it your way."

Chase lifted her up and hoisted her over his shoulders. "Put me down right now!" she screamed at the top of her lungs. He threw her into the closet and quickly slammed the door. She pounded hard until her fists ached. "Let me out! Are you insane?" She heard him insert the key into the lock.

"When you come to your senses, I'll let you out. You need some time to think." Destiny frantically twisted the knob, pounded the door with her fists, and screamed every obscenity she could think of at him.

"You're a hot tempered little bitch, aren't you?"

Destiny sunk down on the floor and started to sob. She had no idea how long he was planning to leave her there. "I'm going out with my buddies. Be back later." No man was going to do this to her. He wasn't going to get away with this, she thought as she sat in the dark, his clothes hanging in her face. She swiped them angrily away. Who the hell did he think he was to do this to her? He had no right to treat her this way. She wasn't a piece of property, she was a human being with rights. She would get back at him for this. She swore it. She would never forget it. She would find a way and would leave him for good.

The next morning Destiny awoke, relieved to find herself in her own bed. Out of exhaustion, she had fallen asleep on the closet floor, and sometime during the night, Chase had come home and had thrown her in bed with her clothes on.

She woke up groggy, her eyes so swollen she could barely open them from all the crying, and she wondered how she would ever escape him. She still couldn't believe that he had done something like that to her. He was severely disturbed, she believed, now more than ever. She wondered how she would ever be free of him. For the first time she realized she was playing with fire, and that she had to treat the matter very delicately. He had even threatened to kill himself if she ever left him, and at the moment she didn't care if he did it.

"Hungry?" Chase stood apologetically in the doorway with a breakfast tray for her.

"No." She could barely look at him she was so angry.

"I'm sorry about last night. I know I got a little out of hand. I'd been drinking. You're not hurt or anything?" He sat down on the bed and placed the tray over her lap.

She shook her head.

"Your favorite . . . black coffee and light toast."

Chase leaned over to kiss her, and Destiny turned her head abruptly away.

He looked down at her sorrowfully, then walked quietly out of the room.

Destiny truly loved her work at the school and hated the thought of abandoning the children who so desperately needed her. In addition, that she had fallen in love with its director. She considered moving to another part of town, but she knew that Chase would never be able to accept that arrangement and feared that he'd come after her, so her only recourse was to move out of the state back to Virginia.

She thought of Jeff more and more each day. In the few months of working together they had developed a strong friendship based on mutual respect, and Destiny found that she could confide in him about almost anything. He had been shocked when she told him about the closet incident.

There was a light snow flurry the morning Destiny drove herself to school in the old Volkswagen Beetle that Chase had bought for her. Tears coursed down her cheeks as the snow hit the windshield. The hypnotic beat of the wipers were strangely in synch with her heart. She and Chase had had another terrible fight and by the time she arrived at school, she was sobbing. She raced past Jeff who was sitting at his desk next to the large picture window. He had caught a glimpse of her as she flew by.

"Destiny . . . are you all right?" Jeff entered her classroom and found her hovering over her desk, her red-rimmed eyes searching for something, a crumpled tissue in her hand.

"Chase and I," she breathed deeply, then looked at him, "had another fight."

"He didn't hit you, did he?" She shook her head, and he breathed a sigh of relief.

"No." She shrugged." He just knocked over a couple of chairs, broke a few plates." Jeff looked at her in concern.

"What was it about?"

Destiny hesitated a moment, then met his eyes. "You."

"What about me?"

"He's very jealous. He thinks something is going on between us."

Jeff shook his head, crossed his arms and looked downward. "He's always been jealous of me ever since we were kids. Did you tell him it wasn't true? That we're just very good friends." He sighed. "I guess it wouldn't matter. Chase is pigheaded, he's going to believe whatever he wants."

Tears welled up in Destiny's eyes. She felt so alone, so desperately unhappy. She didn't know how much longer she could live this way. She began to cry.

"It's gonna be all right." Jeff pulled her into his arms, and she didn't resist.

"Maybe Chase has a legitimate reason for concern," she mumbled softly into his chest.

Jeff looked at her. "What are you talking about?"

Destiny gazed into his eyes. "I think you know. I'm in love with you, Jeff—not Chase. You're the one I think about day and night. You're the one I want." She could feel her heart pound, and she wanted to kiss him.

"You're just upset. You're upset with your husband and your turning to me because I'm here and we're friends, that's all."

"No, you're wrong." Tears streamed down Destiny's cheeks. "I'm in love with you, Jeff. The two of us are alike. Chase and I—we're too different. We could never make each other happy. Our marriage was a terrible mistake from the start. I don't love him . . . I never have . . . I never will."

Jeff exhaled deeply. "Destiny, you and I are good friends . . . and that's all. You know I'm always here for you if you need me." He put up his hands. "We've said all there is to say."

She was suddenly hurt and angry. "I know you feel more. . . . I see the way you look at me."

"Whatever I feel is irrelevant. You're my brother's wife."

"You're the one I want. I've never felt this way about anyone." She moved closer and tilted her face to kiss him. Jeff felt the overwhelming passion between them and found her irresistible and met her lips, kissing her fervently. He ran his fingers through her long dark hair. It was as soft as spring rain. His desire for her mounted; he wanted her more than ever.

"Destiny this is wrong." He pulled his lips away.

"But it's not, Jeff, *this* is the only thing that's right." She kissed him again falling into his eager arms.

He knew that if he didn't stop himself soon it would be too late. To her dismay, he tore away from her. "This is getting out of hand."

He quickly left the room before she had a chance to speak. She scurried into the hallway after him. "Jeff . . . please." Destiny's eyes filled with fresh tears as she watched him walk down the hall away from her.

꙳

Destiny cried the day school ended. Each child had been so special to her, had helped her to discover more about herself. She had seen each one of them make such tremendous progress, and she felt so very proud knowing she had at least been partially responsible. "Samuel," Destiny called out to the twelve-year-old boy who stood awkwardly with his back to her, only a few feet away as if he didn't want to go. She reached out to him, pulled him into her arms and embraced him. "You have a good summer."

Samuel hugged her back, fighting back the tears he felt clouding his eyes. "Thank you, Mrs. Braddon." He looked up at her with his sad, big brown eyes, and she smiled gently. She brushed her hand lightly over his curly dark hair.

"You know I'll always be here for you." A tear escaped and slid down his cheek.

Destiny and Jeff stood side by side watching Samuel. Destiny was fighting back an overwhelming surge of emotion while the young man, about to embark on adolescence, climbed the steps of the yellow school bus. She fell silent as the bus pulled away, then murmured, "I hope he does well in his new school next year."

"You've done all you can for him. Now it's up to him."

Jeff turned to look at her. She was such a beautiful person on the inside, besides being breathtaking on the outside. He had the sudden urge to embrace her, to pull her into his arms, and kiss her as if there would never be a tomorrow. But he restrained himself. Some things can never be . . . as much as we want them, he thought to himself sadly. Destiny was married to Chase. All he could ever hope to be was her friend. Nothing more.

Two of the other teachers were cleaning out their classrooms; one had already left. "I guess I need to go clear out my things for the summer." There was a small breeze, the air was like freshly washed cotton. Jeff had no idea that Destiny was not planning to return in the fall, that she was planning to move back to Virginia. The thought of all of this ending made Destiny overly emotional and she turned and began to head toward the schoolhouse.

"Destiny." She stopped and turned. Jeff approached her and smiling gently, wiping a tear off her cheek. "Don't take it so hard. You'll get to do it all again in the fall . . . but as co-director. I could use the help. What do you say?"

She looked at him in surprise. She met his eyes, a smile illuminating her face. Her smile quickly faded.

Jeff chuckled lightly. "Don't look so surprised. I'm thinking of expanding," they turned toward the building, "adding on an extension. What do you think?"

He pointed toward the house, and they both tried to envision how it would look. She attempted a smile and tried to be cheerful. "Think of all the kids we could help," she said.

"Twice as many." He placed his hands on her slim shoulders and turned her around to face him. They looked into each other's eyes. He wanted her so much, he could barely stand it. He had made up his mind to confess his feelings. He could no longer go on like this. He could no longer hold back. He loved her too much. It was torture. He hadn't asked to fall in love with her. He hadn't done it consciously or deliberately. It had just happened. It had been beyond his control. He wished it hadn't happened but it did and there was nothing he could do to stop it. He couldn't control his emotions or feelings. He couldn't see her every day, work with her so closely, and not tell her how he felt. She was too important to him. He had no choice but to reveal his feelings and then deal with the consequences later.

"Destiny—I—" She looked into his eyes hungrily. *I love you more than I've ever loved anyone. I can't hold back my feelings anymore. I don't know what to do about it, but I'm deeply in love with you.* He had rehearsed what he would say that morning when he was alone.

Suddenly he couldn't say it. The words just lodged in the back of his throat. Every time he tried he thought of Chase. He just couldn't do it. "Never mind, it's not important." Destiny's face filled with disappointment.

"What do you say we close down here, go collect my younger brother and head to Wallowa lake for some fishing? I think we deserve it."

Destiny nodded. "Let me get my things."

Jeff watched her as she walked briskly to the old house, her long ebony hair cascading down her back, as he tried with great effort to suppress what he felt for her.

⁓

Chase wasn't anywhere to be found. Destiny searched the apartment and Jeff looked outside. "Where do you think he could have gone?" Jeff asked, as Destiny stepped outside.

"I don't know." She shrugged, relieved that they *hadn't* found him. "He's probably out drinking with Bobby George. That seems to have become your little brother's favorite pastime."

"Jeff," said Destiny a few minutes later, sitting beside him as he pulled his blue Camaro out of the driveway. She lowered her chin. "Things are not good between Chase and me, as you might have guessed. They never have been. I never should have married him—it was a mistake. I only married Chase to get away from my father."

Jeff looked at Destiny, hurt and surprise filling his face. "Why would you want to do a thing like that?"

"I don't know what possessed me to do it—it was childish and immature. I've thought of leaving, of returning to Virginia. I'm planning to ask Chase for a divorce, but Chase has threatened to kill himself, and I'm afraid he might do it. He's been very depressed lately."

Jeff shook his head and frowned. "Chase is not going to kill himself. He is only telling you that to scare you into staying." He met her eyes. "The school would hate to lose you . . . but you can't stay in an unhappy marriage. Have you considered counseling?"

"I told you . . . I'm not in love with Chase."

Crossing steep mountain roads, they arrived at Wallow

lake an hour and a half later. The glacier-formed lake, located near the high lakes and the wilderness area surrounded by snowcapped mountains, presented the most spectacular view Destiny had ever seen. It took her breath away.

"This is where I come to get away," Jeff said. They parked the car in the designated parking lot and headed toward the lake.

"The water—it's crystal clear."

"And so cold." Jeff feigned a shiver. "Come on, go ahead and stick a toe in it." Destiny chuckled. She walked to the edge, removed one white sneaker and submerged her foot, withdrawing it quickly as Jeff laughed. "See what I mean. It's like ice water. The snow from that mountain," he pointed ahead, "trickles down into the lake. And it's one of the deepest." Destiny gazed ahead in awe. "It's reported to be between three hundred to six hundred feet deep. A friend of mine lends me his speedboat whenever I'm here. It's docked over there." Destiny surveyed the cluster of small boats.

"What kind of fish are we going to be fishing for anyway?"

"Yank, landlock salmon, trout; whatever's hungry enough to nibble on the bait."

꙳

It had been so incredibly serene out on the water, and it pleasantly reminded her of fishing with her father in the pond behind their house. She felt the warmth of the sun on her arms and face. She had dressed appropriately in shorts and a T-shirt. She had caught seven trout, and Jeff had caught only one. She gleamed with pride. "How about a ride on the gondola lift? It's the highest vertical ascent in North America. The view from the top is indescribable."

Destiny hesitated. "I have a confession to make." Jeff

looked at her curiously. "Uh—um—I'm afraid of heights."

"Don't worry about riding on the gondola; it's all enclosed." She looked at him skeptically. "The best way to conquer your fear is to face it. Come on." He took her by the arm.

The ride to the top of Mt. Howard seemed to take forever as the cable pulled the small box that enclosed them grudgingly up the designated path. It was as if they were being pulled up the steep mountain in slow motion just to torment her by someone lacking the strength and who might lose his grip at any second and send her plummeting down the mountain to an early death. A few times the cable car came to a brief halt allowing them to sit and dangle. Destiny broke out in a cold sweat. Throughout the trip her hand remained firmly locked around the metallic pole. Numb with fear, she could feel her heart jump, and she sat so deathly still she could almost hear it and prayed that the ride would soon be over. She tried not to look down or around or anywhere but at Jeff. She tried not to think of where she was or the fact that she'd have to return the same way.

"What a view."

Destiny made a wry face.

"Don't worry. We're over half way there." She attempted a weak smile as the cable car continued its ascent.

Instant relief came the moment she stepped foot on solid ground. Being on the top wasn't as frightening as she expected. The surface was too large for her to find the edge and fall off. She scanned the landscape. The mountain top was blanketed with green grass and dotted with patches of wildflowers. "The air's so fresh." And it was cooler than down below.

"Look out over there." Jeff pointed. "You can see the high lakes and the wilderness area. They took the next half hour to wander around. Suddenly they found themselves all alone. The other sightseers were no longer around. Jeff found himself staring at Destiny. He couldn't seem to take his eyes off her. She stirred feelings in him that he'd never felt before, and his desire for her began to mount. She was so incredibly beautiful with her shiny wind-tousled hair and deep blue eyes. He had suppressed his feelings for her for so long, but all of a sudden he saw her in a different light—it was as if she no longer belonged to Chase. She said herself that she was planning to leave him. He couldn't make her love his brother, and it wasn't his fault she didn't love him. From what she had said she hadn't loved him from the start. He could no longer control how he felt. He wanted her now more than ever.

He knew she only loved him; she had confessed her love for him that day at the school. *Destiny*. He loved the sound of her name. He loved to say it, to whisper it to himself at night. Their eyes met and held and she smiled softly and Jeff moved closer and pulled her into his arms. She didn't resist. He kissed her gently. He loved the feel of her full lips against his. His body began to fill with desire as he kissed her harder. The power of her kiss overtook him and they embraced each other tighter, and he pulled her down with him into the tall grass. Jeff rolled on top of her allowing her to feel his strength and peered into her eyes. "You have no idea of how long I've dreamt of doing this, of being with you . . . but you've always been—" He hesitated, trying to think of the right words to describe exactly how he felt—"the forbidden fruit."

Destiny laughed. But her expression soon turned serious, as she gazed into his eyes while running her fingers through his chestnut hair. "You're all I've thought of since the day we met. Chase means nothing to me. He never has. You're the one I love, Jeff."

"And I love you . . . more than you can imagine, more than I ever thought possible." Hearing her confess her love for him filled him with overwhelming emotion, and he began to kiss her again, this time more urgently. They became lost in each other's kisses and caresses and tore at each other's clothes desperately until they each lay naked, their bodies locked together on the mountaintop. They made the most passionate love as he entered her, and afterward they held on to one another tightly, each one wishing that this moment would never end. "I can't bear the thought of your leaving," said Jeff, as he turned to look at her. "There must be another way."

Destiny sighed. "I wish there were, but I don't see any alternative."

"I can't live without you," he said tenderly.

"Would you ever consider moving east?"

He released her and rolled onto his back and placed his hands beneath his head as he gazed at the clear sky. He mulled over the idea. It had never occurred to him. His whole life had been here in Milltown.

Destiny sat up and pulled her T-shirt over her head, then slipped on her shorts. "Here . . ." she chuckled lightly, tossing his shirt and shorts over his still-swelled member "Cover yourself up before we get arrested."

"There's no one else up here but us." He laughed, slipping into his jeans shorts. "Maybe the best thing to do is to just confront Chase, tell him how you feel . . . tell him about us."

"I don't know." She looked suddenly afraid. "There's no telling what he'll do."

"I wouldn't take my little brother too seriously."

"It's really amazing."

"What?"

"How completely different the two of you are."

"I guess I take after my mother."

"What was she like?"

"I barely remember her. She died when I was very young. She was supposed to be a very special lady."

"My mother died, too." Destiny said. "My grandmother and uncle were murdered right in front of me," she blurted, and Jeff looked completely stunned. "But I don't remember it. This is what I've been told. And not too long ago I learned that my 'adopted' father was my real father. Can you believe he kept something like that from me? I was so hurt. We're still not on good terms. I don't know if we'll ever be."

"How traumatic for you."

"It's okay, really. I don't remember anything."

"It was too painful. You've obviously suppressed it. I'm sure it's manifested itself in other ways—ways you may not be aware of."

"I just wish I knew more about my background." Unwittingly, she began to smile. "I was really quite lucky. I had everything. My father adored me, spoiled me absolutely rotten."

"I think he did a terrific job."

She reached over and hugged him. He began to kiss her lips again softly.

✴

Jeff drove Destiny back home. "I had a wonderful time," she said, gazing fondly into his eyes before climbing out of the car.

Gingerly he took her hand into his. "Are you sure you don't want me to come in and be there when you talk to Chase?"

She nodded, feeling her stomach tighten nervously at the thought of having to confront an irate husband. "I think it would be best if I spoke to Chase alone."

She left him, her heart pounding, rehearsing what she would say, dreading the heated argument that she knew would soon ensue.

~

"Where've you been? I've been waiting for you for over an hour," hollered Chase from the small kitchen. He was retrieving a third can of beer from the frig. The smell wafted into her nostrils as he approached her. "Where you been all this time, Sweet Thing?" His appearance disgusted her. He hadn't shaved in days and his hair was long and straggly. He wore the same sleeveless undershirt and torn jeans day after day. "Baby," he said as he grabbed her, "I've missed you." He planted a wet kiss on her lips.

Destiny pulled away. "Chase, we have to talk."

"About what?" Reluctantly, he followed her to the couch and sat down.

"Chase, I want a divorce." She could feel her stomach tighten. A veil of anger crossed his face.

"You're not going to start that divorce thing again, are you?" He felt his pulse race. He couldn't lose her. She was all he had left.

Destiny took a deep breath, then said, "Chase, it's not my intention to hurt you, but let's face it, we both made a big mistake . . . but it's still not too late to correct it. It's really the best thing for both of us."

"Maybe for you," he glared at her, "but not for me. I love you."

"And don't even think to throw the suicide wrap on me, Chase." She could see that he was becoming more agitated, and suddenly his own self-pity blossomed into full-fledged fury.

"There's someone else, isn't there?" Chase looked terribly proud of himself.

"Chase, I'm not going to sit here and lie to you. I'm in love with Jeff. I didn't plan it . . . it just happened."

Jeff. His brother's name rang like an alarm growing louder and louder until he thought his head would explode. He was livid, and after three beers his sense of reality was clouded. He stood up, looking tall and ominous as he glared down at her, and suddenly she felt physically threatened, fearing that he might lose control and hit her or even kill her. There was no telling what he might do. He was filled with so much pent-up anger, anger that had been fermenting since he was a small boy. "That son of a bitch!" he began to yell. "My whole life he's taken everything from me, everything I ever wanted, everything that shoulda been mine. And now he's taken my wife." All he could think of was how much he despised his brother. He hated him enough to kill him. He could feel his blood boil. He felt so hot he thought his skin would melt. He lost all control. "It's time that I settle the score. I'm gonna kill that no good son of a bitch." Terror filled Destiny's eyes and her heart raced. The thought of him doing anything that awful to Jeff was too terrible to comprehend.

"Chase, calm down. You don't know what you're saying. You're drunk," she said frantically, but he wouldn't listen.

"I'm gonna kill him. I'm gonna kill him," he muttered, as he ran to the glass gun cabinet and pulled a twelve gauge shotgun off the rack. He stopped momentarily and rubbed his hand over the stock admiring the intricate carving. Destiny looked at him in astonishment. He then opened the bottom drawer of the cabinet and took out three shells. He loaded them into the gun, then dropped a couple more into his jeans pocket on his way out of the apartment.

Destiny could not believe what she was witnessing and ran after him begging him to come to his senses. Tears streamed down her cheeks. "Chase, please stop before it's too late. You don't know what you're doing. You are making an irrevocable mistake."

He turned and glared at her. "This is something I shoulda done a long·time ago." He hurried to the pickup, and Destiny tried to block him. She no longer cared what happened to her. All that mattered was Jeff. Forcefully, Chase pushed her out of the way and she fell to the ground. She lost all self-control and began to shout at him, as he jumped into the old pickup and tore out of the parking lot like a madman. She stood there trembling and crying, thinking of what to do next.

Do something, do something, hurry and do something before it's too late, a voice screamed frantically in her head. She must call Jeff and warn him, she thought, as she ran back into the apartment. She had to call him right now. She dashed to the phone, picked up the receiver and, with her hand shaking, dialed his number. . . . There was no answer. Jeff probably wasn't home yet. Destiny began to cry hysterically. She knew even if she got in her car right now there was no way she'd reach Jeff in time. What was she going to do? What was she going to do? Trembling, she tried dialing again. Oh, God, please let him answer . . . please. No answer. What to do next, what to do next. Call the police. Call the police. If anything happens to Jeff she'd die. She dialed 911. She loved him so much. Please, God don't let anything happen to him. She spoke to the operator. She could barely explain what happened. She kept stumbling over her words.

"Unless an actual crime has been committed, there's little we can do."

"This isn't a threat!" Destiny began to yell into the phone. "My husband went over there with a loaded shotgun! Do you hear me?"

"Lady, please stop screaming in my ear. I can hear you just fine," said the 911 operator calmly.

"Then send someone out there before it's too late," sobbed Destiny. "Please . . ."

"I'll see what I can do." The woman hung up.

Destiny attempted to call Jeff's house one more time. There was still no answer. She had to go out there and intercept him. That was all she could think of to do. *Please don't let it be too late.*

～

Chase drove his pickup furiously down the small streets, never in his life feeling such fury. *I'm gonna kill him. I'm gonna kill him.* That was all he could think of. The truck came to a screeching halt in Jeff's driveway, and Chase jumped from the vehicle, carrying his rifle to the front door. He began to pound like a raving madman, holding the shotgun at his left side.

Jeff had arrived a few minutes before. He opened the front door only to discover his baby brother pointing a shotgun in his face.

Chase leveled the gun as he stepped inside and pointed it at Jeff, who looked at him in disbelief.

"Chase, what are you doing?" His heart jumped. "Why in God's name are you pointing that thing at me? Surely you're not planning to use that." Jeff extended a hand as if to defend himself. "Now, calm down, Chase. Get a grip on things. I realize you're upset, but shooting your own brother is not going to help matters any. Let's try and talk this thing out." He tried to remain calm.

Chase glared at his older brother, never feeling such hatred, and his eyes began to fill with tears. His hand trembled as he gripped the shotgun. "My whole life you've always been better than me. You've always been the

165

smarter one, the one everybody liked, the one who was gonna be something, make something of himself . . . and you did just that, DOCTOR P-H-D. Ever since I was a kid you took everything that was supposed to be mine . . . and now you've taken the only thing I have left—Destiny.

"You stole her right out from under me, and now I can't get her back cause she wants *you*. She thinks you're better, too. She was the one hope I had left, and now I don't even have that." Tears rolled down Chase's cheeks. He wiped them away with the side of his bare arm.

"I'm sorry if I hurt you, Chase. Things between Destiny and me just happened. Believe me, I didn't plan it that way. I love you . . . you're my little brother."

"You're no brother. Brothers don't steal each other's women." Chase was filled with such anger. He wanted to see Jeff dead and gone forever. Then he couldn't take Destiny.

"Please, Chase, think about what you're about to do . . . I can help you get your life back on track." Jeff's heart pounded wildly. "I don't want to die," he pleaded. "And I don't believe you really want to kill me. Try to think back to when we were little. We had some good times then, remember? Surely you must remember something good."

Chase thought back to when they were small. He could vaguely recall a fishing trip they went on with their father, how after a beating from Henry which Chase didn't deserve, Jeff had tried to comfort him. That night, bruised and bloody, he had slept curled up against his big brother, who held him in his arms in the back of the pickup.

Destiny suddenly thundered through the door, praying it wouldn't be too late, that she wouldn't find the man she loved on the floor. Out of breath, with tears rolling down her cheeks, she jumped Chase from the back startling him. The gun went off just missing Jeff by an inch. With all her strength she tried to pull the shotgun away from Chase, but his strength overpowered her, and he flung her to the floor causing her to hit her head on the end table. Jeff attacked Chase from the front and tried to wrestle the gun away from him. The two went at it for what seemed like hours but what was in reality only seconds until a second shot went off. Chase reclaimed the shotgun and in a frenzy of anger aimed the gun at an unconscious Destiny who lay slumped over on the floor next to the couch.

❧ *Chapter twelve*

"*A*lexander—" Jack Winslow hesitated. "The tumor is malignant . . . you have nodular melanoma."

"Nodular melanoma?" echoed Alexander, feeling his stomach cramp, his hand tightening on the phone. He instinctively knew it was something terrible. He was in a state of shock. That damn freckle . . . it had been something serious after all. Julia's suspicions had been correct. He would have ignored it altogether if hadn't been for her constant badgering him about getting it checked.

"Alexander, I don't want to alarm you, but I think it would be best if you came in right away so that we can begin a treatment plan."

"It can be treated, Jack, can't it?"

Jack Winslow answered frankly. "As long as it hasn't gotten into your lymph nodes or bloodstream."

"I guess I can only hope for the best."

"Maintaining a positive attitude is essential."

Alexander still couldn't believe it. If they found anything inside him, he was a dead man. He had just had his forty-ninth birthday. He wasn't ready for this. He was much too young for his life to be over. He wasn't ready to die. But who ever was?

After thanking his longtime friend, Alexander lowered the receiver pensively. He suddenly had a lot to think about. Much more than he had bargained for. His mind began to explode with thoughts. He thought of his darling Destiny and how much he missed her. She was more precious now than ever. He hadn't heard from her in months, and it bothered him tremendously. He wondered if he'd ever have the chance to see her again.

✧

Unaware of the ominous phone call Julia waltzed cheerfully into the study. "How about a picnic lunch? I packed some things. I thought we could go down by the pond. What do you say? It's such a beautiful day." Her golden hair was tied into a French twist and she had on an expensive blue sundress with a halter neck and short skirt. She looked absolutely lovely, thought Alexander. Too lovely to receive such horrible news. She carried a small wicker basket with a long loaf of French bread peeking out the side like a giant nose.

Ever since his daughter's departure, their marriage had improved. They went to concerts, symphonies, dined at the most exclusive restaurants, made love in the afternoon whenever neither of them were working.

"Why the somber look?" Julia was quick to observe. "Surely you could afford me at least a few minutes of your valuable time," she teased, guessing the grave look on his face was work related.

"I just got off the phone with the doctor." Alexander took a deep breath.

Julia's heart began to beat harder. "Is it about the mole on your face?"

Soberly, Alexander nodded. "It's malignant."

"Malignant?" Julia's heart missed a beat. She clutched her breast, and her face filled with fear and dread. "I never expected this. After all, it's been three weeks and I thought no news meant—"

Julia embraced Alexander and looked deeply into his eyes.

"I'm scared," he frankly admitted as he met her gaze. "For the first time in my life . . . I'm really scared." She rested her head against his shoulder, feeling his heart beat against hers.

჻

"You must find Destiny. I must see her," said Alexander groggily. The news they had learned was the worst imaginable—Alexander's melanoma had metastasized. They had found evidence of cancer in his parotid gland, the large salivary gland located below and in front of his right ear, after removing it during a lengthy six-hour surgery. The deadly cancer had gotten inside him and there was a good chance he was going to die. Now all they could do was wait helplessly and see where the capricious melanoma was planning to strike next.

Every time Julia thought that he was likely to die from what had started as a barely noticeable eraser-tip-sized freckle she thought it too ludicrous to be true. How could son. thing so innocent as a freckle become something so deadly? She found it difficult to accept. She couldn't believe this was really happening to her. She was much too young to become a widow.

"I'm having difficulty reaching her." Julia had found Destiny's number listed in the Milltown directory. "She must be away or something." Julia sat next to Alexander on their bed. He had bandages all over the right side of his face, and he looked like a mummy. He was taking painkillers by the hour.

He had been permanently disfigured. The surgeon had warned them beforehand that this would be the end result;

and as much as it had upset them both they had no other choice but to allow the surgery. If nothing else it gave them a clearer picture of Alexander's condition. The surgeons had also recommended a neck dissection in addition to the removal of the parotid gland, and as a result, a section of Alexander's neck was missing.

It was a gruesome sight, thought Julia. Alexander looked as if he had stepped right out of a horror flick. Julia hadn't slept in nights. She was so terribly distraught over Alexander's illness, and the fact that he'd be left with a severe deformity made her literally sick to her stomach every time she thought about it. She didn't know how she was going to cope with it all. She couldn't bear the thought of seeing him to the bitter end. She wasn't emotionally strong enough. She'd had no prior training. Nothing as horrible as this had ever happened to her before, and there was a part of her that wanted to run away and never return, leave Alexander to suffer and die alone. At least then she'd be free. She could forget him and start all over, make a new life for herself. She was still vibrant and young. She still had many years ahead of her.

"You must keep trying. I need to see her."

Julia nodded. "I'm doing the best I can." She was under an inordinate amount of stress with this thing and seeing Alex's daughter would only exacerbate matters. If that girl disappeared for good she quite frankly wouldn't care at all; in fact, she'd feel quite blessed—especially at a time like this.

Whenever she thought of Destiny her whole body tightened. Her abhorrence of her stepdaughter was still as ripe as if she'd seen her yesterday.

✧

"These painkillers make me so drowsy," mumbled

Alexander, before drifting back to sleep. He had only gotten home a few hours before and already Julia found the whole situation unbearable. She didn't know if she could stand waiting on him another moment—that's why they had servants and private nurses—but he seemed to want her constantly around. He wanted her to do everything for him. He wanted her constantly by his side.

"Alex . . . please . . . let the nurses help you. I need a break. This is too hard on me," she pleaded. She wasn't used to waiting on anyone other than herself. Alexander told her that he wished to be only in the company of the people he loved. Life had suddenly become so lonely and he felt so vulnerable. "I'll keep trying," she promised.

A little while later as Julia temporarily escaped and lay submerged in a haven of fragrant bubbles, she found herself thinking selfishly that as much as she loved poor Alexander, if he was going to eventually die she wished he would just do it quickly and not prolong the whole affair and make her suffer any longer than she had to. It was the least he could do, she told herself. After all, she was only human. And this was much too hard on her.

𝓍* *Chapter thirteen*

*I*t had only been a week since the horrible incident had occurred. Destiny was still in a state of shock. Jeff was dead. Seeing how devastated Etta was and that awful Henry at his funeral hadn't made things any easier. It was as if time had stood still.

Her mind kept jumping back to that night as if on instant replay. She had attacked Chase and tried to wrest the gun away from him but that was the last thing she remembered before hitting her head and falling unconscious. When she awoke there were policeman all around and Jeff's lifeless body was slumped over hers.

According to what Chase had told the police before they had carted him off, he had regained control of the gun but couldn't bring himself to shoot his brother. Instead he had turned the gun on Destiny who lay unconscious on the floor when Jeff in a last ditch effort to save her threw himself in the way intercepting the bullet. Chase was incoherent and sobbing hysterically as two officers handcuffed him and took him away. "I never meant to kill Jeffie . . . I never meant to hurt 'im."

༄

Destiny sat in her apartment crying day after day assailed with bittersweet memories. She had loved Jeff so very much and she would have given anything to have him back; to be able to wrap her arms around him; to feel the warmth of his body against hers; to gaze into his soft green eyes; and to kiss his tender lips. She longed for him, felt so empty, so sad and lonely without him and she cried for the future together that they would never have, a future that now seemed empty and bleak. And those poor children at the school. She thought of them, too. What would become of them? He had been their only hope.

She thought about staying and continuing his work but she knew that she couldn't—there were too many unpleasant memories. She had to go home, to be with her father, the one person who truly loved her, the only one who could comfort her now.

She hadn't answered her phone in days. It rang continuously but she didn't want to talk to anyone or see anybody. She just wanted to be alone. She needed time to think. She knew she needed to pull herself together and get on with her life.

⌇

The flight back to D.C. seemed endless and Destiny was emotionally exhausted, her eyes so swollen from all the crying that she could barely see out of them. She felt terribly conspicuous the moment she stepped off the jet even with her dark sunglasses to shield her. She knew it was obvious to everyone that something was very wrong by her blotchy cheeks and sullen expression. Even the flight attendant picked up on her distress kindly asking once during the flight, "Are you all right, Miss? Is there anything I can get you?" But Destiny had simply shaken her head hoping she would leave her alone with her grief.

She hailed a cab at National Airport and sat quietly the entire way in the back seat as they sped down the George Washington Parkway to the beltway.

As they approached the estate she felt jittery inside as if she'd had too much caffeine. She thought of Julia, dread filling every inch of her. The last thing she needed right now was a confrontation. She thought of her beloved father and wondered if she hadn't been too hard on him after all. She missed him so much, especially right now when she needed him more than ever before. She knew they would both be surprised to see her there, although she realized that she should have called first.

Destiny tipped the cab driver handsomely and he offered to help her with her small carry-on bag, but she graciously refused his help. The rest of her things were being sent. She had packed only the essentials.

She took a deep breath as she walked to the front door of the mansion. Everything looked so beautiful this time of year. The grass was a lush jungle green, the flowers radiant and in full bloom. There was a slight breeze. The sky was a deep riveting blue similar to the sky that she and Jeff had made love under for the very first . . . and for the very last time. She would never forget that day. She would treasure the memory forever.

Jeff Braddon hadn't left her thoughts for very long; she missed his company so much. She thought again of poor Etta. She was a sweet old lady and Destiny harbored no resentment against her. She never held her responsible for Henry or Chase. A parent could only do so much; Etta couldn't live their lives for them. She was one of the few people who had been especially sensitive and kind to Destiny and she would never forget her.

Fresh tears began to well up in her eyes. She couldn't believe he was really gone. Jeff . . . I miss you so much, she whispered. He was no longer a part of the living, a part of her world.

Destiny knew in her heart that she would never again

love anyone the way she loved Jeff. What they'd had was too special—it only came a person's way once in a lifetime. Against his grandmother's wishes Jeff asked in his will to have himself cremated. He believed it was the most practical thing to do. But whenever Destiny thought that there was literally nothing left of him but her memories it broke her heart.

Nervously, she rang the front doorbell feeling increasingly uneasy about seeing Julia, wondering how she would react to seeing her, dreading the inevitable battles she knew they would have.

Destiny was totally surprised when Julia answered the door herself instead of one of the servants and the two women, arch enemies, stood there, each one astonished to see the other.

Destiny was shocked by her stepmother's appearance. For once in her life she looked like a human being with human frailties. Wisps of blond hair dangled loosely around her lightly made-up face. It was as if Julia had actually done physical labor for the first time in her life. She was wearing white slacks and a casual blue and white striped knitted shirt and no jewelry except for her wedding band. What had happened to her? wondered Destiny. It was obvious that she had been through something dreadful. The same exact thoughts at the same exact moment had crossed Julia's mind about her stepdaughter.

"Destiny . . . why Destiny . . . I had no idea you were coming . . . I've been trying to contact you for days." Julia actually seemed happy to see her.

Destiny looked at her in surprise wondering why Julia had been trying to contact her. The two hadn't communicated since the day she moved out. A chill crawled up her spine and her stomach tightened nervously and she was suddenly afraid. "Is my father all right?"

"Where is your husband?" asked Julia, looking around, a small smile playing on the corners of her mouth.

"That's a long story." Destiny soberly turned her eyes away. Then she looked directly at Julia. "You didn't answer me. Where is my father? Is he okay?"

"He's upstairs resting." She quickly dismissed Destiny. "Are you still married?" She couldn't just leave things alone. She was so damn nosey.

"I'd rather not talk about it right now." Destiny met her eyes. "Can I see him?"

Julia hesitated a moment. "Yes, you can see him . . . but first there's something I must tell you. Come into the study." Destiny followed Julia, wondering what this was all about. All she could think of was that something had happened to her father and she began to panic. The two women sat across from one another in front of the fireplace.

"Julia, stop being so evasive and just tell me." Destiny felt herself losing patience. "What is going on? What is this all about? Has something happened to my father?" Julia lowered her eyes, then looked away.

She took a minute to exhale deeply then said, "he has cancer."

Destiny looked stunned. She could feel her heart rip from her chest and tears filled her eyes. "Cancer?" She swallowed hard. "What kind of cancer? Is he going to die?" All this was more than she could take and she thought she might lose it at any moment and release a hellish scream.

"The most lethal type of skin cancer . . . nodular melanoma. I'm not going to lie to you, Destiny. The prognosis isn't good."

"Why didn't you tell me?"

"I've tried calling you for days . . . no one answered." Destiny turned her head painfully away. Julia exhaled deeply. "I've been going through all of this alone." Julia looked to Destiny for sympathy, but she wasn't about to get it. "I have to warn you," tears rolled down Julia's pale cheeks and her voice trembled, "he's had surgery." She exhaled again. "Half his neck is gone."

Destiny's blue eyes widened in horror. This was too awful to bear. Poor father. Her heart broke for him. Julia tried to regain her composure. She sniffled and wiped her eyes with the side of her hand. Destiny looked at Julia. It made her realize how very fragile people were. She stood up. "I want to see him."

Tearfully, Julia nodded. "He's been asking for you."

With trepidation Destiny headed up the long staircase. She wanted to see her father but there was a part of her that was so terribly afraid of what she might find. She approached his room cautiously and knocked at the door.

"Father, it's me Destiny. May I come in?"

"Destiny." She heard him whisper her name. She cracked the door and peaked inside.

"Father?" She was almost too afraid to look at him, but she knew she had to be brave.

"Destiny." She entered the room. She couldn't see his face; it was hidden by a mound of blankets. Alexander attempted to sit up so that he could get a better view of his daughter. He was groggy from the pain medication and even sitting required a great deal of effort. Destiny couldn't help but gasp as his face came into full view before her. She quickly turned her head away. She couldn't look. She couldn't bear it. He had been such a handsome man and now he looked like a freak.

"It's okay. It's hard to take, I know. I understand. Don't worry, sweetheart."

"Father." Boldly, Destiny edged her way closer, feeling queasy. It was very difficult to look at him. The right side of his neck was all but gone. There was a large ugly scar on that side of his face and under his neck which seemed to go on endlessly, and it troubled her to think of how devastating this was for him most of all. He had been so vibrant and good looking. Now before her lay a man who was frail and deformed.

"Destiny, I'm so glad you came." He watched her as she lowered herself on the bed and took his hand in hers.

"I'm so sorry." She looked at him tearfully.

"I'm so glad you're back." He squeezed her hand. She smiled, gazing sympathetically into his eyes, glad she was there to comfort him.

"Is there anything you need? Anything I can get for you?" She wanted so desperately to do something, anything to help him, anything to make this whole thing more bearable. She wanted to reverse all the bad things that had happened to both of them. If only it were possible. They didn't deserve all that had befallen them . . . but then no one ever did.

"Just be with me. Let me enjoy looking at you. It's been a while." He attempted a smile, but then felt a stab of pain in his face and froze. She surveyed the metal staples on the side of his face and neck. They looked like miniature railroad tracks and all she could suddenly think of was, *The Little Engine That Could,* her favorite bedtime story that her father used to read to her as a child. She imagined the little blue train disappearing behind his right ear.

"I'm so sorry for everything I put you through. I've been so selfish."

"We are all selfish at one time or another. We all make mistakes." He paused and breathed deeply. "As you know I've made my share."

"It's so stuffy in here. Let me open the window. You need some fresh air." The air in the room was thick and smelled medicinal. Destiny crossed the room to the large window. "That's better. It's such a beautiful day." A small breeze sifted in. She took a deep breath of fresh air as she gazed out at the gazebo down by the pond and the garden brimming with summer flowers. In her mind's eye she saw herself as a little girl bending down next to her father, he smiling down at her as she picked a handful of daisies. She remembered putting them up to her nose. She saw herself laughing and running around in circles in a party dress with a full petticoat underneath. She was glad to be home, to be with her father whom she loved so very deeply. She was happy to be with him even under these most unpleasant circumstances.

She admired the garden and the happy times she had playing there and how much her life had changed since then, and tears cascaded down her cheeks.

❧ *Chapter fourteen*

*I*n the two weeks since Destiny had arrived, she and Julia got along reasonably well. Destiny took over the primary care for her father which enabled Julia to take a break from the nursing responsibilities she hated; and she was in turn truly grateful to her stepdaughter.

Over the two-week period Destiny went to visit a lawyer about divorcing Chase. She wanted to rid herself of him permanently and hoped the entire process wouldn't take too long. She hated him for ruining her life; for taking away the man she truly loved and depriving them of a future together; and she desperately wanted to erase that part of her life and begin anew.

Each morning Destiny joined her father in his recuperative walks around the garden. While walking, she gradually confessed all that had happened to her in Oregon. Alexander had been horrified at what he had learned and terribly upset for his daughter and all that she had been through.

"The hardest thing was losing Jeff. I truly loved him. I still can't believe he's really gone." She glanced at her father and smiled softly. "You would have liked him, too. The two of us . . . we were so much alike. We loved the same things. He was the most compassionate man I've ever known." Destiny's voice quivered and fresh tears filled her eyes as she held on to her father's arm during their morning stroll, both of them clad in white shorts and casual white shirts. They stopped by the pond and gazed at the two familiar mallards who'd long ago declared this their home. "I can't get him out of my mind, no matter how hard I try. He meant the world to me. I was hoping someday we'd get married . . . start a family—" Her voice trailed off. She sadly shook her head. "I guess it wasn't meant to be." She breathed deeply. "I miss him. Life seems so meaningless now."

"It's always hard when you lose someone you love." Alexander thought of his beloved Elena. He had never gotten over her, even after all these years. "I was very much in love with your mother. It was very difficult for me to lose her, but as time passes, grief becomes easier to bear." Alexander looked affectionately at his daughter. "It will get easier for you . . . in time," he reassured her. "For now, you must try and get on with your life."

"I suppose getting a job would be a good place to start and finding a place to live," she added.

"Don't worry about finding a place to live." Alexander turned to look at his beloved daughter. "This is your home and you can stay here for as long as you like."

"Thank you," she attempted a smile, "but you know as well as I that that wouldn't work, not as a long-term arrangement anyway."

"Just think about it. You have no money and I know better than to suggest you accept a loan from me. Where would you go?"

"I'll think about it," she said to appease him. At the moment it didn't sound like such a bad idea. She was still shaken from all that had happened to her and being with her father made her feel safe and secure. She couldn't bear the thought of losing him, too, and a lump formed in her throat.

"I've been doing all the talking. It's your turn now. Tell me about my mother. What was she like? How did the two of you meet?" She had been curious about her all this time, and he had said so very little.

Arm in arm they strolled over to the white wrought-iron bench and sat down together facing the water. They were shaded from the sun by a row of trees. Destiny peered at the weeping willow next to them. It's thin limpid arms hung over the grass like long strands of hair. The air was still, not even a whisper of a breeze. A forlorn look crossed Alexander's face as he spoke of Elena. "She was the most beautiful woman in the world," he said softly. "I loved her very much. It's uncanny how much you remind me of her." He turned to look at her. "Your hair . . . the shape of your eyes . . . the resemblance is really amazing." Destiny gazed at him, her eyes filled with tenderness. The way he spoke of her brought her to tears.

"Why didn't you marry her?"

"I wanted to . . . but then she left me. She just disappeared out of my life, and I never saw or heard from her again."

"That sounds awfully heartless."

"Elena wasn't cruel. She was wonderful." He smiled.

Alexander had a faraway look in his eyes as he began to recount the story of how they'd met.

"It was June 20, 1969. After my graduation from William and Mary I didn't quite know what to do with myself. I knew the publishing business wasn't what I wanted. The whole country was in disarray over the war. Nixon had begun pulling troops out of Vietnam. I didn't believe in the war, had demonstrated zealously against it; and my father was able to pull some strings and get me out of it. In retrospect, I regret it. I feel that I should have gone.

"I regret not serving my country, but in those days I was a bit of a radical and was adamantly against it. Of course, none of this went over too well with my father. He had served in the second world war, won medals for bravery, and was very disappointed with me. He thought that I'd at least take over his business. He'd always hoped that I'd be his successor; but then again I was a bit of a maverick in those days. I didn't know what I wanted." He glanced at Destiny. "I'm sorry I'm getting sidetracked. I didn't know what I wanted . . . except for Elena. There was no doubt in my mind when it came to her.

"Anyway, a couple of college buddies and I decided that we would live it up for a couple of days in the big city. The three of us, Marc, Daniel, and I headed to Times Square, and then on to Forty-second street for a little action later that night after we checked into the hotel. We drank ourselves into a stupor, smoked a lot of pot, and then, well, I'll leave the rest to your imagination. We stayed at the Dumois. That's where I first saw her.

"The three of us had gone down to the dining room for breakfast and I had forgotten my wallet, so I went back upstairs to my room for it . . . and there she was." He looked wistful as he remembered.

൸

June 1969

"I—a—forgot something. I'll just take a minute and then I' get out of your way." Alexander awkwardly entered the room scanning the two twin beds, the contemporary night stand, and dresser. "Where did I leave my wallet?" he mumbled. He couldn't remember where he'd set it down last. Elena looked up from making the bed and began to smile. Alexander looked down at the pretty young woman He never expected to find anyone so lovely.

"Could this be what you're missing, sir?" She chuckled. She stood up and reached into her apron pocket and retrieved a leather wallet and the three packaged condoms that had fallen out of it. "I found these on the floor. I was going to put them over on the dresser." She spoke with a light Spanish accent. Alexander felt his face flush and looked away.

He reached over the twin bed. "Yes, that belongs to me. Thank you." He grabbed the wallet and condoms out of her hand.

Elena laughed. "Planning a busy week in the city?" Alexander looked at her wryly. "You'd better be careful. You never know when you might need these . . . you don't want to come up one short."

Blushing, Alexander stashed the condoms back into the fold of his wallet and stuffed it into his back jeans pocket.

Elena stared at him. Her beautiful dark eyes captivated Alexander as she smiled, and he realized just how very pretty she was. He smiled back and found himself at a loss for words. The more he looked at her the more beautiful he realized she was . . . even in her pale blue maid's uniform with the white apron. Her flowing black hair cascaded to her shoulders and her skin was tan, the color of creamed mocha. She didn't look very old, thought Alexander, as full figured as she was. She was somewhere in her teens, he guessed. Much too young for him.

"Thank you." He smiled, feeling like a complete imbecile. His legs seemed to be made of lead and he couldn't budge them. He felt a quiver run through him. He couldn't take his eyes off her. He stalled and tried to think of something to say. "What is your name?"

"Elena," she replied.

"Do you mind me asking your age?"

"Twenty," she lied.

Alexander didn't believe her for a second and sup‐
pressed a grin. "Thirteen?"

She climbed over the second twin bed that separated
them and looked him directly in the eye, smiling impishly
He towered over her petite frame.

"Fifteen," she whispered.

He tried to conceal his disappointment. She had con‐
firmed his suspicions—she was much too young for hi
twenty-two years.

"Don't tell anyone around here, okay? I could lose m
job. They think I'm twenty."

"Trust me." Alexander raised two crossed fingers
"Your secret is safe." He smiled and added, tapping th
back of his pants. "As long as mine is."

Elena giggled and her dark eyes sparkled. She wa
only a child. There was no point in pursuing her. H
turned back around once before leaving the room
"Thanks." He retrieved his wallet and shook it above hin

꙳

Four Years Later

"That's her." Alexander pointed Elena out to his fathe
"That must be her."

"We didn't come here for you to chase some Spani
maid all over the hotel. We have work to do. Remembe
Work?" His thick Kentucky accent had never left hi
Alexander had accompanied his father to New York on
business trip. His father had convinced him to come wo
for him again. He'd just been fired from his job in the sh
department at Garfinkel's and needed the money; he fel
certain compulsion to accept the offer. They had booke
reservation at the Dumois and one morning on Alexande

way down to breakfast he thought he saw the same chambermaid that had found his wallet four years ago. She was carrying a stack of freshly laundered towels into the next room. She can't still be here after all these years. Alexander thought that perhaps it was nothing more than wishful thinking. He'd thought of her off and on over the years, and he longed to see her again.

"Dad, I left something back in the room. Be back in a minute." Alexander rose from the breakfast table in the hotel dining room and took the elevator back upstairs. It stopped on the second floor where he was staying and he stepped off. The maid's cart was midway down the hall and he decided to casually peek into each open doorway. Once he thought he'd spotted her and dashed into one of the rooms like a complete idiot. But it wasn't her. It was a hard-looking chambermaid around fifty. She mumbled something in Spanish. "Does Elena work here?" he asked the woman. She replied in Spanish and he couldn't understand her. Discouraged, Alexander left. He glanced at his watch and knew that if he didn't hurry back down he'd be responsible for his father's being late for his meeting, and that the old man would be irate. He had always been a stickler for punctuality.

During the entire business meeting as the three men, one an old publisher friend of Alexander's father, sipped martinis, Alexander could think of nothing but Elena. He knew that he had no other choice but to find her. She had become an obsession.

Alexander and his father went back to the Dumois later that day. Alexander stopped at the front desk. "Do you have a chambermaid who works at this hotel named Elena?"

"I'm new here. Don't know the cleaning staff." He'd suggested one person that might know—the person in charge of domestic services. It was Alexander's only night in the city and he was gravely disappointed that the person in charge could not be found, and that he hadn't made more headway during his brief stay. Later that night William Raines, dressed in his best suit to attend a Broadway show, looked disapprovingly at his son who was still buttoning his shirt.

"Are you almost ready, son? We're going to be late."

"Go down to the dining room ahead of me, Dad. I'll meet you there shortly." Alexander detected his father's impatience.

"I'll meet you downstairs in five minutes." William exited the room. Fifteen minutes later Alexander left the room and started to head down the hall . . . when he saw her. She was wearing her blue maid's uniform and seemed to be in a hurry. He called out to her. "Elena?"

She stopped and peered at him. It was her. Alexander was elated. She was even more beautiful than he'd remembered. She was older now, more mature looking . . . even more breathtaking. She stared at him with a puzzled look, trying to recall where she'd seen him before.

"How do you know my name?"

"We met a few years ago . . . here at the hotel. You were cleaning my room. I forgot my wallet . . . and something else," he said, smiling.

"I clean a lot of rooms and I find a lot of things." She didn't remember him.

"Don't you remember?"

"I don't mean to be abrupt, but I'm already late for class." She began to walk away.

"Please . . . wait . . ." Alexander jumped in front of her. "Just give me a minute. You're all I've thought about."

"Look, I'm running late. I still have to change my clothes. I have an exam that I can't afford to miss."

"I can wait."

Elena released a sigh. "Okay, we can talk on my way

190

down the hall. But first let me change my clothes. Give me a minute." Elena carried an army backpack full of clothes and textbooks over her left shoulder and dangled brown sandals in her right hand. She looked at Alexander impatiently as she stopped and fished for the utility room key. "Wait here." She slipped inside, leaving him waiting outside. A few minutes later she emerged wearing an ankle length multicolored skirt and white peasant blouse.

"When can I see you when you're not so rushed?" Alexander said, as he walked Elena to the elevator. The elevator door opened, and William Raines suddenly appeared with a look of disapproval on his face.

"I should have known." William Raines's bushy white brows arched into a frown. His son had a passion for the ladies. It was one of his more serious character flaws—one of many. "Did you forget that I've been waiting for you all this time?" William Raines shook his white head disapprovingly. William met Elena's eyes briefly. She looked away. Alexander felt awful. He had become so preoccupied that he'd forgotten about his father. "The dinner was quite good I must say. I enjoyed every bit of it." His father ran his hand through his thick hair. His face was strong and indented with deep lines.

"I'm sorry, Dad."

"Yes," he flashed Elena a second look, "I'm sure you are." William glanced at his gold watch. "If we don't leave now we're going to miss the entire performance." Alexander couldn't have cared less about the show. He wanted nothing more than to talk to Elena, but he couldn't disappoint his father.

"I have to see you." He turned to her and took one of her hands in his—it was chapped and her nails were bitten. He didn't want to let her go. He was afraid he'd never find her again. "Can you meet me in the lobby tomorrow at nine before we leave? Our train pulls out of Penn Station at eleven." Alexander's face filled with hope. Reluctantly, Elena nodded. Alexander didn't believe her. "Promise me."

"I promise." She looked at him with her beautiful dark eyes. "Now if I don't go, I'm going to flunk chemistry and be cleaning hotel rooms the rest of my life." She tore away from him and bolted down the hallway to the stairwell.

Alexander and his father took the elevator downstairs. They crossed the antique-filled lobby and hailed a taxi to the theater.

⚘

"Alexander, we really must be going," said William Raines. It was ten-thirty the next day and their train was leaving out of Penn Station at eleven. If they didn't leave right now they'd never make it. Alexander looked at his father who was equivalent in height and stature and quietly acqui- esced. Elena hadn't met him just as he had feared.

All the way back on the train he couldn't seem to get her out of his mind. And after a week had passed, and Alexander still couldn't sleep or think or eat, he knew he had no other choice but to go back and find her again. He had already lost her once, and he wasn't about to lose her a second time.

"Don't you think it's about time you settled down and do some work instead of chasing after some maid? For God's sake Alexander, when are you ever going to grow up?"

"I know you can't possibly understand, Dad, but I must find her. I can't concentrate. She consumes my every waking thought."

"But what is the point of pursuing her?" William Raines grimaced. "She didn't even show up. Obviously she's not interested."

"Maybe something happened to detain her from com

ing. I must give her the benefit of the doubt."

"Forget her. You're making a mistake, Alexander. I really think you should just try and forget her. There are plenty of Southern women for you at home, women who are much more suitable." William followed Alexander out of the study into the foyer.

"Suitable?" Alexander turned and glared at his father. "And what is that supposed to mean?"

"You know damn well what it means." He swung open the front door of the mansion. "The limo is here. I have to go or I'll miss my train." William shook his head. "Why can't I ever get through to you?"

Alexander, intentionally turning a deaf ear to his father, stepped outside with his one suitcase, and climbed inside the waiting vehicle.

❧

Elena had fulfilled her promise just like she agreed and had come to meet Alexander at the Dumois the morning of his departure; but in spite of her good intentions, she had arrived too late, missing him by only minutes.

Every Friday she went to the library to study. She went early in the morning that day and had gotten lost in her studies. The next time she looked up at the clock she frantically realized that too much time had passed. She had waited in the lobby for over an hour hoping he would still show somehow, but it was too late.

Alexander arrived in the city that Friday one week later hoping desperately to find Elena. He vowed to himself that if he found her again, he wouldn't lose her this time. Upon arriving in the late afternoon he went up to the front desk and asked once again if anyone knew her. "I really *must* find Elena. I don't know her last name. She works for you, has for the last few years. She's one of your chambermaids.

Can you tell me where I can find her?" he asked, his pale blue eyes glimmering with hope.

The old man behind the desk smiled back at Alexander. He knew exactly who he was referring to. "Oh, yes. I know Elena. I'm afraid it's her day off," Alexander looked disappointed, "but she should be in tomorrow."

Alexander relaxed his shoulders and breathed deeply. He removed his blazer and tossed it over one arm. "I'd like a room for the weekend." He signed his name. The old man gave him a key to the room. "Also, would you mind giving Elena a note for me?" The man nodded. "Can I have a piece of paper?" The aged desk clerk found a small pad of paper with the hotel's insignia and handed it to him. Alexander tore off a sheet, retrieved the small pencil on top of the desk, and began to scribble away:

> *Dear Elena,*
> *Please meet me in the lobby at ten o'clock*
> *tomorrow morning. I must see you.*
> > *Yours,*
> > *Alexander Raines*

Alexander folded the piece of paper in half and handed it to the man. He pulled a crisp twenty-dollar bill from his pocket. The clerk's eyes grew wide. "Please see that she gets it."

The desk clerk nodded gratefully.

"Thank you." Alexander grabbed his suitcase and headed to the third floor.

The next morning, unable to sleep, Alexander rose early. He was terribly anxious to see Elena. He was too excited to eat so after showering and putting on a clean white T-shirt, his black blazer and jeans, and splashing himself with aftershave, he went downstairs at nine for a quick cup of black coffee in the dining room. At a quarter of ten he was sitting astutely in the lobby on the gold George III mahogany humpback sofa waiting for her. By ten o'clock she still hadn't come and Alexander's excitement began to wane. He began to worry as he surveyed the room looking for her. At ten-fifteen he approached the desk, but discovered to his dismay the same young man who'd replied on a previous visit that he hadn't known Elena. He glanced at his watch again wondering if she had ever received the note, then went back to the couch and sat down. He picked up part of an old newspaper that someone had left on the satinwood and rosewood tripod table next to him and began to read.

"I apologize for being late." Elena suddenly appeared standing before him in her familiar blue uniform with the white ruffled collar.

"I thought you were going to stand me up again." Alexander smiled, and their eyes met as he stood up. He seemed to tower over her five-foot-two height. He was delighted to see her.

"I'm so sorry about the last time. I got caught up in my studies. I came too late and you were already gone."

"You came?" He looked down at her in surprise. He was elated. So she hadn't stood him up after all.

"I remember you, now. You were the good-looking guy with the lifetime supply of condoms." She smiled.

Alexander laughed. "That's right. You never can be too careful these days." He breathed deeply. "What a hell of a way to be remembered."

"Did you ever use all those things?"

"Of course. Did you really have any doubt?" They both broke into laughter.

"I only have a few minutes. I have to get back to work." She looked nervously around to see if anyone were watching her.

"What time do you get off? I'd like to take you to dinner."

"Dinner?" She looked pleased. "I usually finish my last room at five-thirty."

"Meet me here in the lobby, let's say, at six."

"I'll see you at six then." She smiled, then left to go back upstairs. Alexander hummed with excitement. She was so incredibly beautiful and had a wonderful sense of humor like he remembered. His fantasies of making love to her grew stronger with each passing moment.

All afternoon Alexander could think of nothing but Elena and where he would take her that night—the most special night of his life. He strolled down Fifth Avenue stopping in the elegant department stores along the way. He went to Bergdorf's, then into Bonwit Teller's where he spotted a dress that looked as if it was made for her. He simply couldn't resist it, and he bought it right off the mannequin. It had come straight from Paris; an off the shoulder red taffeta cocktail dress. He imagined how very beautiful she would look wearing it and hoped she would like it.

He had made up his mind to treat her in a way he'd suspected she'd never been treated before. He decided to take her to the exclusive '21' Club for dinner and then for a horse and carriage ride in Central Park.

Six o'clock arrived and Alexander, dressed in a black suit, met Elena in the lobby. She had on the same peasant blouse and skirt she'd worn before. "You look lovely tonight," he exclaimed as he walked toward her and held out his hands, smiling warmly.

Elena smiled as he touched her.

"I have a splendid evening planned," said Alexander with a look of mischief in his eyes, "but first I have something for you." Alexander retrieved a box from the Bonwit's shopping bag he held by his side, and Elena looked at him in surprise.

"For me?" She met his eyes, smiling. She acted as if no one had ever given her a present before.

"Yes, come sit down over here." He gestured, and she followed him to the humpback couch.

She tore open the box like a child at Christmas. Her eyes widened in delight and she squealed as she opened the white crinkly paper and uncovered the red dress. "It's beautiful," she exclaimed, then looked at him disapprovingly. "You didn't have to do this." But she was glad he had.

"I wanted to." Alexander admired her as she admired the dress. He couldn't wait to see her in it. He had been fantasizing about what she'd look like in it all afternoon, and it was driving him absolutely crazy. He reached into the shopping bag again and pulled out a second gift. "And this is also for you."

Her eyes met his, once again with mock disapproval, but underneath he could see how pleased she was. She opened the box and pulled out a pair of red shoes to match. "Shoes." She looked at him in delight. "How do you know my size?"

"I use to sell shoes. I guessed." He looked worried. "Hope I guessed right. Size six."

"Close. Five and a half. But I can wear some sixes."

"And last, but not least." He handed her the last box and when she opened it she discovered a beautiful red purse to match.

"You thought of everything." She laughed. She leaned over and kissed him gently on the cheek. She caught a whiff of his aftershave. He smelled so manly, and his face was smooth as if he'd just shaved. She suddenly had the urge to kiss him again, this time on the lips, but she didn't want to come across as too forward.

She was so beautiful, thought Alexander, and there was such an innocent, childlike quality about her. He had enjoyed the kiss she gave him, her lips against his skin, and he wished she hadn't stopped there.

Elena gathered up her gifts and stood up. "I'll go into the powder room and change." She smiled and his eyes never left her until she was completely out of sight.

A few minutes later she reappeared. His heart raced at the sight of her. She looked even more exquisite than he had imagined. She walked up to him proudly as if she were royalty, truly feeling as beautiful as she looked so that he could examine her completely with his eyes. He would rather have examined every inch of her with his hands, and it was a struggle for him not to reach out and grab her and pull her into him. Her coal hair swept her bare shoulders, and her dark eyes sparkled. Two dimples that he'd never noticed before magically appeared whenever she smiled, and her full ruby lips glistened. The dress fit her perfectly and hugged her curvaceous figure.

"The shoes . . . they fit," she exclaimed, happily.

Her legs were so shapely that Alexander had the overwhelming urge to reach up into her dress as if she were exclusively his, press her against him, and caress her. He almost didn't know if he'd be able to control himself—be the perfect gentleman and keep his hands to himself. He wanted so badly to roam every inch of her skin with the tips of his fingers; kiss her freely with his lips. He wanted to reveal how he really felt about her, tell her how different she was from anyone he'd ever known, how special she was to him, how he'd been obsessed with her for the past four years.

Alexander was speechless as he stared at her. "I can't find the words . . . you look breathtaking." He stood up and held an arm out for her, and she slipped her arm through his. "Have you been to the '21' Club?"

Her eyes widened and filled with delight. It had a wonderful reputation. She had always wanted to go there, but it was more than she could afford. Every penny she made as a chambermaid went to her schooling and to help her mother.

She was a pre-med student at City College. It had been her lifelong ambition to become a doctor and to move out of the slums. She worked lots of overtime. She worked so hard, she almost collapsed from exhaustion.

The doorman winked at her as they exited the lobby, and she winked back at him. Everyone who worked there loved her. She was warm and giving and full of life. She always looked out for everyone. A horse and carriage strolled by, it's noisy shoes clopping against the pavement amidst the traffic, so out of place as if it were lost in the wrong century. They waited in the warm evening breeze for a taxi.

A couple of hours later after a delightful meal, Elena and Alexander rode in a horse-drawn carriage through Central Park, laughing and talking and thoroughly enjoying each other's company. Alexander discovered Elena to be a wonderful listener and found himself revealing every detail of his life to her. She was somewhat reticent about her own life. She didn't seem to like to talk about herself at first. But after a little while she opened up to him and he learned that she was Puerto Rican, worked at the hotel as a chambermaid, lived with her widowed mother and younger brother in the South Bronx, and was a devout Catholic.

The evening had ended much too soon, thought Alexander as he and Elena strolled quietly through the park before returning to the Dumois just across the street. "I need to be getting home. It's getting late," she finally told Alexander regretfully. He stopped along the path under the moonlit sky and without any hesitation pulled her into his arms. He couldn't resist her any longer. He gazed adoringly into her dark eyes. "I wish you didn't have to go." He pressed his lips into hers. He kissed her passionately.

"I'm in love with you," he said.

"But you don't even know me," she replied.

"Come back to the room with me."

"I—I can't . . . I'm sorry."

Alexander looked disappointed, but understood. She wasn't that kind of girl and he respected her for it; but nevertheless he had to try.

They strolled back to the hotel, and she was all that he thought about until he saw her again two weeks later.

∽

Elena had found Alexander very handsome and charming, and she throughly enjoyed their evening out together. No one had ever treated her that way before, so well—like royalty. She couldn't believe he had showered her with all the gifts when he barely knew her; but nevertheless, she appreciated his kind and generous gesture. Every night she opened her closet just to stare at the dress hanging there. Her mother was astonished that he had bought it for her. Elena smiled to herself, recalling the fabulous time she had had, reliving each moment. And she still couldn't believe she'd eaten at the '21' Club.

Alexander was so different from the neighborhood boys that she'd grown up with. She thought about him night and day; fantasized about what it would be like to make love with him. She knew she was bound to lose her virginity one of these days, and she secretly hoped it would be with him. He constantly interfered with her studies; she was worried that she would flunk out if she didn't erase him from her mind, and she counted the days until she would be able to see him again.

Two weeks later, they had a picnic in Central Park, by the pond. They laughed and chatted away the afternoon. Alexander began to chase her around the grounds. He finally caught her, both of them laughing, and he tackled her to the ground. He snatched a blade of grass and began to tickle her nose, showing no mercy.

"Alexander . . . stop." She laughed. He threw away the blade of grass and suddenly became very serious. He gazed into her eyes, and he found that he couldn't resist her any longer. He embraced her and their lips met again and again.

"Let's go to your room," she whispered in between breathless kisses. She wanted him as much as he wanted her. For a fleeting moment she thought of her mother back in the Bronx and how worried she would be if she didn't come home until late and how horrified she'd be if she knew where she had been. But at that moment the desire of her flesh overtook her, and she no longer cared. She had feelings for this man; this man who was older and whom she barely knew. She wanted to be with him more than anything in the world.

"Are you sure? I don't want to push you."

"Yes," she whispered, gazing into his eyes, running her fingers through his golden hair as she kissed him.

Fortunately, they were close to the hotel because Alexander, unable to control himself any longer, was just about to rip off her yellow peasant-style dress right there in the park. The light in the sky was beginning to fade as they hurried back across the street, entered the grand hotel and took the elevator upstairs.

In the elevator Alexander grabbed Elena and embraced her kissing her passionately, caressing every inch of bare skin he could find. The door finally opened, and he lifted her into his arms and went flying with her down the hall as she laughed out loud. He tried to hold her as he fumbled for the key in his pocket. Then, once he found it, he burst into the room carrying her like a baby in his arms. He shut the door with his foot and crossed the room to the bed where he placed her down and eagerly climbed on top of her. "I love you. I love you so much. You're the most beautiful girl I've ever seen," he whispered, gazing into her eyes as he slid the top of her dress off her shoulders and down to her waist. The sight of her bare breasts, so perfect and round, excited him even more and he began to kiss them. He took off her dress, kicked it to the floor with his foot. He removed her panties—sliding them down to her red-painted toes.

She lay before him, her body like a gift, like a priceless work of art, so exquisite—so rare. She smiled as he admired her with his eyes. She eagerly helped him remove his own clothes, and then he climbed on top of her and they made the most passionate love. He entered her with such fervor that they both came together, and he told her again how very much he loved her.

৵

"I want to marry you. Let's run off and get married tonight." Alexander had come back up to New York to visit Elena a week later.

"Alexander, don't you think you're being a little impulsive? We've only been dating for a few weeks. We hardly know each other."

"Time is unimportant. You're the one I want to spend the rest of my life with. There is no doubt in my mind. I've known that from the moment I first saw you four years ago." He pulled her naked on top of him as they lay in bed in his hotel room. They had just made the most passionate love. "Just say yes." He peered into her dark eyes.

"But what about school? I don't want to give that up. I've worked too hard for everything I have."

"No one is asking you to give up your dream. I want you to pursue it. The only thing that matters is that we're together. There are good colleges in Virginia. You can complete your studies there." He kissed her on the lips. "I can't stand another day without you."

"What about Mama? She counts on my income from the hotel. I just can't leave her like that—with nothing."

"I can send her money if you like . . . or we can move her down to Virginia with us." He pulled her head into him. "I love you so much." He pressed his lips against hers.

"I love you, too," she whispered, stroking the sides of his hair. She kissed him passionately. "This is all happening so fast. When I'm with you I can't even think straight."

Alexander laughed. "I'm flattered to have that affect on you."

"I have so many years of school left until I become a doctor. You'll want children and then I'll never finish my degree."

"I do want children, lots of them, but I'm willing to wait."

Elena rested her head on Alexander's chest. "I don't know if I even want them. I don't think I'd be a very good mother."

"What are you talking about. You'd make a wonderful mother."

"I just don't think I'd have the time for children, at least not initially, not with a medical practice."

"We have plenty of time for that. You're thinking too far into the future, Elena. Let's just worry about now—the present. That's all that matters. All I know is that I can't live without you another day." Alexander planted kisses all over her face and neck.

Elena felt her whole body tingle at his touch. "I need time to think. I need more time."

Alexander gazed into her eyes. "As long as we're together, nothing else matters." He wrapped her in his arms and pulled her into him.

༄

"I'm sorry, Alexander. I can't see you next weekend. I need to study for a big exam I have coming up." Elena called Alexander at his Virginia home a few days later. "Please, don't travel to New York. Promise me."

"It won't be easy. You know I can't stand being away from you for even a day."

Elena chuckled. "You're such a major distraction."

"Have you given any more thought to what we discussed?"

"I need more time."

"You have it."

Alexander was filled with disappointment. He couldn't stand to wait another day to see her, let alone another week; but if that's what she wanted he had no other choice.

"You're torturing me. I won't be able to stand another week without you."

"Me neither."

Alexander tried calling her the following week at work since she didn't have a home phone and could never reach her. She never returned his phone calls. He wrote to her and she never answered his letters. Alexander became increasingly concerned and decided that he had to go to New York to see her. He couldn't go on without hearing from her. He couldn't sleep or eat.

Alexander learned her home address from an employee of the hotel and decided to go there directly since he couldn't find her at the Dumois. The taxi pulled up in front of Elena's address and Alexander was shocked to discover that she lived in a broken-down tenement in the worst part of the Bronx. He tipped the cab driver and slid out of the cab and strode briskly in the biting fall air toward the building. He walked up the three flights in the dark stairwell to her apartment. He took a deep breath as soon as he stopped in front of the door, then knocked, and a heavy-set woman answered. He presumed the woman was her mother. "Is your daughter Elena here? I'd like to speak to her." The woman with the short gray hair studied him carefully.

"Alexander?" she guessed. Maria Ortiz, Elena's mother, wearing a loose fitting black dress, hesitated. "Just a minute." She closed the door and Alexander waited while she approached Elena who was sitting on the couch staring into space. Elena . . . there's a young man here to see you. It's your Alexander."

"Tell him to go away," her voice trailed off, as her eyes filled with new tears.

Maria opened the door a crack. "She doesn't want to see you anymore."

"What? Why not? What happened? What's wrong? Please . . ." begged Alexander, "tell her I *must* see her, *just* for a minute. Please." His heart pounded furiously. "Tell her it's me—Alexander."

Maria looked at the young man sympathetically. She sighed deeply. "I'm sorry." She gently closed the door.

Alexander pounded his fists into the door as tears began to form in his eyes. "Please . . . Elena . . ."

৵

Alexander gazed at the serene water. He would never forget Elena and never even begin to understand what had happened between them; why she had left him the way she did. "I kept writing to her but she never answered my letters. I learned that she had quit her job at the hotel. I finally had no other choice but to accept that it was over." Alexander exhaled and started to cough. He looked at Destiny. "In time it gets easier . . . you'll see." He patted his daughter gently on the leg. "I just wish I knew what happened," he said sadly. "That question will probably continue to haunt me till the day I die." He paused and sighed. "Enough of this talk. I think it's about time for lunch, isn't it?" He cupped a hand over a yawn. "I thought I'd take a little nap this afternoon after we eat. I'm afraid I'm feeling a little weak."

Destiny peered at her father in concern as she took his arm and helped him up. She led him back up the small incline mulling over everything he'd just told her. What could have possibly happened for her mother to do that to him?

✳ *Chapter fifteen*

*B*y the middle of October Alexander's health had greatly deteriorated, and he was no longer the man he had once been. He had lost a considerable amount of weight and was burdened with fatigue; he had developed an incessant cough; he ran a fever and had chest pains. It was obvious to everyone that things had taken a turn for the worse. Dr. Winslow, his attending physician and long-time friend, had sent him to an oncologist for a series of tests, and it was discovered that the melanoma, to everyone's dismay, had stealthily invaded his lungs and heart. Destiny and Julia were terribly distraught when they had learned of Alexander's failing condition. They had all been hoping for a miracle.

Of the three of them, Alexander had taken the news the best in spite of the fact that he knew his prognosis was poor and that this was, in fact, going to kill him. He had no other choice but to be brave and spend his remaining days trying to console the two women in his life as best he could. "We all are destined to die . . . it's just a matter of when," he said to Julia, philosophically, as she sat on their bed sobbing into her hands that night after learning of her husband's fate. "I just have the distinct privilege of knowing what's going to cause my demise."

"I can't believe this is happening to us," she cried. She

was overwhelmed with grief; but a part of her was also furious at Alexander for putting her in this horrible predicament. She blamed him for being so damn stubborn about the whole thing, for not taking her advice. If only he'd listened to her in the first place and had gone to have the freckle checked when she first discovered it, then this never would have happened. He wouldn't be dying now. The future would still be theirs.

She loved him more now than ever; more than she thought she could ever love another human being; almost as much as she loved herself. She had never realized just how much he really meant to her and cherished the remaining time they had left. She regretted the pain she'd caused him with her affairs and fighting with his daughter and wished they'd never had happened. She thought guiltily that maybe the additional stress had aggravated his condition.

Tears streamed down her cheeks. "How can you just accept it? You barely seem upset at all. Doesn't it bother you that you're going to die?" She couldn't understand his blasé attitude. If she were the one stricken with cancer, she would have been so desperately afraid. She would have cried constantly. She would not have been able to think of anything else but her impending death and her subsequent funeral; lying still and breathless in a wooden box all alone in the insect-infested ground.

Death was so lonely.

Julia wasn't convinced of an afterlife and was terribly scared of the unknown. She just couldn't imagine the cessation of life. She couldn't imagine a world without Julia Stoneworth Raines, a world where she didn't exist.

She often wondered what her last seconds would be like. She wondered if she would feel much pain and wondered how she'd endure it. She was sure she would have a nervous breakdown. As it were, Julia felt as though she were close to the edge and it wouldn't take much more to push her over.

If she had been the one dying she was sure she would have had to spend her remaining days in a hospice.

Alex was so much braver than she. Perhaps that was why God had chosen him instead. He knew Alex was much more capable of handling it.

She remembered what her grandmother had said to her when she was a small girl: "God does not give us more than we can handle." I can't handle anymore! Julia wanted to scream at the ceiling. I can't handle one more day of this! God, are you there? Are you listening?

"Julia . . . believe me," Alexander looked at her tenderly, "I didn't ask for this, but now that it's happened I have no other choice but to accept it. What good would it do for me to fall apart? It wouldn't serve any purpose. It wouldn't help you or Destiny. It would only make things worse." He exhaled and coughed. Julia lifted her long silky legs onto the bed. "I must in all honesty admit that I've never appreciated life more." He laughed at the irony. "I guess dying has a way of doing that to a person. It makes everything much more vivid as if you've been walking around wearing hazy glasses all your life, and then suddenly someone takes them off your face. It's so much more precious . . . even the little things we tend to take for granted that no one ever thinks of."

Alexander reached for her and pulled her into him like a baby. His body felt strangely thin and frail.

"I know how it is. . . ." He began to rock her gently. "But you'll get through it . . . you'll see." He hated to put her through all of this. It was so terribly unfair and she didn't deserve it. He realized just how much he loved her. It was so different from the way he had loved Elena. He knew he could never love another woman with that intensity again. But Julia was special to him in a different kind of way, and it made him sad to think of leaving her. She was as vulnerable as a child and all of her past transgressions suddenly seemed unimportant. "I don't want to leave you, Julia. Really I don't. If I had my way," the emotion welled up in his throat and he could barely speak, "I wouldn't go." He stared blankly across the room fighting back tears as he pulled her closer.

❧

Alexander had asked Destiny to stay and live with them when he learned how ill he really was, and she promised him she wouldn't leave. She postponed looking for a job, for the time being, so that she could devote all her time to him. Her heart ached for her father, and each time she thought about Alexander lying upstairs in his bed day after day becoming more dependent on them, more hopeless, it filled her with great despair; and at times she found herself slipping into a strange daze. Sleep was her only solace.

The melanoma had invaded Alexander's heart. He was literally dying of a broken heart and Destiny often wondered if knowing *why* her mother had left him, *why* she had taken her own life, would save him, but she knew she was just wishing, looking for something to hold on to—anything.

In her quiet moments Destiny mulled over everything her father had told her that day by the pond. It didn't make any sense to her; she knew there had to be more to the story, and soon it became an obsession, and she was determined to learn the truth. Perhaps she would be able to find out once and for all, quell her own curiosity as well as put her father's mind at ease—at least before he left them. He deserved that much. And she deserved to know everything there was to know about her background.

"My mother, Elena, she went by the last name of Ortiz?"

"Yes, why?" Alexander looked at her from the bed.

"Is the Dumois still in business?" Destiny asked her father one morning as the leaves outside his bedroom window sailed gently to the ground in the soft breeze. She considered making a trip to New York. She handed him a cup of tea and sat down beside him on the bed. It tore at her heart to look at him.

"I believe so. Why do you ask?"

"I was just curious." She hesitated a moment, then said, "Father, I'm going to be gone for a couple of days. There's some business I need to attend to."

Alexander peered at her curiously. "Sweetheart, there is really nothing more to learn about your background. There is really no point in your making the trip. You know everything there is to know. Your mother . . . is dead. She can't tell you anything. I'm sorry." He reached out and patted her hand. She meant everything to him. He was so happy to have his daughter back that he couldn't bear the thought of her leaving again. He didn't know how long he had and every second with her was precious.

She smiled softly, fighting back tears, trying to be brave. "Just a few days, maybe a week at the most. This is something I have to do. I hope you understand." Destiny released her hand from his and rose from the bed.

Alexander knew he could not talk her out of going. Once she made up her mind to do something there was no turning back. That's the kind of person she was.

"The only person who might be able to help you is Pepita Gonzales—if you can find her. I don't know what ever happened to her. I haven't heard from her in years."

"Pepita Gonzales?" She looked at her father curiously.

"She worked as a chambermaid at the Dumois. She

was your grandmother's best friend; she lived across the hall from them. She's the one who brought us together."

"I don't remember her."

"You were too young."

"Do you have any idea where she might live?"

"She used to live in the South Bronx, but that was many years ago. That's all I know. She knew your mother's family very well." Alexander's eyes filled with sorrow. "She could probably tell you the circumstances of your mother's death."

"Thank you, Father."

"Have a safe trip . . . and good luck. Don't be gone too long."

"I promise."

⌇

Destiny took the train up to New York the next morning and arrived at Penn Station around noon. She hailed a cab and asked to be taken to the Dumois, where she had made a reservation. A few minutes later the cab pulled up in front of the Louis XVI style building and an eerie familiarity fell over her as she gazed up at the French windows and balconies. The hotel with its limestone facing and mansard roof was just as she had imagined. She stared at the four concrete steps leading to the glass double doors and could almost imagine her mother as a beautiful young woman waltzing through them.

"Thank you." Destiny took a deep breath and tipped the cab driver. She climbed out of the car wearing her best black suit, carrying her small Hermés suitcase and matching leather handbag. She walked past the red-coated doorman into the antique-filled lobby and approached the desk. She looked around the room and a shiver raced up her back. She felt as if she'd been here before. The clerk, a slender young man with short dark hair, greeted her with a smile.

"Can I help you?" He looked her over.

"Yes. I called last night and made a reservation for Destiny Raines."

The young man scanned the reservation book. "Oh, yes." He smiled at her. "Ms. Raines. We have you in room 230 on the second floor."

She lingered at the desk after getting her key, and asked, "I'm trying to find a woman who worked here in the sixties and seventies. I don't suppose she's still employed here after all these years . . . or if you know where I can find her . . . or someone who might know her. Her name was Pepita Gonzales. Could you possibly help me?"

"That's before my time."

"Doesn't the hotel keep some kind of record of its employees?"

"Hold on a minute. Let me go and see what I can find out." He disappeared behind the key rack. A few minutes later a tall dark haired man in his mid-thirties wearing a gray three piece suit and red silk tie approached the desk. The desk clerk reappeared.

"Mr. Hollin," he said nervously. "I was just helping Ms. Raines."

The man extended his hand and introduced himself to Destiny.

"Andrew Hollin. I'm the owner of this hotel. How can I help you?"

Destiny looked up at him and met his hazel eyes. "This may sound a bit odd, but I'm trying to find a woman who worked in your hotel back in the sixties and seventies. Her name was Pepita Gonzales."

"There must be something on her." He peered at her. "I'll have to check."

"She knew my mother quite well."

"Let me look into it. How long are you planning to remain a guest of the Dumois?"

"For a few days."

"I'll see what I can find out. I'll have to get back to you. What room are you in Miss?—"

"Destiny Raines."

Andrew glanced at her left hand. "Miss? or Misses?"

"I'm in the process of a divorce."

"Oh." He sighed. "I know how painful that can be. I was divorced last year."

Destiny looked at him sympathetically.

"Phone call for you, Mr. Hollin," the clerk interrupted.

"I appreciate your trying to help."

"It's no trouble," said Andrew. "I should get back to you in about a day," he said, before disappearing behind the key rack.

Two days passed and Destiny hadn't heard anything from Andrew Hollin, and she was beginning to wonder if he'd forgotten about her. She dutifully called Alexander each day to check on him. He was in reasonably good spirits. She filled the rest of her time with shopping and art museums; but by the end of the second day she was beginning to go crazy, when she received a call from the front desk around dinnertime that night. Destiny was drying her hair in the bathroom with a fluffy white hotel towel when she heard the phone ring and ran to answer it. She was hoping it was Andrew Hollin and that he had learned something about Pepita. Wrapped in nothing but a towel she lifted the receiver and placed it to her ear.

"Ms. Raines . . . this is the front desk. Mr. Hollin has asked me to invite you to dinner in the main dining room at seven. He has some information for you." Destiny was elated. Andrew Hollin had something to tell her about Pepita, she just knew it. She was so excited she could barely think straight. She glanced at the clock, and as soon as she hung up she began to dress.

Promptly at seven, Destiny, dressed in a red silk dress with a plunging neckline, her hair full and framing her heart-shaped face, clutching her red-sequined handbag strode confidently into the dining room. She met Andrew Hollin at his special table in the corner. The dining room was more elegant than she had imagined, with its antique fixtures and Edwardian mahogany dining chairs and candlelight in the center of each white linen tablecloth.

"You look stunning this evening." Andrew eyed her carefully and smiled as if he approved. "I ordered a bottle of Cabernet Sauvignon," he said.

Destiny smiled back graciously. She was flattered by the compliment. "My favorite." Destiny leaned forward and smiled revealing her dimples, her heart beating in anticipation. Her dark blue eyes glimmered against the restless flame. The waiter poured them each a glass of garnet wine, and Destiny took a sip. She placed the wineglass down on the table.

"I'm dying to know." Her expression became more animated. "What did you find out?"

"If you don't mind, let's place our order first." He summoned the waiter with his hand. "Filet mignon." He gazed at Destiny. "How do you prefer yours?"

"Medium well is fine," she said politely. Eating was the farthest thing from her mind.

The waiter nodded and left immediately to make sure that Mr. Hollin and his guest were promptly served. Andrew brought the wineglass to his lips. He kept staring at her.

She waited eagerly for Andrew Hollin to tell her something. He put down the round crystal goblet. "I went through some files and came up with something you might be interested in. The previous owner kept a detailed record of all his employees." Destiny could barely contain her excitement and leaned in closer. She didn't want to miss a single word he said. Andrew reached inside his jacket and pulled out a small piece of folded white paper. "I wrote it down. Around the time you mentioned there was a chambermaid who worked at the Dumois by the name of Pepita Gonzales. She came from the South Bronx."

"Is there a phone number or address?" she asked, her mind racing with thoughts, her voice urgent.

Andrew handed her the piece of paper. "I wrote it down for you." Suddenly, Destiny felt strangely light-headed and Andrew observed the disturbed look on her face. "Are you all right?" he asked. The waiter brought them their dinners and placed them carefully down in front of them. The steak looked wonderful. It was thick and round and garnished with a sprig of parsley. The baked potato was flooded with warm melted butter and hills of sour cream and sprinkled with chives. The green beans were cooked to perfection. Destiny stared at her plate, but she had lost her appetite. She began to feel dizzy. She held the piece of paper tightly in her hand. Her palms began to sweat and her dress felt terribly tight as if it were choking her.

"I'm terribly sorry, but I'm suddenly not feeling too well. You'll have to excuse me." Destiny rose from the chair as Andrew looked at her in bewilderment and concern. She grabbed her purse which lay near her plate and walked briskly out of the dining room. She flew past the tables and ran to the elevator. Frantically, she pressed the button. Unable to wait any longer, feeling as though she might black out, she ran to the stairwell around the corner. *What's wrong with me?* she thought. I hope I make it upstairs. She felt increasingly dizzy. I must be having some kind of panic attack. She felt as if she couldn't breathe and wondered fearfully if she were going to die. She worried that she would collapse on the stairs and remain there unconscious until someone found her. She tried to think of what had jarred the attack and nothing came to mind. She struggled to remember something from her past but came up blank.

Andrew stood up and the waiter rushed over. "Is something wrong, Mr. Hollin?" he asked nervously.

"No, the meal is fine." He placed his hand on the young waiter's shoulder reassuringly. "Take it back to the kitchen. I'll eat it later." He left the dining room, which was filled with guests, and went after Destiny. "Have you seen a woman in a red dress?" he asked one of the patrons in the lobby.

The white-haired man nodded. "She flew past here," he said in a gruff voice, "and took the stairs."

"Thank you." Andrew attempted a smile. He decided to take the stairway to the second floor instead of waiting for the elevator. When he reached the second floor he walked briskly down the hall and stopped in front of room 230 and knocked. "Ms. Raines," he called. "It's Andrew Hollin. I just came to check on you. Are you okay?"

A few seconds later Destiny answered, her eyes tearful. She invited Andrew in. "Ms. Raines . . . what is it? What's wrong?" he said, noticing tear tracks streaking down her cheeks.

"I don't know . . . suddenly something came over me. I think I had some kind of panic attack." She looked bewildered. "All of a sudden these strange images kept flashing before me . . . and then I felt so light-headed . . . dizzy." Andrew looked at her with compassion. He looked directly into her eyes and told her quite seriously, "I'm going to help you find this Pepita Gonzales. But first, I need you to tell me more about what's going on."

Destiny looked at him, wiped the tears from her eyes,

and laughed. "How many years do you have?"

"As many as it takes." He took off his coat jacket and threw it over the chair next to the small round table by the door. He loosened his tie as he crossed the room and sat down casually on a chair. "But before we start, what do you say we get something to eat. I'm starved."

"I'm sorry I ruined dinner. It was lovely."

"It's okay." He grinned. "It's considerably better than ruining my life," he teased, and she began to laugh. "How does filet mignon reheated sound? I can have them send it up."

Destiny looked pleased as she sat down on the bed across from him. She felt comfortable, as if they were old friends. It was half past eleven when Andrew finally left, astonished by all he had learned, and Destiny hated to see him go. She had thoroughly enjoyed his company and the delicious meal he'd had sent up. She hoped she hadn't bored him to death as she recounted the story of her childhood; her witnessing a murder; her mother's suicide, and the connection she had to the Dumois; even though he appeared interested in every detail of her life and was convinced that he could help her.

He had been equally open with her about his own life and told her about his heartbreaking five-year marriage to Marcia, who had been a manic depressive. "Five years of total hell," he had admitted to her frankly, "mood swings like you wouldn't believe. I never knew what was waiting for me when I got home." Destiny felt complete empathy for him, and understood exactly how he felt after being married to Chase. The union had produced a little boy, now three years old, by the name of Jamie. Andrew had full custody of the boy, and Destiny could tell he was absolutely crazy about him. "Jamie was the only good thing that came out of the marriage. He's been my anchor. He's really mature for a guy so little; sometimes I think he more mature than his parents. He's been through a lot," Andrew said, and shook his head, frowning. "More than I would have liked. He loves the Ninja Turtles and baseball." He smiled gently. "He's a terrific little guy. I just hope that he hasn't suffered too much emotionally. Marcia was a neglectful mother and verbally abusive, and the divorce was very bitter. She has little contact with Jamie now, but I understand she's doing better—her doctor put her on lithium and it seems to be helping. She's mellowed out some. I'd love for you to meet Jamie sometime. I really think he'd like you."

"I'd love that." As soon as her life got straightened out, she'd be happy to get to know Andrew's son. Destiny had told him about her teaching career, and how much she loved kids. Andrew was such a decent man, she thought; caring, and he seemed to be a good father to his son with whom he spent all his free time. He was physically attractive, too, with his beautiful shock of raven hair, warm hazel eyes, straight nose, and spare mouth.

♣

Monday morning at nine o'clock, Destiny met Andrew in the hotel dining room. She saw him break out in a smile the moment he spotted her. "Good morning," he said cheerfully. "You look wonderful, as always," he told her, then took a sip of freshly squeezed orange juice. The waiter came over just as she sat down.

She scanned the menu in front of her. "Just coffee . . . black coffee will be all."

"Eggs over easy," said Andrew before turning his eyes to Destiny. "You look a bit on edge."

"I'm a little nervous." She crossed her arms protectively over her bright orange sweater. She had on an Indian print skirt, brown boots, and big gold-hoop earrings to match. She had tried the number, and it was disconnected. She realized this was a long shot. She sighed.

"We don't have to go if it makes you too uncomfortable."

"No." She put up her hands. "This is something I have to do. But look, Andrew, really, like I told you last night, I can do this alone. I hate to drag you into all of this."

"Let me take you. I'm familiar with the city. Besides, you need me for protection." She looked at him wryly.

"Thank you, but up to now I've managed to take care of myself just fine."

"It's a rough neighborhood, and I don't want anything to happen to you."

"It's where I came from. I'm not afraid."

"Nevertheless, I insist."

"It's really not necessary. You have a hotel to run. I can take a cab."

"I won't take no for an answer."

She put up her hands. "You win." She didn't want to argue. She was too emotionally drained to fight with anyone.

Andrew knew better than to drive his brand-new white Lexus to the South Bronx. Neither he nor Destiny were foolish enough to risk car theft or vandalism, both of which were prevalent in that area; so instead he rented a Rabbit for the day from one of the car dealers he knew in town.

It took them approximately thirty minutes to get to the Bronx as Andrew sped along the Major Deegan Expressway. Destiny was strangely quiet, as she sat beside him gazing out the window. She thought of Jeff and the school, the brief but intense love they had shared, and how he was out of her life forever. She wished that he were part of her life now, that they still had many years ahead. She missed him so very much and wished it were possible to bring him back to life, to turn back the clock to change the course of events. She wanted to burst into tears. She didn't know how she could live without him.

She knew that she would've been content with him for the rest of her life. She knew she never would have stopped loving him. He had been the man of her dreams; everyone she'd ever known—except for her father—had paled in comparison to him. She knew he would have comforted her, shared her pain as her father's health failed. She needed him. She wanted him. Oh, God . . . why did this have to happen? And now her father, too. It was too much too bear.

Andrew was a terrific man and she liked him very much, but she knew she wasn't ready to become involved with anyone. It was much too soon. She didn't know if she would ever be able to love another man so deeply, so completely again.

Her mind then switched gears. She gazed at the boundless blue sky above and listened to Monteverdi's, Domine Ad Adjuvandum, followed by Scarlatti's Sonata in D Major. She wondered what they would find at the end of today's journey. The closer they were to their destination the more wary she felt. Her stomach tightened and she gripped the map in her lap tighter, the moisture from her hands fraying the edges. She wondered if she were doing the right thing, trying to dig up her painful past. She was afraid of what she might find, although she realized that it couldn't be much worse than what she already knew.

She and Andrew conferred over which direction and which street, as they found their way into the slums. A shiver ran up the back of Destiny's neck, as they approached the decaying neighborhood. The buildings were nothing more than rat-infested skeletons, vestiges of a time past, and the whole place seemed eerily familiar. She felt a bit dizzy.

"This is it," said Andrew, as he pulled the small car in front of an empty lot.

This couldn't be it, she thought. There was nothing here. "This is the correct address." He looked at Destiny. Her face filled with disappointment, as tears began to form in her eyes. There was nothing there but abandoned buildings and a playground of dirt. She felt an overwhelming sense of despair. She imagined a building filled with people and wondered if her memory was indeed real.

"Are you sure this is right?" She hoped he was wrong, that somehow he'd made a mistake. This couldn't be it. Her imagination had been flooded with so many images.

"I'm afraid so," he said ruefully.

Destiny tried to pull herself together and sat up more erectly. She refused to cry in front of Andrew. "I'm sorry I wasted your time and had you drive out here." She had envisioned like a child, things that could never be, things that only breathed life into her imagination.

"You didn't waste my time. I was happy to do it." Andrew thought a moment. "I just remembered something." He turned to look at her. "In Pepita's file there were some other names listed. I believe she had children."

Destiny's sullen expression filled with hope and her voice raced. "Do you remember any of the names?"

"No. I should have written them down." He sighed. "I could kick myself."

"Can you get them for me?"

"Yes, they're in the files. I have them back in my apartment. What do you say we go back there and look through them?"

Destiny nodded as Andrew started up the car.

ᜒ

They arrived back at the Dumois, and Andrew took

Destiny up to his apartment, which to her surprise took up the entire fifth floor. He unlocked the door and she stepped in and surveyed her surroundings. It wasn't at all what she'd expected. The furniture was masculine and modern, stark white; the foyer floor which immediately caught her eye was made up of black and white marble squares creating a diamond pattern, and the wall to wall carpet was as dark as her hair. She stepped farther inside and noticed that the tables and lamps were glass and chrome, modern paintings adorned the walls. It was very different from the rest of the hotel, which was old fashioned and decorated with antiques.

Andrew watched as Destiny crossed the spacious living room to the French window and looked out on Central Park, the street barraged in autumn color. She breathed deeply as he opened the window, and a warm October breeze rushed in and tousled her hair. "Fall has always been my favorite time of year. I love it when the leaves change and you can hear them rustling on the ground." She smiled.

Andrew gazed at her and no longer able to resist her, pulled her into his arms. He was about to kiss her when Destiny looked at him apologetically and gently pulled away.

"I don't mean to be ungrateful . . . I appreciate everything you're doing . . . but I'm not ready for *this*." She could see the disappointment in his face. "You're a very attractive man . . . and more than kind." Destiny looked to the ceiling and her voice broke and tears filled her eyes. "But I just lost someone very close to me . . . and I'm about to lose someone else whom I love very deeply. It's just too soon. I've been through too much." She met his eyes. "I hope you understand." She searched Andrew's eyes. "I'm sorry if I led you on in any way." He took her hands in his and kissed her gently on the forehead.

"I had no idea." He gestured to the couch. "Have a seat. I'll get the files."

She nodded gratefully, appreciative that he was so understanding. She felt terribly guilty for leading him on.

"I found it." Andrew returned moments later, looking at her with a smile on his face. "It's listed right here. . . ." He pointed to Pepita's name with his finger. "Let's see . . . she had two sons, Diego and José." Destiny's eyes widened.

Andrew shook his head. "The address is the same." He turned to look at her. She looked disappointed. She thought a moment. "I'll just call every Diego and José Gonzalez in the phone book."

"What if they've moved out of state?" Andrew met Destiny's eyes.

"I've got to start somewhere. What other choice do I have? It's all I can do. I have to try. I'll go back to my room and start calling. Do you have a phone book?"

"Please, make your calls from here."

"I don't want to cause you any more trouble."

"It's no trouble, believe me. You can stay here as long as you like."

Andrew went to get the phone book and returned shortly, tossing it onto the couch next to her. Destiny took the phone off the end table and placed it on her lap.

"I wish I could stay and help you but I have to go back to work."

"You've done more than enough already."

"Please . . ." Andrew looked at her sternly, "stay as long as you like."

"Thank you, Andrew. Thank you for everything. For all your help." Destiny smiled warmly.

࿇

"Having any luck?" Andrew said as he reentered the apartment a half hour later. Destiny sat with the receiver pressed to her ear, her head leaning to one side, frowning. She shook her head.

"May I speak with Diego Gonzalez? Do you know a Pepita Gonzales? I'm sorry, sir, but I don't speak Spanish." She hung up the phone. She sighed. "I need a translator. You don't happen to be fluent in Spanish?"

Andrew shook his head. "Wish I were," he said, then left the apartment again.

"Yes, may I please speak with J. Gonzales? No, I don't want a Jesus—José. There's no one there by that name? I'm sorry to bother you. Thank you for your time." Destiny found herself saying, *Thank you for your time,* again and again to no avail. She cupped her hand over a yawn. She couldn't remember how many numbers she'd called and she'd made up her mind to try only a few more before giving up.

"May I speak with Diego Gonzalez?" she asked warily, prepared to hear that no one by that name resided at that number.

There was a moment of silence on the other end. "This is Dr. Diego Gonzalez."

Destiny began to quiver. She wondered if he were the right one. "Diego Gonzales?"

"Yes."

"You wouldn't happen to know Pepita Gonzales?"

"What is the purpose of your call, miss?"

Destiny felt a bolt of excitement. Was she really lucky enough to have found him? "I've been searching for Pepita Gonzales. She was a good friend of my grandmother's and knew my mother, Elena Ortiz. She took me in to live with her when I was very young."

"Pepita Gonzalez isn't here right now." Destiny could

feel her pulse beating faster. She couldn't believe that she had finally located her. It was too good to be true. Diego paused a moment. "I'm her son." Destiny almost dropped the receiver. She felt her heart almost skip a beat and her stomach tighten. She couldn't believe it. She had found Pepita Gonzalez. She wanted to run and tell Andrew. "What can I do for you?" Destiny was suddenly speechless. Her mind went blank.

"I need to talk to your mother."

"What is your name?"

"Destiny Raines . . . I was born Maritza Ortiz."

"Maritza Ortiz?"

"Yes, that's right. Did you know my mother, Elena, by any chance?" She had so many questions. There was so much she wanted to know.

"Yes, I did."

"I understand she died . . . that she took her own life many years ago."

Diego Gonzalez was silent on the other end. "Where are you? What is your phone number? I'm sure Mama will want to see you."

Destiny was afraid to hang up, afraid she'd never hear from him again. "I'm staying at the Dumois, the number is—"

Diego jotted it down. "Will you be at this number late today?"

"Yes. You can reach me here." She sighed with relief as she hung up the phone.

❧ *Chapter sixteen*

"**M**iss Ortiz?"

Destiny immediately recognized the voice. "Yes, this is she." It was the next morning after breakfast, and Diego Gonzalez had finally called her back. She felt a combination of anxiety and relief. "Dr. Gonzalez?"

"My mother is very anxious to meet with you. Could you possibly come this afternoon?"

"This afternoon?"

"How is one o'clock?" He rattled off the address. In all his time they had never left the Bronx; they had just moved to a better section. "I'll be there." Destiny lowered the receiver and placed it in its cradle, a look of satisfaction crossed her face. She couldn't believe she was really going to meet Pepita. She searched her memory, hoping she'd remember something about the woman, but her mind came up blank. Perhaps seeing her in person would jar her memory. She dressed in a black suit and white blouse, then went downstairs to tell Andrew the good news.

She stepped into Andrew's office. "Andrew, I'm going to see her."

"So, this guy really came through," he said, as he walked around his desk to her side. "I'm so happy for you."

"I'm supposed to meet with her today at one."

"Where?"

"Sedgwick Avenue in the Bronx."

"Would you like me to come with you?"

She shook her head.

"You know you're really something. You amaze me with your determination. You can accomplish anything you set your mind to. How would you like to work here?" he said.

⌖

It was a drizzly October day. The sky was as dim as an unwashed sheet, and the air was frigid. Destiny climbed into the taxi after Andrew wished her luck, and turned to look at him one last time before the car ventured out into the noisy city street.

The drive to the Bronx filled her with apprehension, and Destiny felt increasingly anxious as they neared their destination. She wasn't sure how she'd react to seeing Pepita. She worried that seeing her might jar some painful memories. But then she thought of the brighter side—she would leave knowing more about her background, about who she really was, and possibly learn what had happened between her mother and father. This woman was the key to her past. She was hoping she would be able to put her father's mind at ease at last; hopefully, her questions would be answered.

"You're going to need that umbrella today," said the cab driver, as he pulled in front of the tall building. The wind was blustery and the door practically flew open almost as if it had a mind of its own. Destiny put up her umbrella. By now the storm had picked up and even in her raincoat, Destiny felt the wind whip through her. The wind lifted her umbrella as if to abduct both of them, and she grabbed its handle steadily with both her hands.

The light brick apartment building stood next to a duplicate of itself. Both were across the street from the local reservoir, which was hidden from sight by a high pale-colored wall. Destiny approached the glass doors of the building, closed her umbrella, and entered. She tried to push open the second door, but it was locked. She scanned the registry of tenants off to the left and found the doctor's name and his apartment number listed on the second floor. She buzzed and waited.

"Maritza?" the doctor's voice came on the intercom. She wished he would stop calling her Maritza; it made her feel uncomfortable. She pressed down the tiny black button to speak.

"Yes," she answered and a buzzing sound went off to allow her entrance. The bare lobby had a cold tile floor, and she found her way to the elevator which took her upstairs. She took a deep breath before ringing the apartment doorbell. A man in his late thirties, casually dressed in khaki pants and a white turtleneck, answered. His hair and eyes were dark, his features large; his skin was light cocoa, and he was tall and pleasant looking.

"Maritza?" He kept staring at her. Destiny lowered her eyes, then met his gaze and extended her hand. "Destiny Raines."

"Diego Gonzalez. You probably don't remember me." She looked at him straining to remember, but honestly couldn't. "The last time I saw you you were only two." Come on," he motioned, "I'll take you to see my mother. She just moved upstairs to the third floor. She lived here with me until recently; in a few days I'll be getting married. She doesn't even have her own phone yet."

"Congratulations," said Destiny. "You remember me?" she asked him, as they strolled down the hall to the elevator.

"Yes. You lived with us for a while." Destiny looked at

him bewildered. She couldn't remember. "I'm sorry, but I don't remember you."

Diego cast her a sideways glance and smiled. "You've certainly changed since you were two."

Destiny laughed. "I would hope so." They stepped inside the elevator. "What kind of doctor are you?"

"I'm a dentist. My practice is only a couple of blocks away. My mother assists me." The elevator came to a halt. "This is the floor." Diego held the elevator door back with his hand. Destiny was bothered that she remembered so little, but after all, what did she expect—she had only been two. Diego knocked on the door. "Mama, I have Maritza with me." The peephole latch opened then clicked back into place. A few seconds later Pepita Gonzalez opened the door. She looked to be about sixty-five years old, petite, and had full dyed-black hair teased like a football helmet. She wore a beige corduroy skirt and white button down blouse. Her face instantly brightened and tears filled her eyes. "Maritza. It *is* you. *Dios le bendiga.*" She studied Destiny carefully with her eyes, moved closer, and cradled her face with her hands. "You are so beautiful, just like your mother. I can't believe you're here, that I found you again. Oh, Dear Jesus, this is a miracle. Come in, Maritza, come in." She took her by the arm. *"Es una belleza,"* Pepita said to Diego, and he agreed. She took Destiny by the hand and brought her to the three-seater beige couch. "Sit down. Please sit down. I just want to look at you." She spoke with a Spanish accent. Her voice had the coarseness that often comes with age. Destiny quickly scanned the room. It was furnished well; the couch and three club chairs in neutral colors; the walnut coffee and end tables looked practically new; the carpet was a thick red shag almost ankle-deep, and the drapes a collage of bright flowers.

The strong smell of garlic permeated the apartment.

"What can I get for you? Do you want something to eat or drink? I just made some flan de coco—it's Diego's favorite."

Destiny shook her head. There was something so familiar about this woman. She had an exuberant warmth; there was something about her Destiny immediately liked. She felt as if she could trust her. Pepita Gonzales felt like a close relation; both she and her son felt like family; and strangely, Destiny felt as though she belonged with them. She tried so hard to remember them; some experience they'd shared—but nothing came to mind. It was as if they had been forever erased from her thoughts.

"I'm sorry, but I just don't remember either of you."

"You were only a baby," said Pepita tenderly. She gazed at her.

"Your grandmother, Maria, and I—we were like sisters."

Destiny looked at her searchingly. "I'm sorry, but I don't remember her, either."

"That's a shame. Maria was such a good woman and she loved you very much. She raised you herself for a while." Pepita gulped down a sob and a tear rolled down her cheek as Diego lowered himself into the club chair across from them and listened quietly. She could barely speak. It was still too painful to talk about even after all these years. "It was the most horrible tragedy, such a waste. Maria, she was such a beautiful person, always doing things for others. Everyone loved her. She was the most giving person. She and her son, your uncle Carlos— they were murdered."

"Yes . . . I know." Destiny lowered her eyes.

"Your uncle Carlos had been selling drugs on the street. Your grandmother, she tried so hard to stop him . . . but she couldn't.

"He never gave the poor woman a moment's peace.

God rest her soul. He was always getting into some kind of trouble, always involved with the law. He had gotten involved with the wrong people." Pepita shook her head. "They were both stabbed to death, right in her apartment. I heard Maria scream . . . and then there was nothing . . . silence. I ran over there . . . but I was too late." Pepita lowered her head and closed her eyes. "There was blood everywhere. It was horrible." She exhaled deeply. "They didn't hurt *you,* thank God. I found you there and took you in."

Destiny thankfully didn't recall any of it. "I'm very grateful for everything you did."

"Have you been happy with him?"

"My father?"

Pepita nodded.

"For the most part yes—very. He's been very good to me. He's been a loving father. He's given me everything a person could want."

Pepita glanced at Diego and sighed in relief. "Then I guess I did the right thing."

The right thing? thought Destiny. *What exactly did she mean by that?* She was uncomfortable with the way Pepita said it. "What do you mean by the 'right thing'?"

Pepita took a deep breath and met Destiny's intense gaze. "I didn't want you to go from foster home to foster home; to grow up without love. Your grandmother never would have wanted that. *I* didn't want that. And as much as I wanted to keep you, I just couldn't. I tried to think of what would be best for you, what I should do. I didn't know what to do and I thought and thought. And finally Mr. Raines came to mind. Your mother, Elena, had been very much in love with him."

If that was the case then how could she have left him? thought Destiny. How could she have done that to him?

That didn't sound like love to her, she thought bitterly.

"I was determined not to get social services involved. Elena had told me what a kind person Alexander was, that he loved children, and wanted lots of them with her . . . and that he was a very wealthy man."

Destiny felt her stomach cramp. She became increasingly uncomfortable and was afraid of what she might hear. She didn't like the direction in which Pepita seemed to be headed.

"I didn't know what else to do. I had no one to turn to. I was all alone. I contacted Mr. Raines and told him he was your father—when all along I knew it wasn't true, that he wasn't. It was all I could think of to do."

"You *what?*" Destiny said. She felt her heart pound. "You told him he was my father when you knew he wasn't?" She was momentarily speechless. She couldn't believe it. She stared at Pepita in disbelief. "How could you deceive him like that? How could you do such a thing?" She felt a lump form in the back of her throat. Her father would hate Pepita if he ever learned the truth; found out what she'd done to him. Her father would hate her, too, she thought sadly, for not being his child, for being an imposter— another man's child.

All this time he thought she was his flesh and blood. That was probably the reason why he had treated her so well. If he had known she wasn't his, he would have never taken her in to live with him. Destiny was convinced of that. Her whole life had been a lie. She'd been living an outrageous lie.

She didn't deserve the good life she had had. She didn't deserve her father's love. She didn't deserve anything. Julia had been right—she was nothing, nothing at all.

She was so afraid her father would hate her if he found out the truth. How could she ever bring herself to tell him? She wanted to cry, but she was too angry. She was angry at Pepita for putting both her and her father in this predicament. She glared at the old woman. "How could you do a thing like that? You knowingly lied."

"I had no other choice. What else was I to do?"

"Lying was your only option? I find that difficult to accept."

"Your mother, Elena, had been having a love affair with Mr. Raines, so I thought he might believe it."

"Didn't he wonder? Didn't he ask any questions? Didn't he want confirmation of his paternity?"

"He was very accepting, really. I was surprised myself. He was very happy to learn he had a child with Elena . . . that you were his daughter. He didn't contest it."

What a fool her father had been, she thought, to be duped so easily. "If he and my mother had been lovers then isn't it possible that he might be my real father?" Destiny was grasping at anything she could find. She hoped it wasn't true. She desperately wanted to be Alexander's daughter. Now more than ever. She wanted Pepita to retract her statement, to tell her she had fabricated the whole thing. She didn't want to accept it. "How do you know he's not my father?" Destiny felt her eyes moisten.

"Believe me, I wish he were. I wish he had been. It would have made everything much easier."

"How can you be so sure?"

She looked away. "Your mother will explain everything to you. She would very much like to see you."

"What?" Destiny's head jutted forward, and her eyes grew larger. "What are you talking about? My mother, Elena, she's dead. She committed suicide . . . a long time ago."

Pepita looked away, shamefully. "I'm afraid that was another lie."

Destiny rose from the couch and guardedly crossed

her arms. "What are you talking about? Are you saying my mother is alive?"

"Yes," Pepita said.

Destiny could feel her face flush with anger. "You told my father she was dead. That's what he's believed all these years. Why?"

"Elena had tried to kill herself. Your grandmother had her put in a state institution. She thought maybe there she could get some help. She didn't know what else to do. Elena thought it best if Alexander thought she was dead. She didn't want him to come and look for her. She couldn't face him."

"Why not? Why was she so upset? What happened?"

"I'm sure your mother will be glad to answer all your questions when you meet with her."

"What makes you think I'm going to meet with her? Why does she want to see me now—after all this time? And don't call her *my mother*. She doesn't deserve the title." Destiny turned her eyes away angrily. She met Pepita's gaze. "Did she know that all this time her ex-lover has been raising her child? A child he believed was his?" Destiny's dark brows arched into a frown.

"Yes. She is aware of everything, now. Now that she's better."

"What kind of person is she? How could she allow such a thing?"

"She was happy that you were being well taken care of."

"Is she still there? In the state hospital?"

"No." Pepita shook her head. "She's been out for some time now."

"Where is she?"

"She has her life back, thanks to a young doctor at the hospital. He really helped her. After she was released she went to medical school and is now a physician working at

Mt. Sinai—a cardiologist. She has an apartment on Fifth Avenue."

Destiny felt her fury rise. Agitated, she began to pace. Elena was living a very comfortable life and didn't give a damn about her—or her father. "I'm glad things are going so well for her," she said sarcastically. Her mother was a successful doctor working in New York living on Fifth Avenue, and had never cared enough about her to ever contact her. She and her father could rot in hell for all she probably cared. *The selfish bitch,* she thought. How could she do this to them? If only her poor father knew . . . what would he think? She imagined how hurt he'd be.

She had a mother who clearly didn't love her. Destiny felt worthless. She wished Elena had remained dead; it would have been easier. "Why didn't she ever contact me? Didn't she care at all?"

"Of course. Elena is not heartless, she is very caring." *That's obvious,* thought Destiny. "She thought that what she was doing was for the best."

"Best?" She had a daughter who she refused to acknowledge? "She was going to let me think she was dead for the rest of my life? And my father? Best for whom? Apparently best for her . . . and no one else. She didn't want me to come along and interfere with her brilliant career, to mess up her perfect life."

"No. Maritza, it's not what it seems. She's never stopped thinking about you . . . and neither have I. It's been so hard. All these years I wanted to contact you, but Mr. Raines made me promise never to do so. He thought it best if you forgot your past. It was too traumatic. I suppose your mother thought it best not to disrupt your life also."

"Well tell her thank you. I'm very moved that I enter her thoughts every now and then." Bitch. What kind of woman was she? What kind of woman would have a child and completely abandon her? This is the woman her father had loved so dearly? This is the woman he had described as so wonderful? She didn't know her mother, but from the little she had learned she already didn't want any part of her. How could she have done this to them?

Destiny didn't care what kind of mental state Elena had been in or was in now? She had a child and she had denied her a mother all these years while she selfishly pursued her own life.

"I've known you since the day you were born. You're like my own. Believe me when I tell you there were so many times I wanted to come see you, call you . . . but he and I had made an agreement." She lowered her eyes and looked sadly away.

First Destiny thought Alexander Raines was her adopted father . . . she had grown up thinking that; then he was her biological father—now he wasn't. What were these women doing to her? What gave them the right to play games with her life? She had been caught up in their web of lies and deceit, and she was sick and tired of it. She was so confused and angry at everyone for deceiving her.

"I think I've heard enough. I have to leave." Destiny headed for the front door. She had so many more questions to ask, but she was too infuriated to think clearly. She had to get out of there.

"I'm so sorry. Please forgive me," said Pepita, as she followed Destiny to the door. "I did what I thought was best. I'm so sorry to have upset you. Perhaps when you're feeling up to it we can meet again."

Doubtful, thought Destiny. Right now she didn't want anything to do with any of them. "I suppose my mother did what was best for me. Everyone is always doing what's best for me." And she was the recipient of all their lies. She despised them all.

Destiny quickly left the apartment, glad to be out of there.

~

There were still so many pieces missing. Destiny rubbed her forehead, as she stood in the rain waiting for a cab she had called for at the corner store. She was still in a state of disbelief over all she had learned—that her father was not her father, that her mother was alive and well. She wanted to know so much more about her mother. What had happened to her? What had caused her to break it off with her father? Who was her real father? Why had she tried to kill herself?

Her head began to throb. She needed to go back to the hotel and rest, regroup. She needed to sleep off her anger and start fresh with a clear head. She didn't want to see anyone—not even Andrew. She wasn't up to explaining everything to him.

~

Andrew knocked at Destiny's door. The knock was persistent and finally woke Destiny up from a deep sleep. Groggily, she dragged herself out of bed. "Who is it?" she asked tiredly, annoyed by the interruption.

"It's me—Andrew. Open up."

She wasn't interested in seeing anyone and hesitated, trying to come up with an excuse. "I just stepped out of the shower."

"Can I meet you later? How about a picnic dinner in the park?"

"Fine," she said.

"Meet you in the lobby at six."

"Okay." Destiny combed her hand through her disheveled hair and yawned. She glanced at the clock. She still had time to rest before she had to get ready. She crossed the room and climbed lazily back into bed.

৵

Andrew and Destiny sat by the water on a bench eating sandwiches prepared by the hotel, the skyscrapers peaking over the trees like nosy neighbors all around them. A male jogger disrupted their solitude. Destiny could hear his labored breathing, see the sweat streaming down his left temple, and hear his footsteps pounding the pavement as he passed them by.

"So what are you going to do now?" Andrew asked, after Destiny had poured her heart out to him once again, telling him everything she'd learned. The park was so peaceful, like another place and time, and took her away from the hustle and bustle of the city.

"I don't know. I suppose I'll go back."

"So soon?" Andrew looked disappointed. "You've decided not to contact her?"

Thoughts of her mother kept filling her head. She knew where she worked. It would be easy to find her. But Destiny didn't feel up to making the first move. "Pepita said she's going to get in touch with me. Quite frankly, right now, I'm not in the mood to see her. I'm still too angry . . . too hurt."

Andrew peered into her blue eyes, accentuated by her blue sweater. "You need to do what's best for you." He was so understanding, she thought. In such a short period of time he had become a dear and supportive friend. She met his eyes and smiled. She felt strangely at peace with him. He had a calming effect on her, made her see that no problem was too great or insurmountable.

"Thank you for being here—for listening." Andrew moved closer to her and stroked her cheek gently with his hand. His fingertips made her skin tingle. He ran his hand through her shiny black hair, then leaned over to kiss her.

And Destiny didn't resist. She was so lonely, so distraught, and needed someone, and Andrew was there. She responded to his kiss, surprised by how much she enjoyed it.

"That was nice." She felt a little guilty enjoying the kiss when Jeff had so recently died.

"For me, too."

A crazy lady began to chant something incomprehensible across the murky pond. Andrew looked at Destiny and shook his head. Destiny felt pity for the shabbily dressed woman, clearly out of her mind, and simply sighed. She might end up like her someday. One never knew. She thought of her mother, Elena, the life she must have lived in the state hospital. Andrew took her hand in his, and they headed back to the hotel. She tried to envision what Elena was like now—how she looked, what kind of personality she had, if it were similar to hers. She still couldn't believe that she really had a mother and that she wanted to meet her.

She thought of her poor dying father and tried to imagine his voice in her head, tried to think of what his response would be if he only knew that her mother were alive.

✳ *Chapter seventeen*

*J*ulia called Destiny later that night at the Dumois pleading with her to return home. "You've been gone for almost a week. When are you planning to come home? It's too tough supervising all these nurses alone. I need your help during the night. He only wants to see me and no one else. I'm literally exhausted. It's just too much for one person."

Destiny frowned. She was quickly losing her patience.

"It's just too hard. There's only one of me. I'm not a nurse. And I keep thinking he's going to die on me. Do you know how frightening that is? Do you have any idea of what this is like, day after day? You're off having a great time staying in a plush New York hotel while I'm stuck here working my tailbone off." She huffed. "I've never worked so hard in my life."

A little hard work isn't going to kill you. Destiny wished Julia would stop whining.

"He's becoming more dependent all the time. I just can't cope. If I had wanted to wait on somebody hand and foot I would have become a mother."

Thank God you didn't, Destiny thought. Julia didn't have a nurturing bone in her body. Destiny exhaled and rolled her eyes. She didn't feel particularly sympathetic— she was in no mood to hear Julia whine—but nevertheless she replied, "I'll take the train back in the morning."

"I'm so exhausted. All I do is run up and down the steps all night long. I haven't slept in days. Can't you come back tonight?"

Destiny was becoming more annoyed by the moment. What did the woman want from her? "I'll take the train in the morning," she said firmly. What did the woman expect? It was already nine o'clock at night.

If her father had taken a turn for the worse it would have been a completely different matter. She would have left immediately.

"Very well." Julia's dissatisfaction was evident in her voice. "Maybe we should consider putting your father in some kind of nursing facility or hospital. He'd be able to get the care he needs. I hope you realize that he's never going to get better, he's only going to get worse. And if he has to go," breathed Julia, "I hate to say it . . . but I just wish he'd get it over with already."

"How can you say a thing like that!" Destiny yelled into the phone, her face flushing in anger.

Julia began to cry from sheer exhaustion. Her voice trembled. "I'm much too young to have to deal with all this. It's just too hard on me. Do you understand?"

Destiny bit down on her lip and tried not to lose her self-control, which was becoming more difficult by the moment. Julia's suggestion about placing her father in a home had infuriated her no end. It was the easy way out of a difficult situation, and her father deserved much better. He had given so much to both of them, and she wasn't about to abandon him when he needed her most.

Julia always looked for the easy way out of everything. She was such a spoiled woman. "Let me make something perfectly clear . . . we're *not* putting my father in a nursing home." She knew her father wanted to remain at home. He had expressed his wishes to her on one of their walks—no nursing home, hospital, no life saving resuscitation; and he wanted to be buried next to his father. "I won't hear of it. My father is not going into a nursing home or hospital. *I'll* take care of him myself if need be. I'll be back as soon as I can." She hung up the phone.

~

"That woman is absolutely impossible." Destiny complained to Andrew the next morning over coffee in the dining room an hour before her train was scheduled to leave Penn Station. "Would you believe Julia called me at nine last night and wanted me to take the next available train? 'I just can't cope anymore,'" Destiny mimicked her. "Julia Stoneworth is the most self-centered woman I've ever met. She only thinks of herself. No one else matters." Destiny thought of Chase. The two of them would make a good pair. "The poor thing isn't getting her ten hours of uninterrupted sleep. For the life of me, I'll never be able to figure out what my father ever saw in her."

"You never know what attracts some people."

"That's for sure."

"I'm sorry you have to leave so soon. Is there any way I can convince you to stay awhile longer? Free of charge, of course." Andrew met her eyes and smiled.

"I'm flattered." Destiny smiled back, "but if I don't go back, Julia is going to have a nervous breakdown and that's all I need. Besides, I promised my father I wouldn't be gone too long." She felt the tears form in her eyes. She knew in her heart that she didn't have much time left to spend with him.

The maître d' approached the table. "Ms. Raines, I'm sorry to intrude." He met her eyes, then glanced at Andrew. "There is a woman in the lobby who is looking for you."

A woman? Destiny wondered who the woman could be when suddenly a chill raced up the back of her neck, and she thought of Elena. No, it couldn't be, she told herself. Not here. Not now. She wasn't ready for this. She never really thought she'd come.

"What does she look like?" Perhaps it was Pepita.

"She's around your height, attractive, with shoulder length grayish hair."

It wasn't Pepita Gonzales; the description didn't fit. "Did she say her name?"

"No, but I'd be happy to go and find out if you like?"

"No. That won't be necessary. Where is she?"

"She's waiting in the lobby."

"Thank you. Please tell her I'll meet her shortly."

Destiny cupped her hand over her mouth.

"What's wrong?" asked Andrew.

"That woman out there—" She peered into his eyes "That woman—I think she might be my mother."

Suddenly, like a small child, Destiny wanted to run and hide. She wasn't ready to see her. "I have a train to catch. I can't meet with her now."

"You can always reschedule."

Julia would have a fit if she were even a minute late But quite frankly, she didn't care. Her whole body quiv ered slightly. She knew she had no other choice. She wa curious to see her. There were too many unanswere questions.

"Do you want me to come with you?"

Destiny shook her head.

"Would you like me to ask her to leave?"

She shook her head again. "Would you excuse me?"

She grabbed her coat off the back of the chair an walked slowly out of the dining room. She cautious entered the lobby, scanning the large room with her eye

She spotted a woman standing in a gray wool coat with a black leather shoulder bag who fit the maître d's description. That must be her, she thought, as she nervously made her way closer, feeling her heart pound louder and faster with every step. The woman saw her and walked to meet her half way.

She smiled warmly. "Are you Destiny Raines?" she asked in a surprisingly soft and feminine voice.

"Yes."

"I'm Elena Ortiz." The woman extended her hand, but Destiny refused it. Elena looked surprised.

"I know who you are."

"May we talk?"

"I suppose."

"Are you familiar with the coffee shop around the corner? They serve wonderful food."

"We can sit in the park. I'm not hungry."

"Anywhere you like."

Destiny slipped her arms into her coat, and the two women left the hotel walking side by side, Destiny keeping a safe distance. "It's just across the street."

"I'm quite familiar with the park."

Elena was still beautiful even though she had gray hair, and her face was accentuated by lines. She looked a little different than Destiny had imagined, not quite as glamorous. She looked like someone who had worked hard all her life.

Destiny felt strangely ill at ease in her mother's presence and could feel her resentment mounting.

✎

Elena had detected her daughter's hostility the moment she approached her, but it didn't surprise her. It was what she expected all along. She knew that meeting with her daughter after all these years wouldn't be easy. Nevertheless, she was pleased to be with her daughter and happy to have found her; to see her at last after all this time.

Elena thought of Alexander. She had never stopped loving him, and was grateful that he had taken in her child and has raised as his own. She kept glancing at her daughter along the way. She had turned into a beautiful young woman, more beautiful than she would have ever imagined.

She had waited much too long, not wanting to disrupt her child's life; and it was only when Pepita called to tell her that Maritza was looking for her that she decided the time was right. She had imagined little Maritza at each stage of her life and regretted that she had missed so much; that she'd never had the opportunity to be a part of it.

At first her decision to give away her only child had seemed to her to be the only decision. She and Pepita had consulted on more than one occasion, and they both agreed it was the only thing to do. Pepita couldn't afford to care for the little girl, and Elena, still angry and resentful, and locked away in a state hospital, had been in no mental condition to raise her. When Elena learned that Alexander had taken her in, she was greatly relieved, knowing her little girl would be in good hands. She didn't feel particularly comfortable with the idea of deceiving him, but Pepita had convinced her that it was the only way.

As the years passed and she regained her sanity, she longed for the child, missed her terribly, and realized that she had made a grave mistake by giving her away.

But by then it was already too late. It was too late to be a mother to her daughter. It was too late to be a wife to Alexander, the only man she'd ever loved. The memory of the little girl with the feathery black hair and big blue eyes continued to haunt her. The little girl that should have been *their* little girl together . . . and in a strange sense she was. She had learned through Pepita that Maritza had a good life with Alexander, and she didn't want to disrupt it at any cost. It was the most unselfish thing she'd ever done.

She realized in retrospect that she had been so emotionally distraught by what happened that she had been unable to think clearly. She regretted hating the child at first. If she could have done it over she would have been stronger. She would have kept her child.

Destiny sat down on the bench facing the pond, the same bench where Andrew had kissed her the day before. Elena sat down next to her—closer than Destiny would have preferred—Elena could detect by her daughter's body language. Elena kept staring at her; she couldn't take her eyes off her. She longed to embrace her and reclaim Maritza as her own, but she knew it could never be that simple. She wanted to pull her into her arms and tell her how much she loved her; how a day hadn't gone by without her thinking of her; how she deeply regretted the mistake she'd made by giving her up; how she wished she had seen her all these years; how very sorry she was; and how if she could have only turned back the clock, she would have married Alexander and kept her. They would have been a real family. She had been so weak, and now she was paying the price.

Tears welled up in her eyes as she thought of this young woman beside her. Elena could see the likeness between them. Destiny reminded her of herself in her younger years, and it warmed her inside.

Destiny noticed a striking resemblance between them, too. She *did* resemble her mother. Just like her father had said.

"I've been waiting so long for this." Elena peered at her daughter with her dark eyes. "I've never stopped wondering about you—never stopped loving you."

Destiny laughed. She found it difficult to believe. "You had a very peculiar way of showing it."

"I realize that you're very hurt and angry with me, and I don't blame you. It's to be expected after what I did."

"I didn't even know I had a mother until yesterday. I thought you were dead."

Elena lowered her eyes, then looked at her daughter. "I'm not here to make any excuses. I made a lot of mistakes, and believe me when I tell you that I deeply regret them. I hope that in time you're able to forgive me."

"My father loved you. Why did you leave him? He's never stopped loving you. He's never gotten over you."

Elena's face filled with pain. "I know what I did was terribly wrong. I never meant to hurt him. That was not my intention."

"Then what *was* your intention? My father is dying of cancer." Destiny's eyes filled with tears. "I'm sure he would like to know. Of course, he thinks you're dead."

"Cancer?" Elena looked alarmed. "What was his diagnosis?"

"You're a doctor. Don't you know everything?"

Elena ignored the comment. "What kind of cancer is it?"

"Malignant melanoma in the advanced stage. He's has it all inside him. He's going to die."

Elena looked very distraught. She leaned over, clasping her hands together, closed her eyes, and silently prayed for him. She sat up again.

"Has he tried Interferon? There is also a new injection . . . I recently read a study—"

"It's too late for anything. Why did you leave him? What happened? Why did you give me up?"

"There is so much you don't know."

"Why didn't you contact me all these years?"

Elena looked up to the sky. She was filled with pain. "I never planned to have you." She lowered her head and nervously played with her nail-bitten thumbs. "I don't know any gentle way to say this, so I'll just come right out and say it . . . I—I was raped."

The word rape tore through Destiny like a knife. She felt her chest constrict, and she suddenly couldn't breathe. She had never imagined anything so horrible. She had been the end result of a rape. She had been unwanted. How could anyone love a child like her? She felt like the lowest form of existence. She was devastated. She wanted to shriek at the top of her lungs and run away and never come back. She tried with all her might not to burst into tears.

"By whom?"

"I believe it was the man who raped me first—"

First? thought Destiny, looking at Elena, her eyes filled with horror.

"He was an old boyfriend. I was his girl before I met Alexander. He was a gang member; he lived in the neighborhood. I broke it off with him when I met your father. We were very much in love, and we were going to be married; and he was very angry that I had jilted him. He surprised me one night on the way home from work." She looked away shamefully as Destiny listened in silence. "He held a knife to my breast. He threatened to mutilate and then kill me. He dragged me into the back alley where his buddies were waiting, and they gang-raped me, one by one, and beat me until I blacked out."

Destiny was horrified and felt overwhelming pity for Elena having to go through such an ordeal. She continued.

"And then I became pregnant with you. I knew that if I told Alexander what happened he'd go after them, and they'd kill him, so I broke up with him and decided to never see him again."

Elena would never forget that awful night for as long as she lived. She would never forget how her clothes had been ripped off by all of them; how degraded she had felt by what they had done to her; having to stagger home nude in the dimly lit streets, a spectacle for everyone to see. She remembered climbing the steps to her apartment, wondering if she had the strength to make it.

She would never forget how frightened she had been for her life; how she thought they were going to kill her; how her life had ended that night; how the baby that had been conceived that awful night had been a constant reminder of what they'd done to her.

❦

October 1969

"Mama! . . . Mama! . . ." Elena shrieked as she staggered up the first flight of stairs, her face and nude body bruised and bloody. "Mama . . ." She felt terribly weak and her whole body throbbed with unbearable pain from all the times they had beaten her. Pepita was the first to hear Elena screaming in the stairwell and rushed out into the hallway and pounded on Maria's door across the hall.

"Maria . . . it's Elena. She's been hurt!" Maria's eyes widened in alarm, and the two women bolted down the stairs to meet Elena as she took another agonizing step. Maria put her hands to her face and began to sob when she saw her naked daughter—dirty and bleeding. She tried to cover Elena as best she could with the soiled dish towel she'd had draped over her shoulder.

"Mama . . ." Elena fell into her mother's arms, tears coursing down her swollen cheeks. Maria's eyes filled with fresh tears as Pepita looked on. She lowered herself on a step and pulled her baby girl into her lap. "What happened?" Elena was hysterical. Her whole body trembled and she cried, "They all raped me, Mama." Maria felt her heart stop as Pepita gasped and covered her mouth. Elena buried her face in her mother's chest and sobbed uncontrollably.

"Why did they do this to me?" Elena asked, tears gushing from her eyes as the two women lifted her to her feet and helped her upstairs to the apartment.

॰॰

One Month Later

Elena began to cry into the palms of her hands. "I think I'm pregnant," she mumbled. I feel so sick lately . . . and I'm never late. What am I going to do? Elena looked up at her mother. "What am I going to tell Alexander? I've been cutting him off. I can't tell him the truth and I don't want to lie." Maria and Pepita looked at each other. "I have to get an abortion. I have no other choice. I can't keep it. I won't keep it." Elena rose off the bed in her faded nighty. I must get rid of it. It was conceived in hell."

"Don't talk like that!" yelled Maria. She would hear of no such thing. Abortion was a sin. She would not allow her daughter to do it. "I will not hear of it! You will not commit such a sin." She quickly crossed herself and asked the Lord for forgiveness. Pepita lowered herself quietly into the torn couch.

"I can't have this baby!" Elena yelled back. "You can't make me have it. Please . . . Mama," her voice softened. "Please don't make me have this baby." Sobbing, Elena fell her hands and knees and begged Maria.

॰॰

Maria brought the tiny dark-haired infant to her mother

who lay weakly on the torn couch in the one room apartment. She's hungry, Elena. You must feed her."

Maria placed the beautiful baby girl in her daughter's arms. Elena looked down at her and tears filled her eyes. She was a constant reminder of that horrible night and everything she'd lost; a night she wanted to erase from her memory forever; a night that had cost her the man she loved. She didn't love this child—and she never would She wished the baby didn't exist. She didn't want to take care of her, feed her or see her. She had never wanted her

"The Lord works in strange ways," said Maria. "He delivered this tiny angel to us, and now we must care of her." If only this baby had been Alexander's—though Elena, she would have loved her with all her heart; she would have been happy to have her, to be her mother.

She didn't even know who the baby's father was— there had been so many of them. Tears gushed from he eyes. Each day her mind replayed the rape. She didn think she could go on with her life. She had been s degraded, humiliated. They had taken away her dignit and sense of self and she wished she were dead. Sh couldn't go on living after what they'd done to her. A soon as she was stronger she had planned to kill herself. was all she could think of since that night. She could n longer bear to be a prisoner of her own thoughts.

The baby began to cry. "If you don't feed her, she w die," said Maria, hovering over her.

Elena stared blankly at the window and fantasize jumping out, her bones smashing on the pavement belov as tears slipped down her cheeks. She opened up h nightgown, put the tiny girl to her breast, and the infa began to noisily suck.

"You cannot blame her, Elena. It's not her fault wh happened. You have to take care of her. It is your du

You are her mother. The Lord has given her to you."

Elena turned her head away as if not to listen as the child continued to nurse. She didn't think she would ever be able to love little Maritza.

~

"Oh, my God . . . I'm so sorry. I'm so sorry I ruined your life. I don't blame you for hating me." Destiny burst into tears as she sat on the bench next to Elena. "It's all because of me. I ruined my father's life, too."

Elena looked at her. "It wasn't your fault. I know that now. You were completely innocent. You didn't ask for any of us. No one blames you. I was wrong to ever blame you."

"How could anyone ever love me after I ruined so many lives?"

"Listen to me," Elena faced Destiny and placed her hands firmly on top of her daughter's. "You were not responsible for my rape. Yes, it's true you were brought into the world by unfortunate circumstances. I wish you had been conceived in love. I wish you had been Alexander's child.

"I made a mistake giving you away. No matter how you were conceived—you are a part of me. You always will be. I should have never given you up. I've regretted it every day of my life. You must believe that." Elena released her hold.

"What ever happened to the man who orchestrated all this? Who did this to you?"

"He got what he deserved. He was killed by a rival gang."

"You don't know who my father is?" She was curious to know even though she hated the bastard for what he had done to them.

Elena shook her head. "There were too many of them. Destiny, we must try and put the past behind us. Live for each day; take one day at a time. It took years of therapy for me to understand this. We must go on from here. I'm sorry for all the pain I've caused you. I can see that you've grown into a special young woman. I'll always be grateful to Alexander for raising you."

"Then come back with me and see him . . . before he dies . . . please. It would mean so much to him."

Elena looked away. "I don't know." Elena didn't know if she could face Alexander after what she had done to him, after all these years.

"You could finally put his mind at ease. You owe him that much."

"Destiny," Elena said, "I realize it's a lot to ask, but I was hoping we could start over, that we could have a relationship. I would really like to be your friend."

"I need time to think."

"I understand. I'm grateful that you even agreed to see me. I've wanted to say these things for so long." Elena reached into her pocket. "Here is my home phone number and address. I would love to hear from you when you feel ready."

"I need time."

"I understand completely."

"Will you consider coming to see my father?"

"Yes, I'll consider it."

"I have to go." Destiny glanced at her watch. She had missed her train. She would try and make the next one. She rose and looked down at her mother. Elena smiled softly. Destiny turned to look at her one last time before disappearing down the path.

ᵔ

Destiny's heart felt as if it had been severed and was hanging by one loose thread. She walked briskly back to the hotel. In her wildest dreams she had never imagined anything so awful, so heartbreaking. She felt terrible inside, and a part of her wished she had never learned the truth. It was much too painful.

The thought of facing Andrew and explaining all of this to him filled her with dread. She hoped to avoid him just long enough to gather her things and slip inconspicuously out of the hotel. Right now all she had to offer him was her pain, and she felt as if she had already burdened him enough. He had proved to be a wonderful friend, and she would never forget him and all he had done for her.

She approached the front of the hotel, which once held such enchantment, but now was nothing more than an ugly reminder of her legacy and flew past the doorman. She prayed she wouldn't see Andrew and took the stairs to her room on the second floor. She tore through the drawers and closet and threw her belongings into her suitcase, then took the steps back downstairs. She felt like a fugitive. She stopped nervously at the desk hoping she wouldn't run into him, returned her room key, and quickly paid her bill, then scurried back outside to a waiting cab.

Later that day Andrew stopped by the front desk on the way to his office. "Have you seen Ms. Raines?" he asked the desk clerk, glancing once again at his watch. "She should have been back by now—it's almost dinnertime." His face filled with concern. "I hope everything's all right." He exhaled deeply and shook his head.

"Mr. Hollin . . . Ms. Raines checked out three hours ago." Andrew looked at the desk clerk in astonishment. "She appeared to be in a big hurry."

"Did she say anything?"

"No. She just paid her bill and left."

Andrew could feel his stomach tighten. What could have happened? He wondered why she had left in such a hurry, hadn't even said good-bye. He hoped nothing terrible had happened, although he felt instinctively that something was very wrong. He didn't know her all that well, but from what he knew it seemed out of character for her to depart so abruptly. Perhaps her sick father had taken a turn for the worse. "What is going on?" he mumbled. He was visibly upset. "By any chance did she say what train or plane she was planning to take?"

"She didn't say."

Andrew knew he had no other choice but to find out what happened, and he became lost in his own thoughts.

❧

"You're late. You told me you were taking the early train. What happened?"

Julia made a face and practically flew by her and scurried up the steps to her room.

Destiny wasn't anxious to confront her father and tell him what she had learned, but she knew she had no other choice. She owed him that much, as painful as it would be for both of them. She took off her coat, threw it on her bed, put down her purse and suitcase and crossed the room to the window. It was a beautiful autumn day. Leaves sailed through the air landing delicately on the ground, and the trees were bathed in brilliant color. When she opened the window and took in a breath of fresh air she was surprised at how much warmer the weather was here than in New York.

An hour later, dressed in jeans, a blue turtleneck, and jeans jacket, Destiny walked down the hall to Alexander's room. Her stomach twisted in knots. She knew the moment he saw her he would know something was wrong.

by her eyes—they were still puffy. Even makeup couldn't hide her distress. She took a deep breath then knocked on her father's bedroom door. "Father . . . it's me. May I come in?"

She could hear his voice rise cheerfully as he said her name. She attempted a small smile, then crossed the room and leaned over to kiss his cheek.

"I'm so glad you're back." He took her hand lovingly in his.

"It's such a beautiful day," she breathed, then met his eyes. "Why don't you get yourself dressed and we can go for a walk."

Alexander searched her eyes. He suspected something was wrong in spite of her attempted cheerfulness. She helped him up, and he slowly crossed the room to his closet where he picked out some clothes. "Give me just a few minutes." He carried his jeans and red-plaid shirt to the bathroom while Destiny sat on his unmade bed. A few minutes later he emerged unshaven with matted hair, but smelling freshly washed.

~

Arm and arm, wading through the leaves, they strolled down the small hill past the gazebo to the pond. Alexander kept glancing at his daughter along the way. He was so happy to have her back. "You're wearing that look of yours," he said, "that look you always wear when something's wrong."

"I can't hide anything from you, can I?" she smiled sadly, fresh tears welling up in her eyes.

"I'm afraid I know you too well for that." He smiled gently back as they both sat down on the cool metal bench. "An actress you're not. You've never been good at disguising your feelings." He looked at her wryly and Destiny laughed, because she knew it was true.

She lowered her chin. "I don't know where to begin."

"Anywhere you like." Alexander affectionately took her hand in his as they gazed at the russet water.

Destiny sighed deeply. "I went up to New York—to the Dumois—to see if I could find out what happened to Elena." Alexander looked only faintly surprised. He had suspected she was up to something of that nature.

"And did you find out anything?" He turned his head to her.

Tears streamed down her cheeks, and Alexander put his arm around her. She hesitated. "I found out what happened."

Alexander looked at her in surprise. His pulse began to beat faster. He removed his arm and turned all the way to face her.

Destiny couldn't bring herself to say it. "Please—" He could see that she was reluctant.

"Elena's not dead."

Alexander looked at her, stunned. "She's alive?"

"She tried to commit suicide after she broke it off with you, and she ended up in a mental institution."

"A mental hospital? Why? For God's sake, what happened?" Destiny could see the pain in his face. Elena had so much to look forward to—a medical career, a life with him.

"This is what Pepita told me."

"Pepita?" She slowly came to mind. His memory wasn't very good lately. "Ah . . . yes, Pepita."

"Her mother had her committed to a mental institution. She thought she might try to do it again. She didn't know what else to do." Alexander lowered his eyes and shook his head.

"But why? We were going to be married."

Tears rolled down Destiny's cheeks as she looked

him. "Because she was gang-raped and beaten so severely she almost died." Alexander looked at her, his face filled with shock and horror. Anger coursed through his veins filling every inch of him. He struggled to fight back tears. "Who did it? Who did that to her?" He wanted to kill the son of a bitch who did it, and if he were here right now, he would have strangled him with his bare hands with the little strength he had left. "Why didn't she tell me?"

"That's not the worst of it."

Destiny crossed her arms and rose from the bench. She gazed at the pond. "Then she became pregnant," Destiny stammered, "with . . . me." Alexander looked at her in utter astonishment.

"With you?" He froze, speechless. She wasn't his daughter, his flesh and blood, after all. He couldn't believe it.

"With me," she repeated tearfully, shamefully. "Pepita lied to you, so that you would take me."

He had been deceived. He couldn't believe Pepita had done that to him—make him think Maritza was his.

"She tried to take her own life because of me. She never wanted me." Destiny's voice was nothing more than a whisper. "She never wanted me," she trembled. "I ruined her life . . . and yours. She could never face you after what happened."

Destiny sobbed into her hands.

"Why on God's earth didn't Elena tell me the truth?" mumbled Alexander. We could have found a way to work it out. *Someway. Somehow.*

She turned to face him. "I know you must hate me . . . and I don't blame you."

Alexander wasn't angry at Destiny. He knew it wasn't her fault, and that she had nothing to do with it. It angered him that he'd been deceived, but it didn't change his feelings for his daughter. Flesh and blood or not, he would always love her. She sat back down on the bench crying, and he pulled her into his frail arms. "Don't be absurd. Of course I don't hate you—I love you. You're my daughter. You'll always be my daughter." He had raised her since she was a little girl. She had been a part of his life for so many years, and she would always be his. He tried to catch his breath. "None of us has any control over the circumstances of our birth."

"But I took away the woman you loved."

"You didn't take her," he said ruefully, fighting back emotion, "she took herself."

Alexander suddenly felt as if a tremendous burden had been lifted and his body relaxed. He had at last learned what had really happened. It was finally over.

"You've given me a great gift, Destiny. You've at last given me peace of mind. I know now that she didn't leave because of anything I did. I just wish she'd been able to come to me, but," he looked sadly away, "I suppose she just wasn't that kind of person." He wrapped his arm more securely around his daughter. "I have a part of her. I'm grateful for that. Perhaps it was meant to be this way." Destiny hugged her father back tightly. "Perhaps it was our destiny."

❧ *Chapter eighteen*

*A*lexander lay in bed half the night mulling over everything his daughter had told him by the pond. He still couldn't believe Pepita had deceived him, and that Destiny really wasn't his daughter; that she was another man's child. . . . But nevertheless, he loved her just the same. He never once blamed her.

He couldn't shake his beloved Elena from his thoughts, and it tore at his already frail heart every time he thought of her and the terrible tragedy that had befallen her. Why hadn't she told him? He couldn't for the life of him understand her thinking. Tears clouded his eyes as he envisioned her being beaten and raped, pleading desperately for help. It destroyed him to know he hadn't been able to protect her. He would have done anything for her. He would have willingly given his life for her. If she had only told him, things would have been so different. They could have had a life together—the three of them.

He had never stopped loving her. He would go to his grave loving her—and only her.

Another current of pain shot through him—this one he couldn't ignore—and he clutched his chest and felt as if he was becoming weaker. He couldn't believe he was really going to die; that his life would soon be over. He never thought it would really end. He thought somehow he'd be able to beat it. He knew his time was near, and that he wouldn't be with the people he loved much longer. Weakly, he focused straight ahead. He thought he'd heard someone enter the room. "Mother?" He thought he saw his mother, Cecile, at the foot of the bed, smiling at him. "Mother . . . I knew you'd come back." She had returned to him at last, and he was overjoyed to see her. He had missed her terribly.

Alexander was beginning to hallucinate, thought Elena, worriedly as she watched with her arms crossed from the doorway. Destiny gestured for her to enter the room.

Elena crossed the room and stood at the side of Alexander's bed, sadly staring at him. He looked gaunt and sickly, not at all like the young and vibrant man she remembered and had lived in her memory all these years.

"Elena?" Alexander called out to her. "Are you really there . . . or am I dreaming?" He began to smile. Elena took Alexander's hand in hers as Destiny looked on somberly, gently closing the door behind her. Julia had gone. She had slipped out the front door just as Elena had rung the bell, showing up unexpectedly.

"Great . . . you hired a new nurse," Julia had said to Destiny, passing Elena on the way out. Destiny and Elena had met each other's eyes, both of them suppressing a grin.

Destiny was relieved that Julia had gone shopping. She had wanted her out of the way so that her mother and father could spend time alone without interference. Destiny was truly elated that her mother had come. It meant so much to her, and she appreciated it greatly. She knew it would bring her father great joy. He would at last be reunited with his beloved Elena—for one last time.

"Alexander . . ." Tears filled Elena's eyes. She pressed

his thin hand against her cheek. "I'm so sorry about everything. I never stopped loving you." She was overcome with emotion. She couldn't bear seeing Alexander this way—so frail, so ill, so close to death, knowing there was nothing she could do to save him. He had been so full of life and so handsome. She remembered the first time she had seen him. She remembered the way his strong and youthful body felt against hers as they were making love; the smoothness of his skin; the smell of his cologne; how he'd kissed her with such feeling, such overwhelming emotion and love; love that poured from his very soul into hers.

"Why? Why did you go?" He looked at her with glassy eyes.

"I knew that if you knew I was raped you'd go after them, and they'd kill you. I couldn't let that happen. I loved you too much. I couldn't risk it."

Alexander remained silent. He was losing his ability to think clearly.

"You did a wonderful job with *our* daughter." She smiled gently.

Alexander attempted a smile. The room around him began to slowly fade, and he could feel himself becoming weaker. With his last bit of strength he tightened his grip and squeezed Elena's hand. Tearfully, Elena motioned for Destiny to come over. She quickly went around to the other side of the bed and took her father's other hand, lowering herself beside him.

"You're the best father anyone could ever have." She kissed him on the forehead, then brushed his gray bangs back tenderly with her fingers. "I love you so much."

"Des—Lena." With great effort their names erupted from his throat. Alexander felt another surge of pain. He strained to touch his daughter's face, but couldn't seem to reach her. She grabbed his hand and kissed it.

Alexander had never felt such peace and could feel the intensity of their love, as he felt himself drifting off.

A look of contentment crossed his face. They were a family . . . at last.

❧

Destiny cried herself to sleep that night. She couldn't believe her father was really gone. They were sitting together chatting at the pond just yesterday morning. She'd had no idea he was so close to dying, that they had such precious little time left. It all seemed so strange, like a horrible dream.

Her mother had left shortly after. She was clearly distraught. Elena's heart had been shattered into a million pieces watching Alexander die, and she was overwhelmed with grief and plagued with guilt because of what she had done to him. She went back to New York, but told her daughter she'd be back in time for the funeral. Destiny was glad her mother had come to be with Alexander and would be forever grateful.

Julia had become hysterical the moment she returned home. She had bags of expensive clothes and accessories from Saks and Neiman-Marcus. She was told of Alexander's death. Despite the show, she was secretly relieved that she had missed his passing and that it was finally over—behind her once and for all. She felt as if he'd been pulling her into the grave with him; draining the life right out of her. Her little shopping spree had been a wonderful relief and directly needed, and she had gotten some wonderful buys. She felt as if a great weight had been lifted from her shoulders.

"Destiny, there's someone here to see you," said Julia, sniffling into a handkerchief, as she cracked open Destiny's door later that day. Alexander's body had been removed from the house, and Destiny had fallen asleep for an hour on her bed.

"To see me?"

Julia nodded.

"I don't want to see anyone," mumbled Destiny as she sat up. She touched her swollen eyes and rubbed her aching forehead.

"He said he was a friend of yours. I told him this wasn't a good time; but he said he wouldn't leave until he saw you. I believe he said his name is *something* Hollin."

Destiny felt her stomach tighten. "Tell him—tell him I'll be right down." A few minutes later after making herself presentable, clad in a black sweater and skirt, she went downstairs to meet him. Andrew was standing patiently in the foyer as handsome as ever dressed in a navy suit, light blue V-neck cashmere sweater and tailored blue shirt.

"Andrew—I'm surprised to see you." Destiny walked up to him, combing her fingers through her dark hair. Her eyes were red and puffy, and he could see that she'd been crying. Destiny's eyes filled with fresh tears as she said, "My father passed away this morning." Andrew looked at her sympathetically.

"I'm so sorry. I had no idea."

"Why did you come?"

"You left the hotel so abruptly without any explanation . . and I was concerned."

"Let's go outside," she said, and grabbed her jacket from the hall closet. He deserved an explanation for her quick departure.

The sky was a vivid blue. The leaves swirled on the grass like mini tornados. They strolled down to the pond, and she told him everything she had learned about her background and how devastating it had been. Andrew looked shocked, but was very understanding. He pulled her into his arms as she wistfully stared at the water. "I know it may seem a little soon; we've only known each other a week, but I'm falling in love with you, Destiny Raines. I don't care about your past . . . only about who you are now." Andrew pressed his lips against hers and kissed her long and hard. She felt so alone and needed someone to lean on. Destiny began to sob, then peered into his hazel eyes and realized just how much she cared for him.

"Do you really mean that?" she asked, and her face brightened.

"Absolutely." He kissed her again.

❧* *Chapter nineteen*

*A*fter days of grieving and crying, Destiny decided to begin her work of converting the mansion into a school and safe house for abused children. She knew it was what her father wanted; it had been a dream of his that he'd never been able to fulfill; and it was also a way of continuing the work that Jeff had started back in Oregon. They both would live on through the school. It was a way to keep them both alive in her memory forever. She knew it would take a lot of work and energy but she was willing to give it all she had.

❧

Destiny stood on the back lawn, on this perfect autumn day gazing at the pond through a veil of trees. It had been one year since Alexander's death, and Destiny still couldn't believe he was really gone.

"Miss Raines—" Her reverie was interrupted by a tiny voice. "Look what I did, Miss Raines." Lionel, with the curly dark hair and light mocha skin skipped up to her, flashing his painting.

"Why—that's wonderful!" exclaimed Destiny.

"It's a clown!" he said gleefully, totally centered on his work. "It's for you." He smiled, looking up at her with his big brown eyes and long lashes.

Destiny gave him a great big bear hug. "Thank you. I'll hang it up in my office, where I put my favorite artwork." The little boy looked pleased, then darted off to join a friend in play. Destiny walked down to the gazebo. She thought of her father again. Alexander would have been happy to learn that his favorite room, the study, had become a library for the residents, and that she had turned half of the grand living room into a classroom. With the money her father had left her, she had hired her friend Valerie to assist her with the teaching, and a social worker.

Julia, who had mellowed during her father's illness, had been well compensated for her acquiescence. "Julia will do anything if the price is right." Destiny recalled her father saying once and it proved to be true. Alexander had left his wife a handsome sum of money if she agreed not to contest the will. With it she moved to a condominium on the Potomac with a young gynecologist, ten years her junior, whom she'd begun seeing shortly after Alexander's death.

Destiny, looking out at the water, thought of Andrew. She never thought she'd fall in love again after Jeff. But to her surprise, she had fallen deeply in love with Andrew, and they were planning to be married at Christmas. She absolutely adored his little son, Jamie, and was happy to become his stepmother. And within the next few years they were hoping to give him two siblings.

She thought of all that Andrew had sacrificed for her. He had sold the Dumois to an interested buyer, explaining to her that he needed a change, and that he wanted to be with her more than anything else. He wanted to move to Virginia and run the home with her. Destiny had been thoroughly elated.

She saw her mother, Elena, on occasion, and spoke to her on the phone from time to time, and she could feel their relationship growing stronger.

Destiny smiled as she overheard two of the children as they played on the lawn behind her, just as she once had done. They were so much a part of her. Destiny felt there could be no greater joy than knowing her work enabled her to help others.

She walked up the wooden steps of the gazebo, turning her head as she heard someone coming up behind her. Andrew wrapped his arms lovingly around her, and she snuggled up against him; and they watched two mallards sail by.

✿ ABOUT THE AUTHOR ✿

Jane Garrard was born and raised in New York, and has been writing since childhood. After graduating college she married her fiancé, a graduate of West Point. While following her husband's military career and traveling with him all over the world, she completed a master's degree in education and pursued a teaching career.

For the last three years the author has been a contributing editor at *Longevity* magazine, and a freelance writer for various newspapers and magazines. She has completed three novels.

Jane Garrard lives in Oregon with her husband of eighteen years, her daughter, and two sons.